All that's left to hold Onto

Crystal
Always hold onto
what matters most
xo Elle

ELLA FOX

Ebook ISBN: 9780996189484
Paperback
ISBN-13: 978-1519425126
ISBN-10: 1519425120

Cover Photo & Design by Sara Eirew
Editing by Vanessa Bridges, Prema Editing
Proofreading by Manda Mettlach, Prema Editing
Final Proof by Gemma Rowlands
Formatting by Stacey Blake, Champagne Formats
Teasers by Melissa Ringuette, Monark Design Services
Release Blitz & Blog Tour by Lisa Hintz, The Rock Stars of Romance Promotions
Blurb Assistance: Carol Eastman (The Blurb Bitch) and Tijan
Cover Models: Mike Chabot and Marilou Genest

Dedication

This one is for Tara, Dawn, Nancy, Dena, Sian, Nikki, Dawn C.
and Joni.
Thanks for making me laugh.

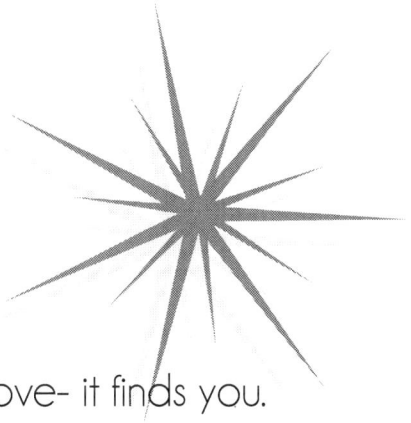

You don't find love- it finds you.

It's got a little bit to do with

Destiny, fate and what's written in the stars.

~Anaïs Nin

Prologue

THERE WERE NASTY LOOKING BRUISES ON HIS CHEEK AND jaw, his lip was swollen and his knuckles were scraped and bloody. The instant I got a good look at his face I knew something was horribly wrong. It only went downhill from there.

My attempts to contain my panic weren't working. Choking back a sob I blubbered, "Why do you have to go?"

The anger was all but pouring off of him. Not toward me—he'd never once been angry with me. I knew anger though, and it was more than obvious he was furious about something. A permanent grimace seemed to have set up camp on his face. For him, it was highly unusual. Even in the toughest of times, he kept his cool.

Suddenly, he wasn't calm at all. He was angrier than I'd ever seen him. It was obvious he'd been in a fight, but it didn't change his status as the most attractive guy alive, in my opinion.

I saw his jaw clenching and unclenching which I figured meant he was trying to control himself.

"Because this piece of shit town is like a fucking cancer," he spat. "I'm so done with the crazy assholes around here. People like us aren't normal—we're the freaks for trying to be good people."

I didn't know how to argue with his words. He wasn't wrong—there was a lot wrong with many of the people in our town. Most of the crazy people were either my family members or his. I knew it and so did he. There wasn't a response to erase the reality of the kind of people we dealt with.

"Are you going alone?"

His hands clenched into fists at his sides as he nodded stiffly. "Yes."

"Even though you live with—"

His hand shot up into a stop gesture to keep me from finishing the sentence.

"Don't say her fucking name. If I never hear it again, it'll be too soon. I don't live with that crazy bitch anymore."

I couldn't stand her so it wasn't like I was going to push. She was an evil troll. If he had to go, I was glad he wasn't taking her with him. It would've made me ill. She pretended to be sweetness and light when he was around but it was nothing but a charade. She was terrible. I was glad he wasn't taking her, but the fact he wouldn't say her name told me his leaving was somehow her responsibility. I hated her more than ever.

"Where will you go?"

He gestured back over his shoulder toward the street with his thumb.

"Wherever my car takes me once I pull out," he said.

I couldn't imagine life without him, nor did I want to. Not only had he been my crush for as long as I could remember, he was the only person who ever really listened to me.

"Will you ever visit?" I asked hopefully.

He was shaking his head in the negative before I'd even fully finished asking the question. I knew he wouldn't. The bone-deep hatred he had for everything about where we lived was stamped all over his face. I wanted so badly to know what, exactly, had sent him over the edge, but when I asked, he'd refused to tell me.

It sucked being fourteen because he treated me like a kid. My age said I was a child, but I was so different than any of my peers it wasn't even funny. Because of this, they teased me often, referring to me as Granny Carmichael. I hated it. It wasn't as though I'd had a choice. My childhood was over the moment my mother got sick.

His expression softened when he looked me over. "You need to get back inside before you get pneumonia."

The frigid Colorado air wasn't even making an impression on me until he pointed it out. I realized my tears were leaving cold trails on my face, but I couldn't walk away. All I cared about was how much I didn't want him to leave.

"I don't care about the cold or getting pneumonia. I don't want you to go!" I cried anxiously.

He hugged me then, his strong arms wrapping around me to give comfort. I hadn't hugged him since I'd been much younger—probably five or six. Those hugs had mostly involved me wrapping myself around one of his legs. This was different. I wrapped my arms tight around him and cried against his chest, holding on for as long as he allowed me to.

"I'm sorry," he said as he ended the embrace and stepped back. "I have to leave."

Knowing my denial and resistance weren't going to make any difference, I swiped at my tears as I nodded.

"I'll miss you," I said on a choked sob. "Take care of yourself."

"I'll miss you too," he replied softly. "You're one of the few good people here."

My heart galloped in my chest. I loved him for saying what he did—but hated that it came at such a horrible price. Losing him was unbearable.

He turned as if to leave, then stopped. Spinning back my way, he stared at me intently for a few moments before he spoke again.

"You're so much better than any of these people. Don't ever let them change who you are. The world needs a lot more you and a lot less them. No matter what anyone tells you—you're perfect. Got it?"

I nodded as I wiped at the tears running unchecked down my face.

He hugged me again, very briefly. My heart skipped a few beats when he dropped a kiss on top of my head.

"Don't ever forget your worth—not even for a minute," he murmured.

When he let go, he said nothing else. He just turned and walked to his car. As he went, the chill in the air suddenly took hold of me. Hugging my arms around myself, I watched as he got into the car, turned it on and then pulled out of my driveway. He looked at me one last time before putting his hand up in a goodbye gesture. I did the same. A few seconds passed before he put the car in drive then sped off into the night.

I stayed outside for two or three minutes, hoping against hope he would change his mind and come back.

He didn't.

Hours later when I got into bed, I prayed fate would bring him back one day. I said the same prayer most nights for a long, long time. Eventually I had no choice but to accept reality.

Hell would freeze over before he returned.

Chapter One

Ronan

THE INCESSANT RINGING OF MY CELL PHONE WAKING ME UP from what had been a deep sleep was at the top of the list of sounds I didn't want to fucking hear. It was the first night in weeks where I'd had the opportunity to sleep for more than four hours at a time. My goal was to ride the sleep wave for as many hours as humanly possible before surfacing again. Clearly, I wasn't so lucky.

The phone ringing came on the heels of several shitty weeks of being spread thinner than an Olsen twin. In addition to working my normal day shift, I'd stepped up to do nights when our manager left because she was pregnant. I'd been lucky to find a new manager relatively quickly, but the need to train the new staffer took time—almost two weeks, to be exact. Since my friend and business partner Lincoln hadn't been around to help, I'd been totally responsible for everything. Saying I was shit-kicked when the phone started ringing is one hell of an understatement.

Less than half awake and already planning the verbal assault I was going to dole out to whoever was waking my ass up in the middle of the fucking night, I sat up and tossed the covers off. I'd been pretty damn sure it was bar shit, which made me feel stabby. It was one thing to be on constant call while Linc was in West Yellowstone helping his dad recover from hip replacement surgery. It was another not to be afforded the opportunity to sleep. I was so exhausted I was struggling to form coherent sentences.

A tap on the base of the lamp on my nightstand bathed the room in a soft light. Regardless of how soft the light was, my eyes struggled to adjust to it. With them at half-mast, I grabbed my cell from its spot next to the lamp and slid my thumb across the screen to answer the call. I expelled a sound of annoyance as my dog jumped up on the bed and started poking into my side with her nose, wanting to go out. Completely ignoring my instruction to lay down, Snuggles began running around the room like a maniac. That had been inevitable from the moment the phone started ringing. My pup was high energy. It was not ideal in the middle of the night.

"This better be damn good," I growled into the phone. By then I was pissed to be awake and damn aggravated since it meant I was going to have to take Snuggles out before I could go back to sleep. She couldn't be hurried, so I knew I was looking at a ten to fifteen-minute window before I could get back into bed.

"Am I speaking to Ronan Sharpe?"

My heart rate instantly quadrupled and the hair on the back of my neck stood on end. My annoyance with being awoken faded instantly. The voice on the other end was familiar, but something about the tone told me the call was about something serious. Something was wrong.

"You are. Who's this?"

"This is a technicality but before we go any further, I need you to confirm you're the brother of William Sharpe."

The feeling of unease instantly gave way to disgust. Being reminded I even *had* a brother wasn't a good thing. I confirmed my sibling status through clenched teeth.

"Yeah, he's my older brother. Who's this?"

"Ronan, it's Chuck West from back in Fort Collins."

Chuck West was my oldest friend Canter's dad. He was also the chief of police. I hadn't seen Chuck in several years, but it sure as hell didn't take a rocket scientist to arrive at the conclusion nothing good was happening. I was less than thrilled to realize the call concerned one of my infamous brother's fuck ups. Will wasn't good at anything practical, but he excelled at being a cruel and fucked-up son-of-a-bitch. I'd thanked my lucky stars many, many times about the fact we didn't share blood. I was adopted and damn glad of it.

"Hey, Mr. West. What did the fuck up do now?" I asked. I made no attempt to conceal the irritation I was feeling.

"I'm so sorry to tell you this, Ronan. Earlier this evening, your brother and his wife were killed in an automotive accident. Will died on impact, but Isabelle lived for a few additional minutes. Before she passed, the doctors delivered their child. You have a niece."

I was rendered speechless for several seconds.

My thoughts went something like this:

Of course they fucking stayed together.

A baby? Really?

What the fuck were they thinking?

If there were two people who should never have considered being parents, it was those assholes. My brain felt a lot like a flickering light bulb just before it gives up the ghost and stops working completely. Seconds passed while I struggled to comprehend what Chuck was saying. I was sick to my stomach, and my hands were shaking. My brother was an asshole and I wouldn't—couldn't—mourn him. It was an inescapable fact. It wasn't as though I'd go dancing through the fucking daisies over his death, either. Mortality tended to make shit real, even when the life in question belonged to an asshole.

Regardless of the fact I'd long suspected he'd been breastfed on Satan's milk, Will had been the last living member of my family. It was something he'd traded on numerous times before I'd finally wised up and stopped letting him.

My brother and I didn't get along for shit because I'd seen his true colors—which meant I knew he was a lying and manipulative monster. I hadn't ever wished him dead, though. Sensing my distress, Snuggles came and set her head on my knee. She stared up at me anxiously as I struggled to make sense of what was going on. I briefly wondered if I was dreaming. I stared at the clock, and noted the time was 12:23 in the morning. Whether due to my eyes still being sensitive to light after waking or because I was still trying to take everything in, the red numbers hurt to look at.

The sound of Chuck's voice brought me quickly back to reality.

"Ronan, I know this is a shock, but there's no time to waste," Chuck continued. "Your niece is in the NICU at the hospital. With the situation as it stands, you're the next of kin, which means you're in charge."

I was like a hamster on a fucking wheel trying to wrap my mind around it all. I wondered what the hell I was supposed to do about a baby. The thought of being responsible for a child wasn't something I could connect with. My hands were trembling and my heart was beating way too fast. I hated not being in control.

"I live in Montana," I mumbled. "I can't just drive on over... What the fuck am I going to do?"

"I know where you live, Ronan. You're going to get yourself together and find the first flight out. The best advice I can give you right now is to focus on what you have to," Chuck counseled calmly. "It's too late for your brother and your sister-in-law, but this child needs someone to be in her corner. I can't stress enough— you need to be here. In addition to your niece, there's the matter of

Isabelle's sister, Keely."

My mind had been spinning out wildly in a million different directions, but the mere mention of her name shrank everything down to the head of a pin. Once upon a time, Keely Carmichael looked at me as though I'd hung the moon. Because she lived with her father on the same street I'd grown up on, I'd known her forever. She'd been my little shadow for a long time. Where I went, she wanted to go. It had been more than obvious she'd had a wicked case of hero worship where I was concerned. It was sweet, but misplaced. I'd been no hero—just a dumb bastard who learned lessons the hard way.

The last time I'd seen Keely was five years prior. She'd been fourteen years old, and I'd felt like a piece of shit when I'd seen the tears sliding down her cheeks as she watched me pull out of her driveway. When she'd come down from her bedroom and entered the kitchen, she'd been happy because I was there. Little did she know it was my last visit on my way out of Fort Collins. I'd stopped to talk to her father. Our conversation didn't go well, to say the least. I left the kitchen angrier than when I arrived. Because of that, I hadn't been as gentle telling Keely I was leaving permanently as I should have been.

By the time I left, she was beside herself, and I'd been too fucked in the head to say anything helpful. I'd tried, but I knew I'd failed. I knew I could've done better. I felt I owed her for caring. It meant something to me. Aside from Canter and his family, no one else gave a fuck when I left—including the person I'd been living with until earlier that afternoon. Funny how sometimes the people you think are important in your life are the ones who hurt you the most. The girl I thought I'd loved, the one I was half considering marrying—had only cared about my leaving in a very shallow way. The reality was I hadn't been so much as a blip on her radar. I found out the truth the hard way.

It put the period at the end of a shit day. The person I'd thought would've cared, hadn't. And then, there was Keely who was devastated. Even though I didn't know it at the time, I'd needed someone to show they cared about me. Keely was the one to do so. For that, I owed her.

The moment Chuck said her name I knew it was time to return the favor.

"What about Keely?" I croaked.

"She was in the car, so she sustained some injuries—nothing life threatening. Right now she's passed out. There's no sign of brain swelling, but they're going to need to keep evaluating the situation as it unfolds over the next few hours. Also—when she comes to, someone she knows should be there for her as we break the news about her sister dying."

I was more confused than ever about what the hell was going on. Why would I be there when an emotional bomb of such magnitude got dropped on her?

"Where's her dad?" I questioned angrily. "Let me guess, crying in his fucking Cheerios about Izzy. What an asshole! Hollis should be the one to be with her. He's the next of kin you should be talking to—"

"Damn, you have been gone for a long time. Hollis died of lung cancer about two years ago. With Isabelle being—" There was a pause as Chuck coughed, presumably to avoid saying the word *dead*. "Keely's all alone now."

His words hit me hard. She'd always been a sweet girl, and fuck knew she deserved better than the family she'd been born to. I could only imagine how she was going to feel when she woke up. For some reason, knowing she was alone was the slap of reality I'd needed to get my wheels turning. I realized right then it was time to get my ass in motion.

"I'm going to get there as soon as I can, Mr. West. I'll call the airline now and get the first flight out from Bozeman. You can call or text me at this number anytime. It won't work while I'm in the air, but I'll be sure to get a Wi-Fi pass. Canter has my e-mail."

"Canter already passed it along—it's how I got this number. I'd imagine you'll be hearing from him anytime now."

"Right… I should have realized. I'm sorry I'm so out of it— clearly I'm not firing on all cylinders right now."

"It's to be expected," Chuck assured me. "Don't beat yourself up for being in shock. Right now the best thing you can do is focus on getting here."

"You're right," I sighed. "I'm going to get on it right now. Thanks for being the one to call, Chuck. I appreciate it more than you know. I'll see you when I get there."

There was no time for me to take even one deep breath after I hung up with Chuck. Instead, I got right on making arrangements to fly out. I was so shaken up I'm surprised I didn't book a flight to Timbuktu. I'm reasonably certain I only wound up making the correct reservations because the agent I spoke to was on point.

There were seats available on an early morning flight, which was great. However, this meant I needed to haul ass to pack and get to the airport in time to get through security and check in.

I texted my neighbor Tara and asked if she could watch Snuggles. After I got a text back saying she would, I headed over to drop my pup off. I'd known she would watch her before I even asked. Tara was always down to take my dog if I needed her to. She did this because she figured she owed me seeing as how I'd adopted the dog from the animal shelter she worked at. She wasn't wrong.

I'd never intended to get a dog, but once Tara came over with pictures of Snuggles she just 'happened' to have, I'd been a goner. It wasn't hard for her to talk me into going to the shelter 'just to see' if I liked the dog. I tried to put her off, but Tara was persuasive, pointing out that the dog had been at the shelter for almost the maximum number of days allowed.

"She's such a sweet girl," Tara had explained in a pleading tone. "I can't let her be put down and I thought of you. You're over here without any animals and she needs a home. I'll share my newest case of wine with you if you just come look at her."

Tara would've adopted every stray animal within a four hundred mile radius if she could, but her husband Mike put his foot down after the seventh beagle puppy came home.

Since she couldn't take the dog, I was up. I agreed to check the dog out, but I had no intention of taking her home. I figured I'd make a donation to keep her place at the shelter and take some pictures to hang up at the bar to find her a home.

When I got to the shelter, Snuggles looked up at me with those big puppy dog eyes, and I'd caved. The next thing I knew, I'd been filling out an application. A few hours later, I was dropping a shitload amount of money at the local pet store for food and toys. Snuggles was a ridiculous name, but I loved her, and she'd become my family. Knowing I was leaving home for God only knew how long didn't make me happy.

Tara was a night owl, so I'd known she would be awake when I called. When I showed up at her house a few minutes later, she opened the door with two of her seven dogs at her feet. They yapped happily when they saw Snuggles, and the three of them ran through the house and quickly exited into the backyard using the doggie door. Tara's house was like Disneyland for dogs, which meant I felt good about leaving Snuggles with her.

Closing the door behind me, Tara gestured to the kitchen and started walking that way. Over her shoulder she asked, "You look like you need a coffee for the road. Come to the kitchen and I'll brew you some. While I do that, you can explain how I never knew you had a brother. You keep that a secret for a reason?"

It was a fair question. She'd been my neighbor for going on

two and a half years. I spent a fair amount of time with her and her husband Mike, so we all knew plenty about each other. I knew it seemed weird I hadn't once mentioned Will.

"My brother was not a good guy," I answered matter-of-factly as I followed her down the hall. "I've spent a good amount of time trying to forget he existed," I admitted. "If it weren't for the situation with the baby and my brother's sister-in-law, I wouldn't consider going back."

She went over to her single serve coffee maker and began brewing me a travel mug of coffee. I leaned against the counter tiredly as the rich scent of the French roast she was making for me filled the air.

"You don't have the look of someone who doesn't care," she commented. "In fact, I'd say you look pretty damn upset."

I rubbed both my hands over my face as I shook my head. "Honestly T, I don't know what the fuck I am right now. Thinking about Keely being hurt and knowing there's a baby… It's fucked up. My brother and I haven't spoken in five years. Now suddenly I'm next of kin? I'm freaking the fuck out."

After putting eight heaping scoops of sugar into my coffee and stirring it, she twisted the lid and handed it to me.

"I can just imagine the shock," she assured me. "It sort of reminds me of this one book I read…"

I tuned her out as I sipped the steaming hot coffee. Tara and her best friend Dawn ran a book blog. Because of this, Tara could— and more often than not, did—compare everything to the plot of a book. My reading consisted of the local newspaper, cookbooks and the occasional biography. This meant a lot of the time she and Dawn were talking books I was lost.

I'd had no idea what the fuck a book boyfriend was before Tara told me. Unfortunately, she and Dawn had also schooled me on what a tug scene was because they were obsessed with them.

That conversation resulted in my being a little bit scared of them both. I needed to know about fictional dudes jerking their dicks like I needed a hole in the head. When I'd mentioned my horror at being told about tug scenes to Tara's husband Mike, he rolled his eyes and told me to follow his lead. That means enacting the SNF protocol—smile, nod and find something to do away from the talk of books.

She was real excited about whatever book she was talking about. I dug Tara and loved her taste in wine, but right in that particular moment, I wasn't up for it. Holding up the travel mug, I cut her off.

"I gotta hit the road or I won't make it to the airport on time. Thanks for taking Snugs. I'll text or call with an update as soon as I can."

"Don't worry about a thing," she said as we walked to the door. "I've got this shit locked down."

After thanking her, I scrambled home to toss shit in a suitcase and throw away all the perishable shit on my counters and in my fridge. The entire time I felt like I was stuck in a fucked-up dream world. My hands clenched, my teeth ground together, and my head pounded as the memory of the last time I saw Will played out in my mind.

It took everything I had to shut the memories down fast and hard. I'd spent such a long time trying to scrub it all from my brain. Only within the previous few years was I finally able to get to the point where I could go months without remembering. I wasn't about to start going backward. There are some things it's just better to forget.

Chapter Two

Ronan

I F YOU'RE ALREADY STRESSED OUT, FLYING IS FUCKING torture. I spent the majority of my flight fighting with the shitty Wi-Fi—which was a fucking waste of twenty dollars if I ever encountered one. I wouldn't have bothered, but I'd needed to send e-mails. My priority was sending an explanation of the situation to my business partner, Lincoln. I alerted him to my complete and total lack of a clue as to when the hell I would be back.

Right then, I gave absolutely no fucks about the bar. Granted, I didn't want to leave Linc in the lurch, but I knew he'd understand. Considering what I'd done for him while he was out of town, I was positive it wasn't going to be an issue.

After I finished writing Linc, I moved on to Canter, providing him with all my flight details. He wrote back quickly, but it took forty minutes for it to show up, which was part of the reason I was so pissed at the Wi-Fi. It should have been called Wi-Fuck, as in why fucking bother trying because this shit doesn't work. When I finally got to open his response, my anxiety spiked. The baby continued to do well, but there was no change in Keely's condition.

I'd stopped and explained my situation to the flight crew at boarding, so the second the plane landed I was let off first. I ran through the terminal of the Denver airport like the hounds of hell were on my heels, and in a way, they were.

The second the electric doors slid open to the outside, I saw Canter leaning against a black Dodge Durango. The only difference in his appearance after five years was the sleeve of tattoos on one of his arms. I was covered in ink on my left arm, so I approved. Just in the few seconds we were standing outside, I saw several women eying him up. In high school, chicks dropped their cheerleading skirts for him on the regular. There was no doubt he was getting even more ass as an adult.

We did our version of a "bro hug"—fast, one arm—before quickly getting into the running car. He peeled away from the curb before my seatbelt was latched.

"Any change?" I asked.

"Dad texted about ten minutes ago and said the baby is doing very well. She couldn't be in better hands," he said reassuringly. "Kristi's on duty in the NICU."

I breathed a sigh of relief as soon as he said it. Kristi was Canter's big sister, and she was good people. She was also a straight shooter, which meant I could rely on what she'd said.

"What about Keely?"

"Still out," Canter answered.

"But she's going to be okay?" I pressed.

"Looks like it. She's got a hell of a gash on her right arm, which needed twenty-three stitches. The EMTs told Dad it was a fucking miracle one of her arteries didn't get hit."

"Fuck," I muttered sickly.

I dropped my head back against the headrest as I tried to harness my thoughts. I was so far out of the loop with anything to do with my old life. I felt half-awake and totally out of place.

"What the fuck happened? Your dad said it was a car accident, but he didn't give me any details."

As I voiced the question, I noticed Canter's grip on the steering wheel was white-knuckled. It was my first clue I wouldn't like what came next.

Normally Canter was a fairly calm guy. The fact I could tell he was pissed was an indicator shit wasn't good.

"Will was fucked up—driving well over the limit," Canter said stiffly. "An eyewitness called in about him weaving all over the damn road about four minutes before the crash. Damn lucky they called, too. It's what saved the baby."

It was like taking a blow to the gut. "Jesus," I sputtered. "Fuck."

Canter continued, "His blood alcohol was six times the legal limit. I'm surprised he was able to drive at all. EMTs said Izzy was dilated, so Dad thinks they must've been headed to the hospital. "

I yelled so loud, I'm pretty sure the windows shook. "Goddammit! What the fucking hell?"

It took a few seconds for me to get myself together enough to say anything else.

"You're telling me Will had his pregnant wife and Keely in the car, and he was driving fucked up? If he weren't dead, I'd beat the…"

I trailed off as my stomach roiled, and it hit me all over again. Will was dead, and he'd been a selfish sack of shit to the bitter end. His actions left Izzy dead, Keely unconscious and the baby Izzy had been carrying lucky to be alive.

"What the fuck was he thinking driving with them in the car when he's fucked up?" I snapped. "I knew he was irresponsible, but this is…"

I ground my teeth together and tried to get control of myself. The way I was feeling had me wanting to lash out hard. Pure rage. Knowing anger wasn't the answer, I forced myself to calm down. I needed to get my focus off the accident or I knew I would implode.

"You never told me those assholes got married," I remarked after a few silent moments.

Canter turned to look at me quickly, frowning my way before setting his eyes back on the road.

"Fuck, Ronan. You think perhaps it's due to the fact we keep in touch mostly by text and email? We talk on the phone about six or seven times a year. You wanted to leave, and you got fucking out. I get it. What happened was fucked up. You think I didn't avoid them and their little hangers on like the plague? I knew some shit because I'd hear people talk, but mostly I purposely kept my head in the sand."

He paused as he cracked his knuckles one by one against the steering wheel. It had long been one of his habits. "What I did pick up wasn't good," he admitted, "but I expected no different. They were whacked—you did the right thing going. There was no way I was talking to you about anything having to do with them. Don't act like you wouldn't have done the same. In five years you've never once asked how they were doing. You didn't want to know."

He wasn't wrong. I was twenty-one years old when I left, and I'd been quite clear about my intent to stay gone. The last thing I said— yelled— to my brother was a vow he'd never see me again. True to my word, when I left, I was gone. I then spent five years pushing away any and all thoughts of that last day away.

"I get it. To be honest, I'm kind of surprised they stayed in Fort Collins. When I left, I was sure it was only a matter of time before people found out."

"I thought so too," Canter agreed, "But it never happened. If anyone else knows, they kept it to themselves."

A part of me was relieved nothing got out. Being related to Will and knowing what he was fucking sucked. I'd been as ashamed as I was angry, and I still was. Nothing changed. I'd only told Canter because I'd been unwilling to lie to him about why I was leaving so suddenly. I'd also known he would never repeat what I said.

As Canter's car ate up the miles between Denver and Fort Collins, I stared out the window but saw none of the scenery. I went over what transpired since Canter's dad woke me up, as I tried to make sense of it all.

I didn't regret cutting my brother and Isabelle off. I was also not upset we never reconnected. Nothing good would have come of it. After what happened, there was nothing left to say. My brother was never a good person, and there was never a bit of affection between us. He'd hated me—and I sure as hell hadn't been his biggest fan. Especially not after what happened the last time I saw him.

I was affected by his death—but not for the reasons I imagine I would have been if we'd had a functional relationship. There was always a lot of bad blood between us.

Pushing those thoughts aside, I tried to stay focused on the issue at hand. I was going to be responsible, even if it was only in a small way, for his child. My teeth ground together as I fought to stay calm. The baby was innocent, and I would do whatever I needed to do not to bring my emotional baggage into the hospital with me. I needed to concentrate on the current reality instead of my past anger.

Put bluntly, I was scared fucking shitless. Even thinking of the baby made my stomach churn. I was in no position to be a father, which meant I was going to need to get the wheels turning on an adoption and fast. The baby needed a real parent—preferably two—and I knew damn well I wasn't a candidate.

By the time we pulled into the hospital parking lot, I'd talked myself into going to see about Keely first. The baby was the healthier of the two, so I figured seeing her could wait. I assured myself I was not hiding from the baby, but the truth is I was freaking out, and I needed the extra time to get myself together.

Canter stayed with me, guiding me through the lobby and up to the fifth floor where Keely was. As soon as we stepped off the elevator, I saw Canter's dad at the desk in conversation with a nurse.

He'd seen us right away, nodding tiredly in my direction before ending the conversation and heading my way. We shook hands as he told me how sorry he was I wasn't home under better circumstances. I tried to breathe through the sick feeling in my stomach at his choice of words. I didn't want to remember thinking of Fort Collins as my home.

I stood straight and swallowed nervously as I tried to hide the anxiety I was feeling being back in Colorado. "How are they doing?"

"The baby is good," he answered. "No signs of trauma. She's breathing just fine and has already gone through two feedings. Kristi says they'll move her out of the NICU and into the regular nursery probably sometime tomorrow. It's a precaution to have her in the NICU at all. They want to monitor her for twenty-four hours before switching it up."

I immediately felt better knowing she was going to be okay. "And Keely?"

"She's been a little restless for the last hour or so, which the doctors say is a great sign. They're hopeful she'll wake up within the next few hours."

I shoved my hands in my pockets and met his eyes tiredly. "Can I see her?"

He nodded as he gestured down the hall. "Follow me," he instructed. "The doctor is in with her now. I'll introduce you."

My eyes traveled right to Keely the second we entered the room. She was as pale as a ghost and her long dark hair was a mess. It didn't matter—nothing could detract from her beauty.

I wasn't surprised to see Keely had grown up to be gorgeous—she'd been beautiful even as a young teen. Again, not a shock considering her mother, Kassidy, was a former Miss Colorado contestant. Just days after her eighteenth birthday, Kassidy got involved with Hollis Carmichael. Hollis was a forty-year-old divorced single dad at the time, but it didn't stop him from making her his trophy wife. Within two months, she was off the pageant circuit, wearing his ring and knocked up with Keely.

Hollis ignored the small-town gossip about his choice of bride without any fanfare because he didn't care. My father talked shit about him, along with ninety percent of our community. Rumors were started—accusations he'd bedded her before she was legal. Hollis kept his mouth shut and let them all talk, right up until the moment he'd heard the town gossip call his wife a gold digger. Once he'd stood up and told everyone to mind their own goddamn business—and reminded them they weren't judge and jury—people shut up for the most part.

The age difference between Hollis and Kassidy was big, but anyone with a brain could see Hollis was obsessed. They'd been all but tied at the hip, right until the moment Kassidy died from skin cancer. This left Keely motherless from the age of eight—and damn near fatherless, too. Hollis wasn't a good dad to her after Kassidy died. He'd not done a bang up job with Izzy by any stretch of the imagination, but at least with her it was always clear he'd loved her. He did not act the same way toward Keely at all. In a lot of ways, it was as if she'd been invisible to him. I wondered if he'd ever gotten his head out of his ass long enough to work on his relationship with her. For her sake, I hoped so.

My thoughts were halted when Chuck introduced me to the doctor.

"Ronan, this is Dr. Smith. Dr. Smith, this is Ronan and my son, Canter."

After shaking hands and exchanging some benign pleasantries, Dr. Smith started going over Keely's condition with me. I could see she was banged up, and the sight of all of the stitches running down her arm made me nauseous. She could have fucking died—and it was all because of my piece of shit brother.

Dr. Smith gave me a thorough explanation of Keely's injuries—in addition to the stitches on her arm there were some huge bruises on her right leg and several cuts on her left. None of it was much cause for concern, he assured me. The real issue was the possibility she'd sustained a traumatic brain injury. While there was no swelling and no reason they could find to think so, until she woke up and they evaluated her, they couldn't be sure.

As the doctor spoke, Keely stirred restlessly on the bed. The doctor nodded his head in approval. "She's starting to move around a bit," he told me as he picked up her chart and started writing something down. "I'm thinking it won't be long now."

Snapping the chart closed, he looked back up at me. "Miss Carmichael is quite healthy. I think it will help her situation tremendously with the healing process."

"So, you think she'll be okay?" I asked.

"The information we have right now indicates there's no reason she shouldn't be fine when she wakes up," he assured me. "However, since she isn't awake, I can't know for sure. I'll re-evaluate her once she's alert."

It wasn't the answer I was looking for, but it wasn't like I could demand another one. I realized he needed to cover his ass in case she woke up speaking in tongues or was unable to remember who she was.

"I know your niece is down in NICU," Dr. Smith continued. "If you'd like to head on over there, I'll have a nurse call in and tell them you're coming. We'd be sure to alert you when Miss Carmichael wakes."

My entire body froze solid as my pulse skyrocketed. I knew I couldn't do it right then. I didn't even care if it seemed weird—I was completely unprepared and totally unable to attempt even going near the NICU. I was fairly convinced my damn legs wouldn't carry me anyway. The idea of seeing the baby seemed as daunting as climbing the worlds' highest mountain without proper gear.

"I'll stay with Keely for now."

Somehow I managed to say it firmly and in such a way there was no room for argument.

Dr. Smith's graying eyebrows shot up toward his hairline as he stared at me like I was some kind of science project. He schooled his face quickly, but before he did, I saw disapproval. It shamed me, but not enough to change my mind.

"After she's awake, and I've told her what's happened, I'll see the child," I explained.

"It's your decision," he responded stiffly. "I'll be in and out to check on Miss Carmichael. If you need anything, or if you change your mind, press the call button for the nurses' station."

After Dr. Smith left, Chuck announced he needed to take care of some work back at the station. "I'll be back in a few hours."

The door closed quietly behind him, leaving Canter and me alone in Keely's hospital room. Feeling pretty shaky, I dropped down on the chair next to her bed as I exhaled loudly.

I hoped Canter would ignore my obvious reticence to see the baby. Of course, he didn't.

"What's up with not wanting to see the baby?"

I avoided looking at him, choosing to keep my eyes on Keely. "Can't go there," I answered gruffly. "I know fuck all about babies, and I'm no one's dad. Unless Keely wants her, which I doubt considering she's nineteen, I'm going to have to put her up for adoption. It's the best thing for her."

He stayed silent for long enough I'd figured he was going to give me a pass. Right at the moment when I was starting to feel relieved he said, "Is it?"

Sitting up in the chair, I crossed my arms defensively as I turned and glared at him. "You think a fuckin' dive bar owner whose most meaningful relationships are weekend flings with tourists passing through town is father material?"

"It might be your lifestyle right now, but you can choose something different. This baby needs someone in her corner. Why not you?"

I couldn't believe what he was suggesting.

Me? A dad? The idea was preposterous.

"I'm not trying to pawn her off on someone who won't give a fuck," I snapped. "You have any clue how many people are ready and willing to adopt a baby? Open up their homes and create a family? Tens of thousands," I assured him. "If you don't think having a family is the better option, you're crazy."

He laughed at me as he shook his head. "Crazy I might well fucking be, but I know you better than most anyone. You aren't going to be okay if you give her up without at least thinking it through. It'll fuckin' eat at you. Especially with your history."

I knew he was right. However, I believed for the child's sake, I needed to keep emotion out of it. Getting involved wasn't the answer.

"Just because I got adopted by a family that wasn't ideal, doesn't mean it happens to every adoptee," I said stiffly.

"*Wasn't ideal* is an understatement," he retorted dryly.

I shrugged and looked away. There was nothing I could add that would make his words less true.

"You're right," he conceded. "It doesn't happen all the time. But what happened to you should give you pause to think it all the way through before you make any rash decisions. You'd always wonder if you chose right if you weren't certain she was in a loving environment."

I knew that to be true.

"Fine," I answered gruffly. "I'll think it through."

By thinking it through, I meant I'd find out what the best adoption options would be. I intended to make damn sure the baby had a great home to go to. I couldn't do much, but I could make sure she got a family that would love her.

"I'm saying really think it through, Ronan. You've been behind your damn wall for a long time. You have to stop letting what she did—what *they* did—"

I'd pinned him with a glare, a clear indicator he needed to shut up. He was a good enough friend to know he'd reached my limit, so he backed off.

Chapter Three

Keely

66 **I**'VE GOT SOME MORE BABY STUFF," MY SISTER announced in a singsong voice as she breezed into my apartment for yet another impromptu visit. There was a big box in her hands, and I barely contained a groan. My teeny-tiny studio apartment was damn near bursting at the seams. Having my sister load it to the gills with things for the baby she was carrying meant the walls were closing in on me.

There were boxes on top of boxes stacked everywhere—a few piles were darn near touching the ceiling. A car seat, stroller, some weird diaper trash can, cases of diapers, cases of formula, boxes of clothes and God only knew what else everywhere. It was hard for me to get around without bumping into a box. It looked a lot like I'd been holding up Babies 'R' Us delivery trucks in my spare time.

"I don't get why you're buying all of this when you're a surrogate," I said for at least the hundredth time in the last few months. My sister told me she was having a baby for a couple who were unable to carry a child to term. Her explanation raised red flags in my head left and right, but I knew better than to think I could

26

get the truth from her. The constant buying of clothing, baby toys, seats, diapers and every other manner of infant apparatus taking up space in my apartment was a pretty good indicator I was right to be suspicious. Something was fishy about the surrogacy thing.

Waving her hand through the air in a dismissive gesture, Izzy rolled her eyes dramatically. "I told you—the couple adopting her gives me money to buy all of this."

I didn't believe her for a second—no logical person would. My sister was a consummate liar, which meant I constantly kept my guard up around her. Izzy could sell toxic wasteland to an environmental group with a totally straight face and zero effect on her conscience. Lies came easier to her than truth, and they always had.

I was all but positive she was lying, and it annoyed me. She always treated me like I was daft. No matter what she said or how wild of a tale she'd been weaving, I wasn't stupid. It was highly improbable the couple adopting her baby was having her buy all of the things the baby would need. It didn't make any sense whatsoever.

"You don't think it's weird they have you buying everything?"

She set the last package where she wanted it before looking back over her shoulder at me crossly.

"It's not *weird*, it's nice. This is my way of playing a small part in the baby's life. It's all I get and I plan to enjoy it."

Every time Izzy made a comment to indicate affection for the child she carried, my heart broke a little bit. Other than Will, our dad, her mom and her best friend Tiffany, she never seemed to genuinely care about anyone.

"If you want to keep her, you should. You can still change your mind."

Dropping onto my recliner, she sat back, put her feet up and rubbed at her belly.

"I don't want to change my mind," she assured me.

No matter how many times she said she didn't want the baby, I didn't believe her. My sister hadn't done one selfless thing in her entire life. Whether she wanted to admit it to me or not, she felt something for the child she was carrying.

I sat down on the bed next to the recliner and set my hand on the arm of the chair. "Izzy…"

I startled when she put her hand on top of mine and squeezed gently. Izzy didn't do affection.

"It's okay, Kiki. This isn't just what I have to do—it's also what I want to do. I didn't come to this decision lightly."

It was a real moment—a *sister* moment. We'd never had one before, which made it special. I didn't trust Izzy—and many times I didn't like her—but deep down inside I'd always yearned for a real relationship with her.

I had to swallow past the lump in my throat in order to speak.

"I just want you to be sure. It's such a huge decision."

She stared at me intently for a few seconds, tilting her head to the side as she considered me.

"Would you give your baby up, Kiki?"

I stiffened and started to pull away.

"You don't want to hear what I would do," I answered.

Izzy went from simply laying her hand over mine to holding it firmly so I wouldn't pull away.

"I do want to know," she said. "Answer the question. Would you ever give up your baby?"

I didn't want to answer because it felt wrong. I wasn't trying to shame her for the decision she was making.

"I don't want—"

"Answer. Me," she commanded.

My shoulders slumped as I let out a heavy sigh.

"No. I have nothing but respect for anyone who makes the decision to help someone create a family, but I couldn't do it."

I startled when she put her free hand under my chin and lifted it up so I was looking at her.

"That isn't something to be ashamed of," she said quietly. "There are a lot of ways to show love. Letting go is one way—holding tight is another. You and I have always been on opposite ends of the spectrum. I wouldn't have expected this to be any different. When the time comes, you'll be a great mom."

Part of me was wondering what the heck was happening to my sister—pregnancy hormones, I assumed. The other half of me wanted to cry. I'd never known this side of her.

"You could be a good mom, too," I assured her. "If you made some changes."

"The *change* you would have me make isn't one I could live with," she said stiffly.

I braced myself for her anger. Things tended to go poorly when she went into defense mode. I was surprised when a few seconds passed without her tossing out a curse-filled rant. I stayed silent, waiting for her to say something else.

"We don't choose who we love, Kiki," she said calmly. "Will isn't perfect, but neither am I. No matter what goes on between us, I never feel as if he doesn't love me. I know, without a doubt, he does. Our love isn't the kind of thing you'd read about in a book, but it's the only thing I've ever been able to count on. He's mine and I'm his, forever."

I honestly had no idea *how* or why she loved Will. It's said everyone is deserving of love. I don't believe that to be true. Some people are just plain rotten, end of story. Will deserves a lot of things, but love isn't on the list. What he's earned is karmic retribution for the havoc he's wreaked. If my sister were smart, she would leave. Heck, she would've never started anything with him. He was never worthy of her time, much less her affection. He had it regardless because Izzy loved him to the point of insanity.

Izzy sat up straight in the recliner and let out a gasp. Grabbing my hand, she set it on her stomach.

"Kiki, she's moving! Do you feel it?"

My brows knitted together as I held my hand against Izzy's belly and waited. A few seconds went by—long enough for me to think nothing was going to happen. When I went to draw my hand away, I felt movement against my hand. My eyes flew up to meet Izzy's as I let out an excited squeak.

"Yes! I feel it!"

When I looked up at Izzy, her eyes were filled with tears.

"I know you don't get it, but it doesn't make it less true. This is me being a good mom," she said quietly. "I get to make this one decision and it's the most important of all. I've made a lot of shitty choices I'll have to live with forever, but this isn't like that. With this, I know I'm doing right. I'm hoping it counts for something."

I moved so fast to jump up and give her a hug I even surprised myself. Izzy and I didn't hug, but I felt the current situation called for it. Even more shocking, she hugged me back. I was just getting used to the feeling when she pulled back.

She set me back with her hand and then stood up.

She wrinkled up her nose as she gestured to my recliner. "That thing is just awful. Someone should burn it."

I knew changing the subject was her way of declaring the conversation to be over. I followed along behind her as she walked into the kitchen.

She headed for the fridge, opening it up and peering inside to the mostly empty shelves. Taking one of the small bottles of water on the bottom shelf, she twisted the cap off and took a sip before closing the door and turning back to me.

"I'm officially in the weekly doctor visit portion of the pregnancy," she announced. "I've got an appointment tomorrow. You should come with me."

It was then I understood what her show of affection was about. Whether she could admit it or not, Izzy was scared. Our sisterly bond might be weak, but I'd always been softhearted. I figured she needed someone capable of actual emotion, which was why she'd come to me.

I chewed at my lip as I pondered her request.

"What time?"

"Nine in the morning. Can you do it?"

I let out a relieved breath as I nodded. If she'd said any time after one in the afternoon I would've struggled to say yes. I'd gotten lucky and pulled a shift with overtime stocking hours and I really didn't want to walk away from that. Having my car die was a setback I hadn't anticipated. In order to be able to adhere to my plan, I needed to work as much as humanly possible.

"Great! I'll pick you up around eight thirty," she chirped enthusiastically. "Afterward we can go to Babies 'R' Us and pick out a bottle system. I can kill two birds with one stone and drop you off with the bottles so I don't need to make an extra trip."

I let out a groan as I looked around and tried to figure out where anything else could fit. Her house was three or four times the size of my apartment. I really didn't get why she kept bringing everything to me.

"Why are you keeping it here?" I questioned. "Why not keep it at your house?"

She laughed—a fake sound, which set my teeth on edge. After having shared a moment with her, I hated the fake version of her personality coming back.

"You know Will and his OCD. He couldn't have all of this laying around."

My body went rigid at the mention of his name and I forced myself to breathe. I knew a lot about Will. He was an asshole, a liar, a bully and a sick son of a bitch. However, I'd never seen any signs

31

of OCD.

"I don't think Will has OCD, Iz."

She brushed me off with a dismissive wave and then picked up her purse from the counter. "You don't know him well."

I'd venture to say I knew him pretty damn well—and a lot better than I'd ever wanted to. I knew him and I hated him. Nothing he did was for the benefit of anyone but himself. He treated Izzy like she was his territory and she did everything he told her to, and then some. It was insanity the way they stayed together. Their relationship was obviously dysfunctional and utterly contaminated—but neither could or would let the other go, no matter what.

It drove me nuts, but it wasn't like I got a vote. Izzy and I weren't the type of sisters who did the whole heart to heart talk thing. How could we, when she would never miss an opportunity to remind everyone who would listen I was just her *half* sister?

We'd been doomed from the beginning to have a crappy relationship. Izzy's mom was my father's first wife. Estelle, or Ettie as she was called, was an angry, bitter woman, to say the least. When I was about six years old, she hitched her wagon to a cross-country trucker and left town without any real warning. Her contact with Izzy once she left town was sporadic at best and the lack of contact caused Izzy's behavioral issues to escalate. By the time Izzy was graduating high school, Ettie had been out of touch for at least three years.

Izzy always had issues with my mom—Ettie saw to that by swearing up and down dad had been having an affair with my mother before he left Ettie. It was not true—my parents hadn't even met until a year after the divorce—but Ettie and facts weren't acquainted with one another. It was clear the apple hadn't fallen far from the tree because Izzy didn't deal in facts either.

Since Ettie was such a wretched bitch about my mom, Izzy followed suit. She was an absolute nightmare to my mother from the minute she met her. Dad said Izzy had always been tough—she wouldn't be forced to do anything she didn't want to do, and this included being nice. For my mom's sake, he'd ground Izzy, spank her, and at one point, even put her in therapy. None of it did a damn thing about her attitude toward my mom, and it didn't genuinely improve her attitude toward me, either. I blamed a lot of it on my dad—yes, he made all the right noises about Izzy needing to behave, but the rubber never met the road. Next to my mom, Izzy was the person my dad loved best.

Despite her abysmal behavior, she didn't hate our dad. In fact, she worshiped him. There was tension between them when my mom was alive—mostly because Dad kept trying to get Izzy to behave. But once my mom died, everything was right as rain with them again. Dad dropped all pretense of disciplining Izzy, so they'd gotten along like a house on fire.

It sucked for me because watching them get along as well as they did was depressing. Dad was the master at avoiding me after Mom died, which made me feel completely unwanted. I knew he'd done so because I looked like my mom and it upset him, but it hadn't hurt any less to understand it. Izzy practically ate it up with a spoon, never failing to rub her status as the favorite in my face.

Izzy was the adored and doted upon daughter, while I was second string. The only common ground Izzy and I ever shared was Dad. Once he was gone, so too was our tenuous connection. After Dad died, I was forced to live with Izzy and Will for eight God-awful weeks. I was supposed to stay with them until I was eighteen and a high school graduate—but I'd escaped long before that. I wound up renting a room in the home of an elderly woman I found via an ad on Craigslist. It wasn't exactly legal, seeing as I was a minor, but it was far preferable to staying at Will and Izzy's.

What I'd learned during my stay was that Will was a monster and my sister was his enabler. He'd turned her into someone it hurt to look at, but she didn't want to change. She'd attempted to keep their secret from me, but Will had shown me the truth with glee. After he did, I couldn't get out fast enough. Once I left, I knew I wouldn't be hearing much from my sister. Whether she could voice it or not, she had been ashamed.

To be blunt, I didn't want to hear from her. Instead of going to college, I went to full-time at my job as a cashier in the local supermarket. During my senior year I'd worked twenty hours a week in order to save money, so I'd been close to full time to begin with. It left me without a pot to piss in, but with more hours and a small raise, I made enough to get a tiny apartment and have some left over. I then got busy putting as much money aside as I could to get myself the hell out of Fort Collins. My plan to leave was taking forever to implement, but every paycheck got me a little closer.

Almost a year and a half went by without any contact after I left Izzy's house. Out of the clear blue, one day she started texting and calling me. I was understandably quite hesitant to answer her calls and texts. I couldn't imagine any scenario where my sister would make contact that wouldn't involve her or her husband doing something shitty to me. She knew damn well I didn't want to see Will, so the fact she kept trying to get in touch didn't bode well. We lacked a familial bond and I didn't see it ever being any different.

The bottom line was my sister was not there for me, ever. I knew it and accepted it, so I'm not sure I ever would have answered her calls if the choice were left up to me. I lost the option to decide whether to deal with her or not when she showed up at my apartment one night.

I'd been in the process of telling her to leave when she lifted her shirt and showed me her ever so slightly rounded stomach. I'd been surprised. Hell, I'd been beyond shocked, if I was honest. It wasn't any kind of a secret that Will didn't want children. I couldn't believe he'd changed his mind.

Of course, once she explained she was merely acting as a surrogate in order to make money, it made more sense.

At least, I thought it had.

My head was pounding and I didn't know where I was or how I got there. Everything around me was pitch black and covered in a thick layer of fog. I stumbled forward with my hands held out in front of me in an attempt to find something to hold onto.

"Dammit," my sister hollered. "I need you here with me right now! I can't drive like this. Tell your dumb bitch of a neighbor to give you a ride and get here now!"

My heart started beating funny—hummingbird fast—as my stomach roiled in panic. I didn't want to go to her house. She knew it, too.

"Please," I whimpered.

"You have no choice! I need help, Kiki!"

I wanted to say no, but nothing happened when I opened my mouth. I shut my eyes for a second and tried to calm down. When I opened them, I was still unable to see anything around me. Everything was gray.

"It's fine." Izzy said from somewhere very close to me. "He's busy. We can go now."

"Izzy? I hear you, but I can't see you! Where are you?"

"I need to go to the fucking hospital! Get in the car. I need to push. Drive me, goddamn it!"

So much for the nicer, softer version of my sister.

"What car? Izzy! Why can't I see you?"

I spun helplessly in a circle, still unable to see anything at all other than the fog and the dark. Something bad was coming. I wanted to run, but my feet didn't move.

And then, I heard the one person I'd hoped never to be near again.

"Fucking bitch! I knew you were going to try to get away! I'll carve you like a fucking pumpkin before I let you leave me!"

I shivered uncontrollably at the sound of Will's slurred voice. My brother-in-law was evil with a side of crazy. Nothing good ever happened when he was close by.

"Please honey," I heard Izzy begging from what sounded like a faraway place. "I have to go to the hospital. I'm not leaving you. Not now, not ever. Let me go and I'll be back."

"You want some fucking help?"

"It's why she's here," I heard Izzy say. "You know this."

"What I know is this fucking stinks like bullshit," he slurred. "I'm not fucking stupid, Isabelle."

"Honey—"

"Move the fuck over," Will spat angrily. "I'm driving. Let's get this little runt out of you so we can get back to normal. I want my wife back."

I tried to yell no, but nothing would come out of my mouth. I couldn't see him, but I was able to hear how drunk he was.

"You've always had me," Izzy answered. "Just let me go deliver the baby and it will all go back to normal," Izzy assured him. "I've got this. I'll come right back home after it's over."

"You don't move the fuck over, you're not getting out of this driveway alive," Will yelled. "You don't get to leave me, Isabelle. I'll fucking cut your heart out right here before I let you go."

"Honey—"

"Move. Over."

I needed to run. Getting into a car with him was a death sentence. I didn't get a chance to run. Izzy was suddenly right up on me, shoving me into the back seat. When I tried to scramble out of the car, she pushed me back in.

"Stay with me," she pleaded. "You have to be there!"

I tried to scream to get her neighbors' attention, but my mouth was still not producing sound. We were headed for disaster, and I knew it. My stomach churned as I felt the car weaving back and forth on the road. Will needed to stop the car before something really bad happened.

"Think you're so fucking clever," Will slurred from the front seat. "Think you're going to get away from me now. You think wrong, Isabelle. The little baby bitch isn't going to ruin my life. You're mine! Been mine for a long fuckin' time. I'll never let you go and I won't share you with a fucking kid."

"I would never leave you, and you won't have to share me because we won't see her after this," Izzy assured him. "I love you, honey."

I heard the sound of skin hitting skin, and I knew my sister had been slapped. Will always liked to talk with his hands.

"Think I'm fucking dumb?" he raged. "Think I was going to let this happen? I told you to get rid of it, Izzy. Told you the devil was in your belly. You didn't listen because you NEVER fucking listen. This is your fault! Gave me no fucking choice. I'm taking you to hell with me. It's where we belong. Together, forever. Won't breathe a fuckin' day on this earth without me."

Everything suddenly snapped into focus and became crystal clear. Izzy looked back over her shoulder at me. The expression on her face seemed as if she'd been expecting something terrible to happen all along. As we stared at each other, I heard the car accelerate. I grabbed onto the side of Izzy's seat to hold myself steady.

Her face softened as she looked at me and nodded.

"This isn't what I thought would happen. I thought I'd made a deal... I'm sorry—"

Before she finished speaking, we went airborne. The sound of metal twisting and glass shattering was almost deafening, but it was the pitch of my sister's scream that scared me the most.

I tried to reach out for her, but my arm felt like it was on fire, and my head was throbbing more painfully than ever. There was a chemical-like acrid stench mixed with the coppery scent of blood. Both were so overwhelming I needed to swallow past the bile inching up the back of my throat in order to continue breathing.

I was jammed on the floor of the backseat between the passenger and rear seats, unable to move. My right arm was trapped between the door and the spot where I had my hand clutched onto Izzy's seat when Will hit the gas. I couldn't see her face, but I could see Will's head was on his shoulders wrong—turned more to the side than what should have been possible. His eyes were open, but vacant. The eyes of the dead, I realized.

I startled when I heard the sound of my voice rasping Izzy's name. I could talk! She didn't answer, but I could hear her taking shallow breaths. I said her name again as I wondered if she was unconscious.

"Thought...he would let... you take her... I really... am... sorry...."

*Her words sent a chill up my spine. There were many things I wanted to say, but I couldn't get any of them. What did she mean she thought he would let **me** take her?*

*"Promise... me," she whispered slowly. "The baby, please... tell... her... I did... love her. You need... to...do this... **for her,"** she emphasized. "Do you promise?"*

I felt sicker than ever as I realized what she thought was happening. Will was dead—Izzy could finally be free, even if she didn't understand how badly she needed to be away from him. I was certain help was coming—she just needed to hold on.

"Don't let go, Izzy," I pleaded desperately. "Don't leave me. He's gone! You can do anything you want now."

"I don't want... to live... I can't... **be** without Will. This... is a job... for you."

"Please, Izzy—"

"Promise me... now," she rasped.

"I promise, but the adoptive parents—"

"Look in... diaper bag."

I didn't know what to make of anything. My brain felt like it was full of rocks. I was scared shitless, and I didn't want my sister to die.

"She's your baby Izzy. Keep breathing and you can take care of her," I choked out brokenly. "You need to try," I said as firmly as I could.

"YOU... are... my... try."

"Izzy!"

"Will needs... me now."

"No! Stay here!"

Suddenly there was bright light surrounding us. I was able to hear what sounded like dozens of voices.

"... Won't survive if we don't get it out now."

"Can't believe she's still alive at all—"

"There's no time!"

"She's fading fast ..."

"...Heartbeat?"

"This one is completely out of it. Just missed an artery—"

"She's out!"

I couldn't breathe past the boulder, which seemed to be lodged in my throat. It was all wrong, so damn wrong. I felt cold and scared, and I couldn't figure out what was happening all around me.

Once again, I was floating through the darkness. After a while it dawned on me—I wasn't awake. I'd been dreaming about what already happened. My sister, I realized, was dead. I wondered why I wasn't waking up. Was I dead and trapped in some sort of purgatory?

I started to panic—and then I heard Izzy's voice, strong and

clear as a bell.
    "Wake up and keep your promise."

Chapter Four

Ronan

THE HOURS TICKED OFF SLOWLY AS I ALTERNATED BETWEEN prowling the room restlessly or sitting and staring at Keely's face while I held her good hand. It made no sense at all, but I'd been compelled to touch her. It was as though I couldn't stand not to be physically connected to her in some way.

The doctor and several nurses were in and out of the room what felt like a thousand times, and each time they indicated she was closer to waking up. By the time I got to the six-hour mark of sitting beside her bed, I'd lost faith in their word. I was glad Dr. Smith was pulling a twenty-four-hour shift because the care was consistent. Every time he came in, he reassured me Keely was closer to waking up. He said she would come to when her body was ready.

"Her mind just shut down," he informed me. "When you go into shock, the mind does what it needs to do."

His reassurances helped but the fact she wasn't waking up was making me nuts. I'd been trying to work up the balls to get my ass down to the NICU to see the baby. I was so focused on waiting until Keely woke up, but by then I realized it sure didn't look like it was going to go down the way I wanted it to. And then, as I was sitting forward to get up and go see the baby, Keely started making noises of distress. It got me up and out of the chair in a heartbeat, hanging over her anxiously as I waited for her to wake up.

She mumbled Izzy's name several times as she raised her arm as if to reach for something. I pressed the button for the nurse and then set my hand gently on her so she couldn't move her arm around anymore. I did this because I knew it was going to hurt like a bitch when she woke up, and her moving it around wasn't a good thing for an arm that was already fucked up.

I knew when she was awake and alert Chuck was going to tell her what happened, and I wasn't looking forward to having to see her reaction. When her eyes started to flutter open, I felt as much anxiety as I did relief.

The nurse came in around the fifth time Keely opened her eyes. Each time, she kept them open for a second or so before closing them again. It was obvious she was struggling to wake up. I wanted to stay right at her side, but the nurse and then the doctor each took a side of her bed, forcing me to retreat to the bathroom doorway at the side of the room. My heart slammed against my chest as I listened to them talking to her.

"Keely, I'm Dr. Smith and this is Nurse Davies. You're in the hospital—"

I damn near fell over when Keely interrupted him and choked out, "Baby?"

Her throat sounded like it was full of sandpaper. As the doctor answered her, Nurse Davies gave her a sip of water. Keely's eyes never left Dr. Smith's face. It was weird watching such a private moment when I knew she didn't have a clue I was there.

"She's temporarily in the NICU," Dr. Smith answered. "She'll be moved out soon."

Pulling away from the straw, she whispered, "How long was I out?"

"Almost sixteen hours," he answered.

"I need to see my niece," she said. "She needs someone to be there. With my sister gone—" Her voice was weak, but she'd said it pretty damn emphatically, all things considered.

It was clear she remembered whatever happened in the car. I wondered how long she'd been alert after impact. Obviously it was long enough to know her sister was gone.

"As soon as we check you over and get you up and moving a bit," Dr. Smith interrupted. "I'll allow Mr. Sharpe to take you to the nursery."

Keely lost every ounce of what little color she'd acquired since waking as her eyes rounded in clear terror. I wasn't close to her, yet even from across the room I could see she was trembling. The heart rate monitor she'd been wearing as a precaution jacked right up, too.

"He's alive?"

It was very clear she needed reassurance. I stepped forward quickly, appreciating the nurse stepping back in order to allow Keely a clear view of me.

"No, Keely," I reassured her as calmly as I could. It was hard to restrain my anger right then. Had my brother survived, shit would've gotten real between the two of us. What the fuck had he done to terrify her so badly?

"He's gone, sweetheart. When Dr. Smith said Mr. Sharpe, he meant me."

Her already widened eyes damn near bugged out as she looked at me. I swallowed past the Sahara, which sprung up inside my mouth the instant our gazes locked. I tried to put it down to exhaustion, but the way her aqua-colored eyes studied me caused a sensation I imagined was the equivalent of holding a live wire. All my emotional fuses were being blown to smithereens while all she was doing was fucking looking at me.

I reminded myself of her age and did my best to shake off the crazy desire I experienced to pull her into my arms. Contrary to the way I'd been acting since arriving at the hospital—spending hours at her beside all while holding her hand—I wasn't a tactile guy. I especially wasn't tactile with teenagers. Ever.

"Ronan?" she questioned huskily. The sound went right to my dick, a reaction that mortified me, given the circumstances. She'd been awake for five seconds and I was eying her up like she was on a runway. It was fucked up.

When I didn't answer immediately—mostly due to the fact I wasn't sure I could coherently string words together, she spoke again.

"Are you really here?"

She asked like she expected me to evaporate in a poof of smoke. I guess turning up after five years without a word was pretty shocking.

I approached her bed like the floor of the room was littered with landmines. For hours, I'd been willing her to wake up. Once she did, I was faced with something other than the girl I remembered. Sure, while she was asleep I'd been able to see she was a fucking knockout. But when she woke up and started talking, my memory of her as a child evaporated into the reality of her as she was—which was a woman.

She never took her eyes off of me as I crossed the room. The young girl I remembered would have blushed and looked away nervously. The new version of Keely was unashamedly curious about me.

When I got back to her bedside, I dropped back down onto the seat I'd occupied for endless hours since I'd arrived. I did this not because I needed to sit, but because I was having trouble controlling my response to her. Another minute or so of eye contact and I was fairly certain my dick would've busted out of the zipper of my pants.

"I'm really here," I assured her hoarsely. "Got the call from Chief West late last night and I flew in as soon as I could."

Her eyebrows shot up in confusion. "Why?"

It stung like a fucking bitch when she asked. I wondered if she thought I'd turned out like Will.

Cold. Uncaring. Monstrous.

"Chuck called and told me to get my ass here," I explained. "You were out, and they wanted someone to be here to make decisions for the baby, just in case..."

Her good arm shot out lightning fast and she grabbed onto my wrist. My skin tingled where she gripped me.

"But... she's okay, right? The doctor said—"

"The baby is good," I assured her.

She let out a sigh of relief but didn't let go of my arm as she stared at me. I thought her eyes fucked with my head, but it was nothing compared to her touch. I tried putting it all down to needing some fucking sleep, but it sure as fuck didn't feel like it was a one time feeling. Exhaustion and emotional stress were making me feel things that weren't real. At least I damn sure hoped so.

"Tell me what she looks like," she implored softly.

It was like being thrown into an ice-cold lake wearing cement shoes. She would undoubtedly be unhappy with my answer, and I wasn't okay with letting her down.

"Haven't gone to see her," I admitted gruffly, avoiding having to look into her eyes. "I felt you were the priority, so I stayed here."

She inhaled sharply as she yanked her hand back. I immediately missed her touch.

"She's a baby who needs love and she's all alone in the world. You should have gone to see her!"

45

Her tone made her disapproval clear. If there were any doubt, the appalled expression on her face when I looked up would've cleared it up for me. It made me feel shame about my actions or lack thereof.

I didn't have a chance to respond since Dr. Smith started speaking. I was not upset with the interruption. If anything, I felt I owed him one.

"Keely, I need some time to evaluate you," he said calmly. "After I've cleared you, I'll allow Mr. Sharpe to take you to the nursery. I'll let Chief West know you're awake. I know he'll want to speak to you, but I'm going to suggest he do it tomorrow. "

Gesturing my way he continued, "Mr. Sharpe, please wait out in the lounge while we finish up here."

I saw no sense in disagreeing, seeing as how I knew Keely was disappointed in me. I needed to get away and fast. Knowing I'd let her down didn't make me feel good—in fact, I felt like a shit sandwich with a side of rotten fries. At twenty-six years old, I should've been able to ball up in order to see the kid. I could admit it to myself, at least. It wasn't as though I didn't have a good amount of time to sit there and berate myself about what a pussy I was, too. It was at least thirty or so minutes later when Nurse Davies came and got me from the lounge.

"Miss Carmichael is in the wheelchair and ready to go. She's clear to spend fifteen minutes with the baby, and not a minute more. She needs her rest."

I raised a brow in confusion seeing as how she'd been asleep for damn near twenty-four hours.

"Even though she was out for almost a day, her body is exhausted," Nurse Davies explained. "Don't be alarmed if she falls asleep before the visit in the nursery is over. Only pure determination is keeping her up right now."

"Should she even go?"

"If you're asking if it will hurt her, the answer is no. Normally we wouldn't consider letting someone get up this soon after waking up, but in this case, Dr. Smith is making an exception. It will help her to see the child."

At least one of us would get something positive out of it.

Chapter Five

Keely

THERE WAS TOO MUCH HAPPENING FOR ME TO MAKE SENSE
of anything. I was out of my mind worried about the baby,
but I couldn't stop thinking about the last few moments of
my sister's life. My memories of the crash seemed like a dream and
I wasn't certain I could trust them. Had Izzy and I actually spoken
as much as I thought? I couldn't be sure. I felt as if we did, but I
couldn't be positive. I tried to remember everything I could, but
the memories came and went before I could really comprehend
them.

On top of it all, Ronan was back. The shock I felt when I saw
him wasn't only surprise to see him in my hospital room, not to
mention Fort Collins. I thought I was long over my teenage infatu-
ation with him, but the way my heart skipped a dozen beats when
he'd walked toward my hospital bed told another story entirely. It
left me on my ass. I was lucky I was already lying down because if
I hadn't been, I think I'd have fallen.

After they got me into the wheelchair and the nurse left to get
Ronan, I found myself wondering how bad I looked. Almost six-

teen hours in la-la land and no shower upon waking was a pretty good indicator I wasn't at my best. Normally this would not have bothered me at all, but I hated Ronan seeing me look so broken down.

Eventually, I forced those thoughts right out of my mind. The bottom line was I couldn't do a damn thing about it. Also, him spending countless hours at my bedside meant he already saw me at my worst. I was thankful, however, when Nurse Davies helped me brush my teeth with a disposable toothbrush. It wasn't as though I had a choice about looking like crap, but at least I didn't have bad breath on top of it.

I was sitting in the wheelchair when he came back into the room with the nurse. My breath caught as I took him in for the first time in five years. He'd been gorgeous the last time I'd seen him, but the years added something to his appeal. His boyish cuteness wasn't there anymore—Ronan was all sexy *man*.

My eyes wandered over the tattoos covering his left arm, and I wondered when he'd started getting inked. Whenever it was, it was a good move. The tattoos were sexy and added to his appeal. The clean cut twenty-one year old I remembered gave way to a man with sexy written all over him.

My eyes flew up to meet his when he cleared his throat. Realizing I'd been busted ogling him, I forced myself to shrug it off instead of looking away meekly.

I was thankful he didn't call me on it. Instead he asked, "You ready to see her?"

My answer was a resounding yes, with one caveat.

"Do you have a cell phone with you?"

His brows knitted together as he nodded. Patting his back pocket he answered, "Yeah, right here. What's up?"

"Will you take pictures of her when we get there? I don't even know where my phone is at this point, so—"

Reaching out, he touched my shoulder gently. "I got it," he assured me. "Don't worry about a thing."

I was nervous and excited as we made our way to the NICU. The nurse pushed my wheelchair as Ronan walked alongside. No words were spoken along the way, but I could see his tension. I naturally assumed this was because he didn't want to see the baby. Clearly the fact he hadn't made any effort during the hours he'd been at the hospital before I woke up spoke volumes about his frame of mind.

We came to a halt in a sterile looking room outside of the NICU. There were sinks lining one wall. Nurse Davies opened a packet, which contained a bar of hand soap with bristles on one side. Reaching out, she handed it to Ronan as she instructed him to scrub his hands for at least sixty seconds. She pushed my chair forward to the handicapped sink, opening a bar of soap to wash my one free hand. She then helped Ronan into a gown before she put shower caps and gloves on each of us.

"This level of precaution is less for your niece than it is the other babies in the unit. You'll see everyone in there is dressed the same."

After she enlightened us about what to expect, she attached identification bracelets to my hand and Ronan's as well.

"The baby has one too," Nurse Davies explained. "It's for security reasons."

We both nodded our heads in understanding, neither of us asking any additional questions. As we got to the entrance of the NICU, it all hit me. My hand—the one not tucked in the brace keeping my entire right arm immobile—started shaking as the nurse pushed the wheelchair through the sliding glass doors. I was about to meet my niece. I'd seen her ultrasound photos and had felt her kick in my sister's stomach, but knowing I was about to touch her for the first time was huge.

As I looked around and saw several small incubators, my eyes filled with tears. Almost all were decorated with hearts, pictures, prayer cards, rosaries, and mementos. To my left, I saw a man and a woman hunched over one of the more decorated units, talking softly to the tiniest baby I'd ever seen. Across the room there was an elderly woman—likely a grandmother—rocking a baby back and forth. The baby in her arms was hooked up to what looked like a half-dozen tubes. The fragility of the infants I was seeing hit me hard, and I said a silent prayer for them. As sterile as the room was—because it needed to be—there was a lot of heart in it. Signs of family, hope and love were blended into the sterile hospital atmosphere. It was overwhelming how many tiny lives hung in the balance in one room.

A new nurse came walking toward us with great purpose. When she got closer I recognized her as being Canter West's older sister. I hadn't seen her in years, and I knew she wouldn't remember me at all, but I wasn't surprised at her career choice since I knew she'd been a volunteer at the hospital while she was in high school. I knew this because I'd seen her several times toward the end of my mom's final hospital stay.

She greeted Ronan first. "Hey, stranger. Glad to see you again—sorry it's under these circumstances."

The look of affection on his face as he smiled at her caused me to feel a wave of jealousy.

"Thanks. It's good to see you, Kristi. I was relieved when Canter told me you were one of the nurses."

I plastered a fake smile on my face when he gestured to me. "Kristi, this is Keely Carmichael. Keely, this is Kristi West."

She shook her head at him as she laughed softly. "I'm Kristi Harrison now."

My jealousy abated immediately. She was off the market, which was good. It shouldn't have mattered to me, yet it did. It wasn't like Ronan and I were—well, anything at all.

"Oh yeah," Ronan chuckled. "Guess I gotta get used to the changes around here."

"Guess so," she agreed. Looking at me, she smiled. "Hi, Keely. You ready to meet your niece?"

"I am," I said nervously.

"Follow me," she instructed.

Nurse Davies began rolling me forward again, and my eyes flitted around the room as I tried to figure out which baby was my niece. My focus narrowed down dramatically when the wheelchair stopped moving. I found myself in front of a machine with what looked like some kind of sun lamp at the top and a clear bassinet at the middle.

"This is a radiant warmer," Kristi explained. "It's not on because she doesn't need it. Since she's not hooked up to monitors anymore either, the doctor will be having her transferred down to the maternity nursery in the morning."

It was the best news I could have hoped for. Just knowing she was going to be okay took a huge weight off of my shoulders.

I sat up straight and tried to peer into the bassinet, but I couldn't see the baby's face at all—she was all swaddled up. All I wanted was to hold her, but I knew it wasn't a possibility with my one arm out of commission.

"Ronan, you'll need to sit in this rocker," Kristi instructed. "I'll hand the baby to you and then wheel Keely forward. She can't hold her with her arm the way it is, but with you holding her, she'll be able to touch her."

His eyes darn near bugged out of his head. "I don't—hold her? Me?" he sputtered. "Shouldn't you do it? You're the nurse!"

He'd sounded as if Kristi told him he was going to cuddle with a live grenade.

"No, you big baby," Kristi answered sternly. "She's your responsibility which means you're going to need to man up. Take a seat in the rocker."

He grasped at straws. "I can't do it," he said. "I promised Keely I'd take pictures—"

"Not gonna happen, genius. Give your phone to me and I'll take the pictures."

I was in awe of Kristi for being such a ballbuster. I had no clue why Ronan was so reticent to see and touch the baby, but I wasn't in any position to do everything myself which meant he needed to get over it.

He pulled his phone from his back pocket, handing it to Kristi before he dropped on to the chair she pointed to without further comment. I noted he looked a little green, and I could clearly see his forehead was suddenly a little shiny. I couldn't believe Ronan Sharpe was afraid of an infant. He was an unbelievably attractive man who definitely looked as if he could handle himself, but he was terrified of a baby. It was certainly unexpected.

After setting the phone down on the counter next to her, Kristi went to get the baby. As she reached into the bassinet to pick the baby up, I got Ronan's attention by touching his hand.

"You're going to be fine," I assured him.

I saw his throat moving as he swallowed and then nodded. "Yeah," he said weakly. Another swallow followed by a stronger, "Yeah—I'm okay."

When Kristi brought the baby toward Ronan, I caught sight of some spiky dark hair. The baby wiggled in Kristi's arms, letting out a frustrated cry about being disturbed.

"It's okay little one," Kristi crooned softly.

"Shouldn't we wait?" Ronan interjected in a panicked voice. "She doesn't seem happy right now. You hold her or put her back until she's quiet again. She's telling us this isn't a good time for her."

Kristi laughed at him as she shook her head. "Oh my God,

Ronan! You're killing me here. Babies cry, dummy. She'll be fine. Right now, she needs to meet her family. Hold out your arms and I'll settle her in," she instructed.

The baby started wailing louder, making her anger at being moved around quite obvious. Unlike Ronan, the cry caused me no alarm. Instead, I was relieved. She had a good set of healthy-sounding lungs, which wasn't a bad thing at all.

I held my breath as Kristi laid the baby into Ronan's arms. He looked so overwhelmed I feared he was going to have a panic attack. I felt terrible since I was physically unable to hold her myself. The pitch of her cry escalated, which was definitely making his anxiety worse. I fully expected him to throw in the towel right away. Instead, he surprised me—and probably himself, too.

There was a moment where it looked like he was going to hand her right back. He went so far as to look up at Kristi imploringly as the baby wailed loudly and wiggled inside the blanket she was swaddled in. Instead of letting him give up, Kristi shook her head at him and raised her shoulders before grabbing his cell phone and bringing up the camera.

"I've got pictures to take, so pull out your tampon and man up," she instructed him matter-of-factly.

He glared at her for a second or two, probably expecting her to cave in and help. She laughed as she took photos, completely ignoring his annoyance. She was stubborn and not about to cave in. Realizing no one was going to step in to save him from the screaming baby in his arms, he maneuvered her closer to his chest, right over his heart.

"Hey, baby girl," he said softly. "You're okay. I've got you."

She stopped crying immediately. It was so abrupt I leaned forward in my wheelchair in a panic because I was worried she'd passed out from crying. My heart stopped beating for a few moments when I saw her face for the first time. She hadn't passed out at all—she was wide-awake and totally alert, staring up at Ronan intently. She was the most perfectly beautiful child I'd ever seen. Her mouth was a perfect little Cupid's kiss, her cheeks round and rosy. Continuing to stare at Ronan, she opened her mouth. I assumed she was about to start crying again, but instead she let out an adorable little yawn as she tried to snuggle closer to him.

"What a surprise," Kristi snorted. "You've still got a way with the ladies."

Ronan never took his eyes off the baby as he shook his head in denial. "I think she's just tired," he answered.

She didn't look tired to me. She was alert and busy studying Ronan like there might have been a test afterward.

I leaned in closer, running my finger across her cheek. I hated wearing gloves since it left me unable to feel her skin. Ronan maneuvered to the edge of his chair so I could see her better. Unhappy with being moved from her position against his chest, she let out a sound of distress.

"It's okay sweetheart," I said softly.

It was beautiful the way she stopped crying as her head shifted around so she could look at me. I smiled at her lovingly, and my heart melted when she let out an adorable little coo.

"What a beautiful picture," Kristi said happily.

I couldn't wait to look at them later. Right then, I was too busy getting my fill of the baby.

Looking up at Ronan I said, "Can you bring her closer so I can kiss her?"

He came in close, so close I could feel his cheek against mine as we both stared down at the baby. For a few moments, I felt like I was in a bubble of safety—just Ronan, the baby and me. I knew Kristi was still taking pictures, but it didn't interrupt what felt like our private moment.

"Isn't she beautiful?" I whispered to him.

He was silent for a second before he let out a cough. "Yeah," he said gruffly. "She's real pretty."

She looked so content staring back and forth between the two of us. When he lifted her closer to my face, I gave her forehead a kiss before I nuzzled against her cheek and inhaled.

My voice was soft as I murmured, "My God, this smell could be bottled."

Ronan leaned in closer and looked at me like I was having a stroke.

"Smell? What smell? There's no smell in here other than hospital disinfectant."

I heard Kristi mumble, "Clueless," as I struggled not to laugh.

She was right—he obviously knew nothing about babies.

"Smell her little head," I instructed.

He pulled back a little as he raised an eyebrow at me as though I were six doughnuts short of a dozen. I smiled at him as I gestured toward the baby with my head.

"Trust me," I said.

He leaned back in close so he could run his nose against her hairline. His head came up a second later, and he turned to me with a look of surprise.

"She smells like—" he paused for a second, swallowing before he spoke again. I wondered what he'd been about to say.

A few seconds passed and then he mumbled, "You're right. She smells good."

I smiled, happy he 'got' it. We each turned our attention back to her. Ronan held her securely as I traced my fingers over her face and enjoyed the moment. I hadn't seen him in years, yet as we sat there looking at the baby, I couldn't help but wish we were her family.

A few minutes passed and then, completely out of the blue, Ronan asked, "Did they have a name picked out for her?"

I shook my head. "Izzy said she was a surrogate."

Ronan was not in any way happy with my answer. He went tense all over as a look of thunderous rage crossed his face.

"You're saying there's a chance someone they chose is going to come in here and take her? We won't have a say in it?"

I shook my head and shrugged my good shoulder. "I don't know how true the surrogate story was. She kept buying stuff for her and storing it at my apartment—none of what she said added up. I don't even know how to go about finding the truth," I said.

"I'll talk to Chuck," he responded firmly. "There's no way we're handing her off to some fucked up assholes. She needs real parents. I wouldn't trust Will and Izzy to—"

He stopped abruptly, pulling back from me with a look of guilt. "I'm sorry," he said. "I shouldn't have said—"

"Trust me," I answered. "I know just what you mean. Don't censor yourself – it's not as if I don't have the same feelings."

It was easy to see he was relieved.

"I'm glad we can talk to each other," he said.

I nodded once and then watched as he returned to staring at the baby. He seemed fascinated.

"While we wait for answers," he murmured, "she should have a name. Can't have her being the only baby in the nursery without one. It isn't okay."

I knew he was right—she absolutely needed a name. I stared at her for a few moments before looking back up at him. "What should we name her?"

He didn't answer for about a minute, instead staring down at the baby almost as if he were willing her to say what name she wanted. Naturally, she didn't do so. Finally, he looked up at me and said, "I can't think of anything good enough for her. You got any ideas?"

What I wanted to name her came to me in a split second, and I felt a flush spreading over my cheeks as it did. In addition to having the mother of all crushes on Ronan when he lived in Fort Collins, I'd also had a rich fantasy life. It was my escape, the place I went to when life was chaotic. My dreams included planning our wedding and choosing names for our future children. Of course, he didn't know about my dreams. But right then, the name I'd chosen as a young teenage girl for our daughter was right there on my lips.

"Emma," I said softly.

He looked away from me and back down to the baby. After staring at her for a few seconds, he nodded.

"A beautiful name for a beautiful girl. It fits you, baby girl. You're an Emma."

The way she stared up at him, it was as if she got it and agreed. Like she understood it was a big moment. I swallowed past the lump in my throat, willing the gathering tears in my eyes not to fall.

"Hold her up so I can get some pictures of the three of you," Kristi instructed.

We smiled for the camera a few times before Kristi stepped away. I couldn't stop looking at Emma's beautiful little face. I wanted to stay there forever. I was sad when Nurse Davies spoke up from behind me.

"Doctor's orders, Keely. We need to get you back. You'll be able to see her again in a few hours."

I nodded my head in understanding, even though I hated to go. "Lift her so I can kiss her again."

Once she was up at my lips, I dropped soft kisses on her face. "I'll be back, Emma. I love you."

She made another soft little coo sound, which made me even more emotional. I wanted to stay and spend time with her, but I knew Nurse Davies was right. Even though I didn't want to admit it, I was exhausted. My arm also ached badly and it was making me nauseous. I needed to go back to my room.

When Ronan handed Emma off to Kristi so he could go back with me, she protested immediately. Her angry cry pierced the room as Kristi tried to calm her.

Looking at Ronan, I could see he was torn. It was obvious he didn't want Emma to be upset, but he felt obligated to go with me.

"You should stay with her," I told him over the sound of Emma wailing. "Once I get back to the room, they're going to give me a pain pill, and I'll be out. She needs you right now."

The relieved expression on his face warmed my heart. He cared. I suspected he hadn't wanted to, but it was clear he did.

"Are you sure?"

"Yes," I answered honestly. "I'll feel better knowing she's happy."

"Alright—then I'll stay until she falls asleep. Afterward, I'll come back to your room to check on you. I'll need to give Chuck a call so we can get the ball rolling on getting to the bottom of this surrogate thing."

"Sounds good."

He took Emma back from Kristi, and once again, she stopped crying immediately. I let out a relieved breath, relaxing into the wheelchair as Nurse Davies started pulling me backward. Ronan and I stared at each other silently up until the moment when the nurse turned my chair and wheeled me away. I was so exhausted I nodded off before we even got out of the NICU.

Chapter Six

Ronan

THE CLOSER WE'D GOTTEN TO THE NURSERY, THE MORE certain I was I wanted no part of the whole meet the baby thing. I knew there was no other choice but to go through with it since Keely needed support, but I was deep into the process of writing the experience off. I didn't want to be there and I sure as hell didn't want to be involved.

My certainty lasted right up until the moment Kristi put the baby in my arms. When the tiny baby went from crying her little lungs out to silent in a nanosecond as she stared at me with those big, dark, blue eyes. I hadn't wanted to attach at all. I was positive it wouldn't be an issue. But the way the baby looked at me—like I was someone she felt safe with, which made it my job to protect her—was like a deep kick to my heart.

I was completely thrown by the way the baby seemed to know me. I wasn't sure if I was having such a reaction because I was fucked in the head where Keely was concerned, and then a baby got added to the mix. I tried to tell myself my emotions were right at the surface due to Will's death and the exhaustion, but it felt like bullshit to me. Whatever it was I was feeling about my brother's death, it wasn't nearly as big as what I was feeling about Keely—and the baby.

With the three of us in our little cocoon, I experienced something completely new to me. It was a feeling of connection as though we were a family. I would have laughed if I'd been able to get it past the lump in my throat the entire time we were staring at the baby's angelic little face.

What I knew about family could be described in one sentence: you couldn't rely on it. In my personal experience, it was an epic miss. My family was a dysfunctional horror story. My mother endured a rough pregnancy with Will, which was followed with a traumatic birthing experience. She was unable to carry any more children afterward. Personally, I suspect the universe was trying to tell her something. She didn't listen.

According to both my parents, their marriage was going south for quite a while before my mom up and decided expanding the family would be a cure all. My father was a cheating son-of-a-bitch, and my mom thought having a second child would keep him at home. They called me the Band-Aid baby.

Adopting me exacerbated an already shitty situation. My dad continued to cheat which in turn infuriated my mom. She felt foolish and trapped, so she turned to the one man who would always be there for her—Jack Daniels. Growing up with a drunk for a mother and an asshole of a father was pretty damn far from ideal. Having to deal with Will on top of it all was a nightmare.

Both of our parents being completely fucked up meant Will's hatred of me was allowed to fester and boil. My first memory is of him pushing me into the deep end of the pool and walking away. I was about three years old. Twenty-three years later, I still remember the terror I felt as I sank like a fucking stone. If there hadn't been a landscaper walking into our backyard at the exact moment

Will did it, I wouldn't have survived.

Will blamed me for ruining his life. He swore until he was blue in the face that before I came along, things were perfect. Even as a child, my brother was always a master of revisionist history. The marriage was already irrevocably fucked. My arrival was nothing more than another nail in the coffin.

I'm sure there are those who would probably classify my parents' marriage as a success, seeing as how they never got divorced. The truth is divorce would have been a blessing. Instead, they stayed chained together until the bitter end. Their end came when my dad died when I was eighteen. His heart stopped while he was balls-deep inside of Robin Ford—our family physician.

My mother was beside herself. Not because her husband cheated, mind you, but because she lost her doctor because of it. Seventeen months later, my mom died of an accidental overdose of medication, which had been prescribed by Dr. Ford years before. It was a not so subtle *fuck you* to the good doctor on my mom's part.

Growing up watching my parents destroy each other—as they fucked up my brother and me in the process—wasn't what one would call inspiring. As toxic as their relationship was, the issues Will and I had with each other were worse. We'd filled the space where brotherly affection should have gone with hate and rage. Most of it came from him—but once I saw what a lying sack of shit he was, I added my fair share to the mix. I'd goaded and mocked him in continued efforts to get a rise out of him. It wasn't like it was hard—Will had a hair trigger. Only later would I realize all I'd done was guarantee he'd hit back at me in the cruelest way possible. I should've been more observant, but back then I'd been a damn fool. I'd known Will was a motherfucker. What I hadn't realized was how truly evil he was.

In all honesty, a large part of the reason I hadn't wanted to see the baby was because I wasn't eager for involvement with anything relating to Will. Nature versus nurture is a tricky thing, and I'd be lying if I didn't admit I wondered if she'd be like him. I'd been as prepared as I could be to see Will when I looked at her.

My guard was up, right until she looked at me. Right then, it became crystal clear it didn't matter if she was biologically Will's daughter. I knew down to my marrow it was my responsibility to do everything within my power to ensure she had a good life.

It was completely unexpected to find the thought of her being raised by strangers bothered me. With the baby between Keely and me, it felt like she was ours. I hadn't seen Keely in years, but I couldn't deny it—I was drawn to her. I had a sense I was supposed to be right where I was. When we talked about naming the baby, and she came up with Emma, it felt perfect. As if it had always been destined to be the three of us together as a unit—a family. Since I knew it wasn't going to be forever, I did my best to put the brakes on my train of thought real fucking fast.

After Keely was wheeled out of the room, I stayed with Emma for quite a while. Kristi sat with me for a bit as she walked me through how to bottle-feed. The bottle was a tiny little thing, holding only a few ounces. I watched in awe as Emma sucked it all down like it was nothing. Once she finished, Kristi showed me how to burp her. I wasn't a natural, to say the least.

"Ronan, you're going to have to be a little firmer," she laughed. "Right now you're barely tapping her. It's not going to help her burp at all."

I tapped a little bit harder, but not by much. "I can't whack away at her back," I said nervously. "I don't want to hurt her."

"It's a common fear," Kristi assured me. "Babies are a lot tougher than you think, and this one is going to need a good burping. She sucked down her bottle fast, which means she got some air. You need to be firm."

I tapped again, a little harder.

"Dude, you're not going to send her into orbit by putting a little power behind it. She needs to burp."

She reached out and hit me on the shoulder a half dozen times. "This is how you want to do it," she said.

I swallowed past the bile creeping up the back of my throat and did as she instructed. The whole time, I was freaking the fuck out. I kept waiting for her to start screaming in pain, and the very thought made me sick. Emma was so tiny; it went against every instinct I had to be firm with her.

This lasted until thirty seconds after Kristi declared I was finally doing it right when Emma let out nothing short of a champion burp.

"You see? She needed to let one go. She would've been very uncomfortable with all of that gas trapped inside her tiny belly," she explained.

I let out a relieved breath as I nodded. "I think I get it now."

I was barely over the stress of having burped her when Kristi threw another bomb at me. "It's time to change her diaper."

The look of absolute panic on my face caused her to laugh out loud.

"It's okay," she chuckled. "I'll do it, but you should carry her over to the table. She's calm with you—if I take her, I think she'll start to cry."

There wasn't anything I wouldn't do to keep the baby from crying. I got out of the rocking chair gingerly and then walked to the changing station slowly. Kristi looked back at me exasperatedly.

"There some big reason you're making a six-second walk take a minute?"

"I'm being careful with her," I answered testily.

I could feel Kristi staring at me, but I was focusing on getting Emma to the table safely so I didn't look.

"She's tougher than you think," she said kindly.

When I finally got to the changing station and put Emma down, her mouth immediately twisted up in displeasure. Leaning over, I stroked her cheek with my finger as I reassured her it was okay.

"We can't leave you in a wet diaper, baby girl. Don't you worry, this will be fast."

Just knowing I was there seemed to reassure her somehow. Once she saw I wasn't going anywhere, she was easy to soothe. She stayed calm as Kristi changed her diaper and then swaddled her again. Once she was ready to go, I picked her up and took her—slowly—back to the rocker I'd been in before.

"I'm going to leave you for a few minutes so I can work on my charts," Kristi explained. "Since she's eaten, it shouldn't take long for her to fall asleep. As soon as I'm done we can move her into the bassinet."

I rocked back and forth with the baby on my shoulder for quite a while. From time to time, I would rub my nose across the top of her head so I could enjoy her baby smell. Keely was right—it was beautiful. When I first got the scent, I almost blurted out that I thought the baby smelled like an angel. Fortunately, I kept the thought to myself.

As I rocked, I tried to make sense of what was happening. Decisions needed to be made. I knew Emma deserved the moon—and I silently vowed to make sure I found someone who would get it for her. I wouldn't stop until Emma had the perfect parents for her.

I wasn't sure if she was asleep or awake until Kristi came back.

"She's sound asleep," she whispered. "Stand up slowly and walk over to the bassinet."

I reluctantly did as instructed. It didn't feel right to leave her. I would've argued for more time, but I was anxious to check in on Keely. Since I couldn't take Emma with me back to Keely's room, it was best I left while she was sleeping.

I set her down in the bassinet carefully, making certain to put her exactly in the center.

"She'll be okay, right?"

"She's going to be fine," Kristi assured me. "You don't need to worry."

She was wrong. I did.

After I finally was able to walk away, I headed back to Keely's room. I stayed and watched over her for a few hours before I broke down and got a cab to Canter's. I didn't want to leave her at all, but I knew unless I wanted to start smelling, I had to shower. I also wanted to follow through with Chuck in order to make sure figuring out what was going on with the surrogate situation was his top priority.

Over my dead body would I be handing Emma off to a couple that felt comfortable with my brother and his wife. Emma was going to have the best and only the best. I wouldn't allow anything less for her. Having been placed with two fucked up assholes—I wouldn't allow the same thing to happen to Emma.

Chapter Seven

Keely

I WOKE UP THE FOLLOWING MORNING FEELING SLIGHTLY MORE with it mentally. On the other hand, my body felt as though it went through a meat grinder. I ached and my arm itched beneath the bandage. It wasn't a pleasant sensation.

I'd been disturbed by nurses checking on me every so often through the night. The first few times it happened, Ronan was there and watching me. When I woke around one in the morning, he was gone. I'd felt reassured just knowing he was there, and when I saw he'd left, I'd been unable to get back to sleep for a while as my mind raced. I was anxious he wouldn't return. I feared having to deal with me and Emma was too much for him.

There was no need for me to have thought anything of the sort. When I woke up for the day, he was back. The first thing I noticed was Ronan staring at me like my face held the secrets of the world on it. Next, I realized he was freshly showered. I knew this because his hair was still a little damp. I probably would've stared at him all darn day if my senses hadn't picked on something that made my mouth water. His hand was wrapped around a large Starbucks cup and whatever was in it smelled amazing.

"Mm," I sighed longingly. "I'll give you all of my worldly goods for a taste."

His head jerked up and he looked at me like a deer caught in the headlights.

"Just a sip—just for a second," I joked.

The look in his eyes made me shiver. It almost looked sexual, but I figured I was just seeing what I wanted to.

After another few moments of silence I prodded, "Ronan?"

He snapped to attention and shook his head as if he were trying to clear it.

"Huh?"

Using my left hand, I gestured to his cup. "The coffee. You can't bring Starbucks near me and not expect me to want some. I'm a caffeine junkie, and they're my supplier of choice. I get a Venti Mocha Latte every Friday when I get paid. It's my big splurge."

He looked down at the cup in his hand as if he was surprised to see it there.

"Oh," he laughed huskily. "Right. Sure. The coffee. Of course. Drink up. I have to warn you, I'm big on sugar."

"Is it decaf?"

"Hell no," he answered emphatically. "Decaf shit's not fit for a cup."

I realized he was a caffeine fiend, same as me.

"Then it's all good."

"Cool. First things first though," he said as he stood and came to the side of my bed. "I have to sit you up."

I felt my stomach flutter as he pushed the button and moved me into an upright position. I expected him to hand me the cup and return to his seat. Instead, he put it in my hand and stayed at my side as I drank, close enough for me to be able to feel his body heat.

"You okay holding it?"

I nodded dumbly as I took another sip. I was unable to speak due to him smelling so damn good. Suddenly my mouth was watering for something other than coffee. He smelled fresh, a bit like whatever soap or body wash he used. The rest of his scent was all man. I wanted to breathe him in forever.

We were in a stare-off for a good minute or two as I greedily drank half of his super-sweet coffee. We may have kept right on staring into each other's eyes in silence if a nurse hadn't strolled into the room and interrupted us.

Instantly, I couldn't stand her. This was because she was chipper—and by this I mean perky and super bouncy—and she looked like she wanted to eat Ronan alive. Also, she was a fake bitch.

"Oh look," she chirped as she waved her clipboard toward me dramatically. "You're *finally* awake. I told Ronan the last time I came in I've never seen anyone sleep like you do. The joys of being a teenager!"

My teeth gnashed together as I gave her a death stare. She didn't even notice.

"I'm Savannah, and I'll be your nurse today," she giggled.

Yes. My nurse giggled like a damn schoolgirl. When she finished giggling, she settled into a duck-lipped pout. You know the one. It was clear she was performing for Ronan. It was a good thing my right arm was out of commission because I wanted to strangle her.

She hardly glanced at me as she came to the bed and started checking my vitals. At least she acted as if she was. She made the motions, but the entire time she was eye-fucking Ronan and sticking her ass out in an attempt to entice him. He'd returned to his seat so she could check me over while she was doing her best to put on a show. At no point in time was I, as the patient, her focus or priority. My jaw ticked as I tried to keep my annoyance in check.

Things got worse when she inflated the blood pressure cuff so much it was painful.

"Ouch," I yelped. "Stop!"

Ronan jumped to his feet and rushed to my side.

"You're hurting her," he snapped.

Behind her cheerful façade, I could tell she was annoyed.

"I'm so sorry," she giggled at Ronan. "This cuff is still being broken in."

"You shouldn't be using it then," he said stiffly. "She's in enough pain without shit equipment making it worse."

"You're right," she agreed. "I won't use it on her again."

When she finished taking my blood pressure, she finally deigned to look my way. Even when I'd complained about the cuff, her attention had been entirely on Ronan.

She raised one of her perfectly shaped brows as she looked me over. "Your blood pressure is a little higher than the last time it was taken. Are you feeling okay, hon?"

I wanted to say her shitty nursing was making me angry, but I bit my tongue. Everything about her was insincere. From the baby girl tone of voice to the orange sherbet colored tan and even the concern she was pretending to have for me. The girl was a total phony.

"I'm fine," I snapped through gritted teeth. "Where are Dr. Smith and Nurse Davies?"

Her face pinched up fast, and she glared at me for a second before realizing her mistake. She quickly schooled her features back into what I can only describe as Nurse Barbie.

"They're not on right now, hon. You've got Dr. Dena and me. She starts her rounds in about an hour."

I guess she felt as though once she answered my question, she no longer needed to speak to me. After closing my chart, she turned back to Ronan.

"I'm going to have one of the food service girls bring breakfast up for her. Would you like me to bring you anything?"

I wanted to get up and throw something at her for blatantly flirting with him in front of me the way she did. Meanwhile, Ronan seemed to have no reaction to her antics. I assumed being hit on was nothing new to him.

"I had a breakfast sandwich."

Her collagen-filled lips tried to form a pout. "You're a big man," she said in a wannabe sexy baby-doll voice. The sound made my skin crawl. "A teeny-tiny sandwich won't hold you over for long. You come out and find me if you think of anything else you want. I'll be waiting."

The only reason I didn't tell her to get the hell out of my room was because I saw the annoyance stamped all over Ronan's face.

"*I'm fine*," he said firmly. "You're supposed to be worrying about Keely. She's who matters here."

It was obvious she was annoyed because he wasn't paying her any mind. For a second I thought she was going to stomp off in a huff without another word. Instead, she slapped on a big fake smile and giggled as she sauntered toward the door and pulled it open.

"'Kay, well let me know if you change your mind."

After the door closed behind her, I couldn't keep my commentary to myself.

"I find it hard to believe *Savannah* passed enough exams to be a nurse," I snapped. "I wouldn't be surprised to find out she's a stripper play-acting at being a medical professional."

I knew I was being catty, but I didn't care.

"Oh Ronan," I mimicked as I batted my eyelashes. "You're such a big man. You need to eat. She couldn't have been more obvious. Skank."

Ronan threw back his head and laughed.

"Yeah," he agreed. "She was a bit much."

"A little bit."

"She's shit at her job, too," he snickered. "You feel okay? 'Cause it didn't look to me as if she checked you over near good enough."

"I'm good," I assured him.

He smiled the ridiculously hot smile that made me feel stupid giddy inside.

"Glad to hear it," he said. "You tell me if that changes at all and I'll get a real medical professional in here."

My heart skipped a few beats as I bit back a smile. I loved how protective he was. A few seconds passed where I stared at him adoringly. When he cleared his throat, I realized I needed to say something. Wanting to get his attention off of me and the fact he'd just caught me staring at him like a lovesick puppy, I changed the subject.

"How long did you stay with Emma last night?"

His eyes softened when I said her name, which made my heart melt. I'd been so worried when I first woke up, and he said he hadn't seen her. I feared the Ronan from the night before—the one who wasn't enthused about seeing the baby—had returned. Knowing he still cared was a relief.

"I think it was about an hour," he said. "I stopped in and checked on her this morning, but she was asleep. The on-duty nurse told me they were waiting for the doctor. They'll clear her to move to the maternity floor nursery once he signs off."

I was thrilled to hear it. "What great news! I can't wait to see her again."

He agreed, but his expression looked troubled as if something was bothering him. I decided he needed to lighten up.

"I think Maury's on," I said as I gestured to the TV hanging on the wall across from my bed. "Wanna watch some? Are they or aren't they *the father* drama?"

My question made him laugh out loud. "You watch train

wreck TV?"

"Don't be a hater! Maury's doing a service."

"A service only the crazy use," Ronan chided. "You have to be pretty fucked in the head to go on national TV and have a talk show host tell you whether or not you're a dad."

"Oh, stop." I chuckled. "If the choice is to buy a DNA test from the pharmacy so you can get a swab and send it to a lab, then get the results at home a few weeks later... Or you get to fly to New York and do it on TV, obviously you choose Maury. Imagine the guys who have been swearing up and down they know the kid isn't theirs, but no one believes them. After they're on Maury everyone knows what happened. Saves time too. Instead of having to spend time composing e-mails and text messages, you tell people to watch, and it's done."

His eyes went wide and his jaw dropped. "You can't be serious. There's no way they sell DNA tests at the drugstore now. Right?"

The look of utter disbelief on his face was priceless.

"I saw the commercial while I was watching Maury one day. The next time I went to Walgreens I checked it out. Sure enough, it's a thing."

"So there are so many people with no idea who the father is— you can now buy a test anywhere? The world's a fucked up place," he said with a shake of his head.

"It is. You know what's even more screwed up?" I asked.

"What?"

"When Izzy told me she was pregnant, before she got to the surrogate part, I wondered if she would need a DNA test. The relationship she and Will were in... it wasn't normal," I confided. "But when I asked Izzy, she said she was a thousand percent certain he was the father. I was sad to hear it."

I immediately regretted voicing my thoughts when everything about him went tense. He took a breath and let it out slowly.

"Trust me," he said darkly. "I know how fucked up they were."

Before I could say another word, he grabbed the remote and turned the TV on. Instead of Maury, we wound up choosing to watch *Cupcake Wars*. The only talking we did during the show was completely innocuous—*Looks delicious* and *Gross, the recipe sounds terrible*. There was no more mention of Izzy or Will.

About twenty minutes or so later, Dr. Dena came in. I'd been nervous about meeting her after what a letdown Savannah was as a nurse, but I had no reason to worry. She was as good of a doctor as Dr. Smith, and I felt a lot better after she looked me over and declared I was healing very well.

"Please tell me I can shower," I pleaded desperately. I needed to use the bathroom badly, but hadn't wanted to be caught with my pants—or hospital gown—down when the doctor came in.

"Your stitches look great, and there isn't any tearing or further swelling," she said. "This means you're in luck. We kept your arm out of commission for well over twenty-four hours, which means you're fine to shower. You'll need to favor your left arm, leaving the right at your side. You can get the arm wet, but don't let the water beat down on it. Shouldn't be a problem here. The water pressure on this floor isn't great. Many of our patients all but skip out of the hospital to get to their home showers," she chuckled. "When you get out, don't rub at the stitches. You'll need to pat them dry gently."

Her mention of patients going home made me think.

"When do you think I'll be leaving the hospital?"

"I believe we can discharge you in the next few days," she said confidently. "You lost a lot of blood and you were out for a long time. For those reasons alone, Dr. Smith signed off on monitoring you for at least another seventy-two hours. I don't anticipate any problems, but we're erring on the side of caution just to be certain."

I was relieved but nervous. Sleeping in a hospital room sucked so much I actually missed my tiny studio apartment. Still, the bigger concern right then was Emma. I couldn't leave the hospital and go on my merry way. I needed to get the ball rolling on finding out exactly what the situation really was. She was the priority, full stop. I needed to know what was happening—almost as much as I wanted to see her. I was chomping at the bit to hold her.

"This means I can spend some real time with Emma today, right?"

"You can," Dr. Dena assured me. "However, we don't want you over-exerting yourself, so take it easy. I'll be back to check on you during my afternoon rounds. You're cleared to visit your niece after breakfast. You'll be happy to know she was moved into the nursery on the maternity floor early this morning."

I was relieved to hear it, but I still needed answers about the long term. Before I could say anything else, Dr. Dena said something that stopped me short.

"I'll be on my way then. I'll send Nurse Savannah in to help you get into the shower."

"No!" I yelped. "I'd rather do it myself."

Dr. Dena raised an eyebrow.

"I didn't care for her at all," I mumbled.

I was embarrassed to having admitted my dislike for Savannah for all of one second before Dr. Dena nodded her understanding.

"Trust me, I understand," she reassured me. "But," she continued, "Someone needs to be right here in case you need help."

Turning to Ronan she asked, "Mr. Sharpe, can you handle it?"

I could feel the flush spreading over my cheeks. "I'll be okay," I promised.

"I believe you will," she responded. "Still, I wouldn't feel comfortable if he left the room, and you were in the shower by yourself."

"I got it," Ronan assured her.

Satisfied with his answer, Dr. Dena said her goodbyes and left the room.

The second she left, I started to question Ronan about what was going on with the baby so we wouldn't have to discuss my showering needs.

"Have you heard anything from Chuck yet?"

"He's going to get to the bottom of it. He was heading to Izzy's OB/GYN this morning, so hopefully when he gets here, he'll have some answers."

We were interrupted by the arrival of my breakfast. I was excited for all of ten seconds before I realized it was all gross looking. There was plain oatmeal with a few dinky looking raisins, two pieces of wheat toast, a yogurt and a glass of milk. The meal was as tasteless and unappealing as it sounded, but I was so hungry I ate every bite.

While I ate, I worried about whether or not the surrogate situation was real. I was in a panic because if Izzy had really been a surrogate, the couple involved couldn't possibly be fit to raise a child. It wasn't a stretch to imagine Will selling the baby to someone who should never be around children. He'd certainly had no moral compass.

Will hadn't been a genuine—or sane—person. He cared for himself first, always. I damn well knew he wouldn't ever have given a damn about Emma. Hearing the way he spoke about her in the car was all I needed to know about how he'd felt about her.

There was no way I was going to let Emma go with anyone he'd done business with. Without a doubt I knew my job was to fight for her future. Even feeling like ten miles of bad road, I felt I was up to the challenge. Having Ronan at my side made me feel invincible because for the first time ever, someone had my back.

I wished he would have it permanently.

Chapter Eight

Ronan

THE LITTLE BIT OF SLEEP I MANAGED TO GET AT CANTER'S didn't make a damn bit of difference regarding my reaction to Keely. If anything, I found her even more appealing than I had when I left the hospital the previous night. So much for my theory on sleep being the key to waking up feeling different.

When I arrived at the hospital in the morning, she was still asleep. After I managed to get the nurse from hell out of the room, I sat and stared at Keely for a long time. It was a relief to see her coloring was better than it had been the night before.

I was pretty sure I'd stooped to full creeper mode sitting there and staring at her like I did, but I'd been unable to force myself to look away. Over and over again I reminded myself of her age. The thing was, other than the date she was born, nothing about Keely said teenager. I don't only mean her appearance either. From the way she held herself to the way she spoke, there was no doubt she was a woman instead of a girl. Even asleep, Keely's hold on me was worrisome. I hadn't been able to stop thinking of her since the moment I arrived.

I was still staring at her when she woke up. The jolt I felt when her gaze connected with mine was nothing short of electrifying, the same as it had been the day before. The flash of heat in her eyes suggested she felt something as well, but I told myself it was wishful thinking. My reaction to her wasn't normal, at least not for me. I didn't know why it kept happening. *Fuck, this really isn't going away*, I'd thought to myself anxiously.

Before I could open my mouth to say good morning to her, Keely let out a sound, which was half moan, half delighted excitement. I think eighty percent of the blood in my body flooded to my dick right then and there. I wanted to hear the sound—and others like it—over and over again. When she'd said she wanted a taste, I almost let out a moan of my own. Of course, she hadn't been asking for a taste of my cock. She'd been referring to the Starbucks cup clutched in my hand. Fucking coffee.

Being a Private Investigator meant Canter had some leeway with his schedule. He'd taken me to get a rental car in the morning so I'd have wheels of my own to get around with while I was in town, which pleased me to no end. I hated being beholden to other people for shit like rides or food. After getting the rental car I'd swung by Starbucks to grab some much needed caffeine. Going off of Keely's enthusiastic reaction, I'd done the right thing.

I'd been attempting to be helpful when I helped her sit up to drink the coffee. It was a tactical error on my part. All I'd succeeded in doing was bringing us closer together. I came damn close to touching her then. Only the arrival of the nurse from hell stopped me.

It should have been a relief, but in addition to being annoying, the bitch was a shitty caregiver. It made my blood boil watching her prance around like a damn model, all the while ignoring Keely—the most important person in the damn room.

It took restraint I wasn't even aware I possessed not to throw her skanky ass out of the room. Sure, she'd been ridiculously flirtatious when I arrived, but treating Keely the way she did was a step too far.

Not long after Nurse Nightmare left, the on duty doctor arrived. I'd watched with narrowed eyes as the doctor examined her, right up until I was certain the doctor knew what the hell she was doing. Savannah hadn't instilled confidence in me about anyone other than Dr. Smith or Nurse Davies being competent. I was relieved to find this wasn't the case.

The doctor approved Keely spending a good chunk of time in the nursery with Emma. That was encouraging. She also gave the go-ahead for Keely to shower. It was good for Keely, but bad for me, seeing how I immediately regressed to creeper mode, fantasizing about lathering her up myself.

The entire time she was in the shower, all I'd been able to focus on was her being naked, wet and less than fifty feet from me. Only a door separated us, and I was both relieved and annoyed with it.

I prayed she wouldn't fall while also hoping she would need my help in some way. The night before, I'd convinced myself my attraction to Keely was nothing more than an anomaly. The dawn of a new day showed the thought for the bullshit it had been. I'd have written my reaction off as being too horny to function, but it had only been a few weeks since the last time I'd taken a woman to bed. I'd gone months without sex before; a few weeks sure as hell shouldn't have been an issue.

She was in the bathroom forever, or so it felt like. I'd heard the shower go on and then heard it go off sometime later, so I knew she was out. I'd heard some shuffling around after, followed by silence. At one point, I thought I heard her muttering.

When it hit the fifteen-minute mark after she had disappeared into the bathroom, I couldn't take it anymore. I knocked on the door, anxious to make sure she was okay. My hand was raised to knock again when it opened.

"Hey."

Her voice was soft, and she looked embarrassed.

"I didn't mean to hurry you," I explained. "I got worried thinking there could be a problem—"

"There kind of is," she admitted. "I need—"

I jumped right to the conclusion something medical was wrong, and she needed help. Naturally, I panicked.

"I'll get the nurse," I said as I spun around and went to press the call button.

"Stop!" Keely cried out. "I don't want Savannah in here."

I'd turned back around ready to tell her if something was wrong, it needed to be handled. Before I could say a word, she took a step out of the bathroom.

"I'm not sick or hurt. It's this stupid gown," she muttered. "Getting it off wasn't an issue—I untied it, and it basically fell off. Once I started trying to get dressed, I realized it's like a freaking Kimono, and I can't reach back far enough to bring it around."

It didn't sound like such a big deal.

"Okayyyy… "

I didn't get why she looked so embarrassed.

"I need help getting it on right," she blurted.

I cocked my head and raised an eyebrow. "You want me to pull it around the back and tie it for you?"

She was beet red as she nodded. Biting her lip, she stared down at the tile beneath her feet before she dropped the bomb on me.

"I don't have any of my stuff which means no clean underwear. I can't put the old ones back on," she said. "I'm…you know, naked under here."

When she announced she wasn't wearing any underwear, a decent sized portion of my brain melted. Then she added in the whole she was naked thing, and at least a dozen brain cells exploded. Before she could see my reaction, I quickly schooled my expression. By my estimation, I'd seen dozens of naked women from behind. It shouldn't have been an issue. The problem was, I'd never seen *her* naked in any way, shape, or form.

"It's no big deal," I assured her. Obviously, I was lying. It was a very big deal.

"I'll do it so fast, I won't see anything. Not like I'll be looking," I babbled.

Yeah. I fucking babbled. It was awkward and pathetic. I was damn lucky Keely didn't pick up on it. Or, if she did, she did a great job of hiding it.

She blushed as she nodded her head. "If you wouldn't mind, I'd appreciate it."

"No sweat."

I'd said this even as I could feel myself starting to sweat. Keely needing help trumped my issue, so I walked across the room to her with what I hoped was a fairly normal facial expression.

As she turned, I was met with the shower-fresh clean scent of her. I barely managed to keep a tortured groan from escaping me. I'd been using the bathroom in her hospital room, so I'd had the opportunity to see the toiletries Nurse Davies brought in the evening before. It was all travel-sized stuff, nothing fancy. Somehow on Keely, it smelled like a fucking delicacy.

I decided to take shallow breaths through my mouth to avoid her mouth-watering scent. This decision lasted for all of two seconds because when I took in the perfection of her naked back, it immediately resulted in my taking a deep breath. Huge mistake. I wanted to bury my face against the side of her neck and breathe her in.

My teeth gnashed together as my gaze dropped to her amazing ass. It was a work of art—sexy and high. She was rounded in all the right spots, and I couldn't help wondering what it would feel like beneath my hands. I wanted to grip her perfect ass in my hands as I thrust into her. I was appalled at my lack of control. She'd been pretty much comatose only the day before, but my dick didn't seem to give a shit.

Forcing my gaze up, I reached out with shaking hands to grab hold of the side of her gown. I wrapped it around her quickly before looping the fabric ties together. I stepped back and away from her the second I was done.

My voice was gruff when I said, "All good."

She let out a relieved sigh as she spun around slowly. "Thank you. As soon as my hair finally dries, I think I'll feel something like normal."

"No hair dryer in there?"

"There is," she responded. "The problem is I can't hold it and brush my hair at the same time, the way I normally would."

"You should've said," I told her. "Get back into the bathroom—I'll do it for you."

I figured I could handle hair drying. How hard could it be? If I'd had a functioning brain cell, I'd have realized the problem before I even suggested it. The bathroom was the size of a small closet. Therefore, when we got inside, and I plugged in the hair dryer by the sink before positioning myself behind her, I was left damn near grinding up against her ass. The very perfect and ridiculously sexy ass I'd only moments before fantasized about gripping while I fucked her.

Taking the travel-sized plastic hairbrush from her—more child's toy than useful hair tool, in my opinion—I'd turned the hair dryer on hoping to get it over with quickly. Several times as I brushed her hair, our eyes met in the mirror. She was flushed and looking more beautiful by the second while I was pretty sure I looked like a deranged maniac. I'd never gotten my kicks by tending to a woman before, but with Keely, it felt borderline erotic. The way she trusted me to take care of her felt like some kind of gift.

It took longer than it should have for me to dry her hair because I wound up drawing the process out. Right or wrong, I enjoyed it. When I finally turned the hair dryer off, her hair looked like a rich dark chocolate waterfall.

She sounded breathless when she looked back over her shoulder and said, "Thank you."

"No big deal," I assured her.

Again, it was a lie. It was huge. I didn't stand around in bathrooms drying hair, ever. I'd never panicked about seeing a woman naked. I knew I was losing my shit, and I had no idea how the fuck to deal with what I was feeling. The fact that I was feeling anything at all was unusual. As a rule, I didn't do emotion.

We left the warmth of the bathroom and returned to the sterility of her hospital room. About thirty seconds after we got back in the room, a nurse we hadn't met yet walked in. She wasn't as nice as Nurse Davies, but she wasn't Nurse Savannah, so she was good. She made quick work of putting ointment on Keely's arm. Right as she was finished, Chuck showed up.

"Glad to see you looking more like yourself," he remarked happily to Keely as he took the seat next to her bed. "How're you feeling?"

"Better for having a shower. I'm sore as all get out, but otherwise I'm doing fine. Glad to be alive," she answered honestly.

My jaw clenched at her words as it hit me all over again. What the fuck had Will been thinking to drive in the condition he'd been in? Dropping down into the hard chair against the wall across from Keely's bed I watched Chuck pull a clipboard out of a leather bag he'd carried in with him.

"Hate to do this to you, I know it's not pleasant to think about, but I've got to get your recollection of what happened the other night.

Keely raised her left hand and began twirling a piece of her hair nervously. "Okay," she mumbled.

"Don't worry," Chuck said reassuringly. "This should be over pretty quick. After we finish, I'll bring you both up to speed on what I found out about your niece."

I was damn proud of her when she pushed the button to sit up as straight as possible in the bed. I could see her steeling herself for what was to come.

As soon as she was comfortable, she nodded at Chuck.

"Let's do this," she said. "I'm ready."

I admired her backbone. Life had just kicked her in the ass, but she wasn't letting it get her down.

"It's best for you to tell me what you remember," Chuck said.

She nodded stiffly before closing her eyes and taking a breath. "Some of it's hazy, especially toward the end. To get you to where we wound up, I need to take you back to how this all started."

Her face took on a faraway look as she continued. "Izzy and I, we were never close. We'd stopped talking not long after our dad died. Out of the blue, she got in contact about three months ago to tell me she was pregnant. She said she was acting as a surrogate for a couple who wanted a child. According to her, Will was support-ive of this because it was a financial boost, but he wanted no part of the 'nasty shit.' She asked me to be with her in the delivery room so she wouldn't be alone, and I agreed."

She rolled her neck on her shoulders, seeming to gather her thoughts before continuing. "I hated my brother-in-law, refused to be anywhere near him. If Izzy had come to my house when she went into labor the way she was meant to, none of this would have happened."

"She was supposed to come to your house?" Chuck asked.

"Yes—my car broke down a few weeks ago, and I didn't want to waste money fixing it because unless I spent a fortune, it was never going to be reliable. The plan was whenever she went into labor, Izzy would drive to my house and then I'd drive the rest of the way. It should've been fine since my apartment is on the way to the hospital. But she called in a panic and said she was in so much pain she couldn't possibly drive. I begged one of my neighbors to give me a ride to their place so I could drive Izzy from there. When I got there, Izzy was already out at the car, ready to go. And then he came out of the house."

She'd gone pale, her eyes shiny with unshed tears as she swallowed. "He came out of nowhere," she said in a scared sounding voice. I knew she was remembering the way everything had gone down.

"He was screaming and yelling like a maniac and then he announced he was driving," she explained. He was hammered, but he didn't care. Izzy begged him to go back inside, but he wasn't having any part of it. She knew—dammit, she knew—I would never get into a car with him. I don't know what she thought when she shoved me in. I started praying right away—it was a ten mile drive at the most, I hoped he'd stop…"

She broke off abruptly, wiping at a tear as it rolled down her cheek. I hated to see her cry.

After taking a deep breath, she continued. "Will was not a good man, Chief West. But as bad as he'd ever been, this was worse. He was out of his mind with rage, telling Izzy he'd never let her leave him. She kept swearing her love to him, but it made no difference. He said if he couldn't have her, no one could. He threatened to cut the baby out of her and was saying the most horrible things. He said they were going to be together forever. And then he floored it and everything went to hell."

My heart constricted painfully in my chest and my jaw dropped. It felt as though someone punched me in the stomach.

"He crashed on purpose?" I asked hoarsely.

Chuck answered for her. "Everything Keely told me confirms what I'd already concluded. There were no tire marks, no sign of the brakes being engaged. He meant to crash the car. A motorist saw him careening all over the road and called 911 about three minutes before impact. She said she could see the driver waving their arms around so she knew whoever it was, they were awake."

I'd known my brother was a piece of shit. It wasn't a secret. But realizing he'd *intended* to kill everyone in the car destroyed me. Everything hit me all at once, like a thousand pound cement truck. I was emotionally rocked to the core as I realized Will could have—*would have* had he succeeded—killed Keely and Emma.

I dropped my face into my hands as I struggled to breathe. Even thinking about their possible deaths made me feel ill. If Will would've still been alive right then, I believe I would've killed him with my bare hands.

The sound of Keely saying my name softly got my attention. "You okay?"

I stared at her in a sort of shock. I was blown away to realize Keely was worried about me. My brother almost fucking killed her, but she was concerned for me. I felt like an enormous asshole.

"Sorry," I mumbled hoarsely. "I'm okay."

It was as clear as the nose on the end of my face—she knew I was full of shit. Still, she let me get away with the lie, and I appreciated it.

Chuck got things back on track pretty quickly. "I don't have any further questions for you about the accident, at least for now. As for the other situation, I went and saw Isabelle's doctor and met with her this morning. To Dr. Cipressi's knowledge, Izzy was *not* a surrogate. The only person Izzy had brought in with her or put down on her HIPAA form was you, Keely. If she had been a surrogate, there would be a trail, but there's nothing."

Keely let out a sigh as she lifted her good hand to rub at her forehead. "I didn't think she was telling the truth. Izzy's story never added up. In the shower this morning, I think I remembered something. When I asked Izzy about the surrogacy issue before the ambulance came…"

Trailing off, Keely looked up at the ceiling, appearing to hold back tears. I couldn't watch her break down and do nothing. I was up and out of my seat in a flash, standing right next to her bed and rubbing her shoulder. "It's okay, Keely. Take your time."

She leaned her head against my arm in a way that said she needed the comfort.

"I've got you," I assured her. "Take your time, sweetheart."

She took a shuddery breath before nodding her head.

"It's hard. Everything about what happened after impact is so fuzzy, but I can see her face so clearly in my head. I knew she was dying. She knew it, too. I remember her telling me to look in the diaper bag. I'm not sure if it was real or not, but—"

Chuck interrupted. "Is there a diaper bag? We didn't find one in the car."

I'd made no move to leave her side so when she nodded, I felt the silken glide of her hair as it passed over my hand. I quickly pulled my hand away and crossed my arms in an attempt to look unaffected.

"Yes. Izzy brought it over the other day. It should be hanging on one of the hooks by my front door."

"Sounds like I need to get the diaper bag," Chuck said.

"I don't even know where my keys are," Keely admitted. "I have no idea what happened to my purse or anything I had the night of the crash."

Chuck raised an eyebrow as he stood up. Without a word he walked across the room to open the built in closet against the wall. After opening the door, he took out a black purse.

"I dropped this off early this morning. I told the overly perky nurse to tell you I was here," he said dryly. "Guessing she forgot to pass the message along."

I bit my lip in order not to go off on a tirade about what an asshole the nurse in question was.

Keely made a disgusted sound. "Can't say I'm surprised," she said.

"You good if I get the diaper bag?" Chuck asked.

"Of course," Keely assured him. "Grab the keys from the front pocket of my purse—it's the key with the red top. I'll give you my address."

He pointed to his head with a laugh. "Got it all right here. Your apartment is just a few miles down the road, so this won't take long," he told her.

I watched the door shut behind him, and silently hoped what he came back with were answers we could all live with.

Chapter Nine

Keely

I WATCHED RONAN PACING THE ROOM AFTER CHUCK LEFT TO get the diaper bag. Everything about him was on edge from his posture, clenched fists and right on down to the look on his face.

I didn't know what to say or do to make him feel any better, so I settled on asking a simple—and obviously foolish—question.

"Are you okay?"

The answer was written all over his face. It wasn't a surprise when he shook his head in the negative.

He dragged his hands through his hair angrily. "He could've killed you," he croaked harshly. "He could have killed you both. Jesus, Emma came within minutes of never taking her first breath—"

"But she did," I assured him. "We both survived. We're alive, and it's a blessing. The worst didn't happen."

He gripped the back of his head with both hands as he stared down at me with wild eyes.

"How are you so calm? The mere thought of what could have happened…"

"I'm not as calm as I look," I admitted. "It makes me sick to think about it, so I'm trying to focus on the positive."

He looked incredulous. "The positive?"

"Emma will never know him," I replied.

He let out a harsh breath as he dropped down onto the chair next to me. He said nothing for several long moments as he mulled what I'd said over. I wondered if I'd gone too far in telling him how I felt. When he looked up at me, his eyes were blazing with raw emotion.

"I'm glad he's dead," he said bitterly.

His voice was low, but he'd said it with such conviction I felt every word. I knew he meant what he'd said down to the depths of his soul.

"Emma deserves a beautiful life," he said quietly. "The only thing Will knew about beauty was how to destroy it. Everything he touched turned to shit, because he got off on chaos. I know what it says about me, being glad he's dead, and I don't care."

Reaching over, I grabbed his hand with my good one. "It says you would choose good over evil," I told him. "I think the only positive contribution Will ever made to the world is Emma. If he lived, he would have found a way to ruin her life. I'm glad he's gone, too. I'm not ashamed to admit that, either."

I could see his relief of my understanding. I expected him to let go of my hand. Instead, he held on like it was the most natural thing in the world. I wanted to be connected to him because it made me feel right. Therefore, I didn't make a move to pull away, nor did I say anything about it.

The lethargy I'd felt the day before had worn off, and I was anxious as we waited for Chief West to return. I wanted to get some answers and then I wanted to get to Emma. I missed her desperately. Needing something to focus on to make waiting a little easier, I started asking Ronan things I'd wondered about for years.

"So tell me about you," I said. "Where did you go when you left?"

He blinked a few times before rubbing at his temple with his free hand. I realized he was trying to switch gears from talking about Will to talking about things that weren't negative. He was silent, seemingly locked in his memories.

After a few seconds he chuckled. "I found a home," he smiled. "And all because of a shitty ride. You remember the used Mustang I left town in, right?"

I nodded my head in the affirmative. Of course I remembered his car. It had been almost as sexy as he was. As a fourteen-year-old, I'd enjoyed many a daydream about getting to ride in his car. He'd bought it about a year or so before he'd left. I'd gotten to take a spin in it once or twice, but it wasn't like in my daydreams, where I was his girl.

"I saved for the damn car for going on two years," he mused. "Couldn't have been prouder of it. I figured I'd hit the open road, drive across the country and explore America until I found a place, and it felt like home. I drove for one day. Got to Montana—nine hours away. Then the Mustang died on me because the transmission was shot to shit."

Leaning forward, he looked at me and smiled as he continued.

"With no car and no options, I was pretty well fucked. There was a little under two grand in my bank account, which wasn't going to fix the 'Stang. I sold it to a scrapper for five hundred bucks, which I used to buy a twenty-year-old station wagon. The thing was ugly as hell but reliable enough to get around. It took me a couple of days to figure out the car situation. While I waited, I got to know the town. It was a good place—solid. I liked the people and the vibe. Decided it was as good a place as any to set down some roots, so I did."

Just like that, he'd set up roots. I envied him.

"Where in Montana?"

My curiosity about where life took him after he left Fort Collins was nearly endless.

He smiled warmly, squeezing my hand as he did so. "Belgrade. I lived in a run down two-bedroom apartment with three guys I met at work for the first few years. Rent was cheap—less than three hundred a month with all the utilities. Since I had no overhead, I saved a good chunk of change. I became real good friends with one of my roommates—his name's Lincoln. We got the opportunity to buy the dive bar we were working in, so we took it. Been running it for the last few years."

I was surprised. The Ronan I'd known was a foodie who worked in restaurants from the time he'd been of age to work.

"I can't imagine you as a bartender. I always thought you'd be a chef," I mused.

He cocked his head to the side and looked at me in surprise.

"I don't think anyone else ever put together the fact I wanted to cook." He chuckled dryly. "I don't think they gave a crap, either. Obviously Canter knew, but he's been my best friend since first grade."

I felt my face heat with embarrassment. I'd noticed everything about Ronan because I'd cared.

I still did.

"Our bar serves lunch and dinner," he explained. The tone of his voice and his body language made the pride he had in his business clear.

As he spoke, he ran his thumb across the top of my hand. I wondered if he realized he was doing it.

"I don't love being behind the bar, so I avoid it as much as possible. I work the day shift, taking care of the lunch and dinner crowd. When we took over, the place was a dive. The only things on the menu were microwaved Buffalo wings, chips and salsa and chicken fingers. Lincoln and I did a total revamp over the course of the first year. Now, it's the coolest place in town and people line up for the food."

I didn't enjoy my job—it was just a place to go to earn money so I could get out of Colorado. Everything about my life was temporary because I wasn't willing to tie myself to Fort Collins for any longer than I absolutely needed to. I envied him the pride he had in his work. On the other hand, I was thrilled to see how happy he was.

"Do you have someone to cook when you're not there?"

He nodded with another smile. "Lincoln is a hell of a chef, almost as good as me," he joked. "We've got a bunch of kitchen help. They'll be fine without me for a while."

"What's your specialty? I remember you used to make the most amazing roasted lemon chicken. You were always the hit of the block parties."

Even thinking about the food he used to cook made my mouth water.

He grinned widely at the memory. "Those block parties were like my test kitchens. I loved that shit, even though so many of our neighbors didn't give a shit about the food. I still make the lemon chicken, but my specialty is a buffalo and blue cheese chicken burger."

The way he lit up when talking about food and his business made me happy for him.

"One day I hope to have a job I'll love as much as you love yours," I told him honestly. "You're very lucky."

His eyebrows rose as he focused on me. "What do you do?" he questioned.

"I'm a lot like you were, I guess. I couldn't afford college, so I got a full-time job. I work at the Stop 'n' Shop Grocery as a cashier. I like my co-workers, and the job itself is fine. It's just not what I want to do forever."

His eyebrows knitted together as he stared at me intently. "Then what's your passion?"

I looked away as I shrugged my shoulders dismissively. I'd always hated that question. During my junior and senior years of high school, it almost felt like it was asked on a daily basis. It made me feel somehow less than because I didn't have a good answer. I enjoyed doing a lot of things, but I'd never felt called to one profession. I was envious of people who knew what path they needed to be on.

Eager to divert the attention from my lack of direction I joked, "What I know for certain is my passion isn't food. Unless it's Ramen noodles or made from the almighty potato, I don't do it justice. Cooking has always been a chore to me as opposed to a pleasure."

You could've knocked me over with a feather when Ronan squeezed my hand in his. It made my stomach feel like there was a rollercoaster inside of it. I'd expected him to ignore the fact I hadn't really answered his question, but he didn't.

"There's no shame in not knowing what you want to do," he assured me. "I knew I wanted to work with food, but I didn't have a clue how I'd make it happen. I should've gone to college after high school, but I didn't have a pot to piss in, and I was afraid of student loan debt. At the time, it was a tough nut to swallow."

"And yet you wound up where you were supposed to, doing what you've always loved," I reminded him.

The smile he gave me warmed me from the inside out. "You're right," he agreed. "Life has a funny way of placing you where you belong. Without a doubt, getting out of here was exactly what I needed," he shared.

I was glad to hear it. I'd never forgotten what happened after his parents died, or how hard it was for him. Like most people in our neighborhood, the Sharpes were middle class. His father was a realtor, and his mother stayed at home. After Mr. Sharpe died, Ronan's mom seemed to have been on a one-woman mission to spend ridiculous amounts of money. It hadn't been a wise move, for obvious reasons. Without Mr. Sharpe alive and working, there was no money coming in. There was life insurance, but the policy was just enough to pay the house off.

Mrs. Sharpe burned through their savings within a year. The last few months of her life were spent avoiding bill collectors demanding she pay the outrageous credit card debt she'd run up. She'd staunchly refused to get a job. It wasn't as if she could have worked, not really, considering her alcohol problem. Will hadn't wanted to get involved with his mom's issues, so he didn't. Between Will's lack of involvement and Mrs. Sharpe's complete denial of the issue, Ronan was left with no choice but to work two restaurant jobs. He'd done this to support himself all while keeping the basics paid for at the family home.

Both of the Sharpes had favored Will. I'd known this for as long as I could remember—way back into my childhood. It wasn't something anyone needed to tell me, either. It was blatantly obvious. I remembered how sick I'd felt hearing Izzy talking to our dad after Mrs. Sharpe's will was read. She'd left everything to Will. Because she'd burned through the money, it essentially boiled down to him getting the house. To satisfy the debt Mrs. Sharpe left behind, the house was sold and all the leftover money went to Will. It was enough for him to buy a house of his own. It was wretched the way things always seemed to work out for him.

According to Izzy, Ronan was left some furniture and a watch, which belonged to his father. The watch, meanwhile, had been worthless, not to mention broken.

Back then, knowing I didn't hold the monopoly on dysfunctional family dynamics helped me continue putting one foot in front of the other. There were so many things about Ronan that shaped who I was, yet he had no idea.

"What about you? Would you ever want to leave Fort Collins?"

I didn't get a chance to answer because Chuck opened the door and walked into the room with the diaper bag in hand.

Chapter Ten

Ronan

EVEN AS A YOUNG GIRL, KEELY HAD ALWAYS BEEN EASY TO talk to because she knew how to listen. It's a sad fact— many people don't possess the patience. Think about how many times you've been talking to someone, only to realize they've checked out on you. Keely stayed present and focused, taking it all in. I'd thought it was cool when she was young, but having her focus solely on me as an adult was very, very different. I felt a connection with her I had never experienced with anyone else.

It didn't give me a warm fuzzy feeling when she deflected from talking about herself. It left me with questions about why she hadn't been able to afford college, but I didn't want to upset her by asking. I made a mental note to ask Canter what, if anything, he knew about where all of Hollis Carmichael's money went. Hollis hadn't been rich by any stretch of the imagination, but there should've been enough money from the sale of his house to send her to college. Then again, the insurance policy my father left behind should've lasted my mother years. She was flat broke within months. I knew better than most how shit could get derailed.

I'd long since forgotten Keely and I were holding hands, but it all came back to me when Chuck got back. As the door shut behind him I saw that he glanced down and made a mental note of our linked fingers. As controlled as he was, I'd still seen the flash of surprise in his eyes. Severing the connection to Keely, I ran my fingers through my hair as I looked at the pale pink diaper bag Chuck carried on his shoulder.

"Did you find anything inside of it?" I asked.

He shook his head. "It's Keely's bag to open."

I couldn't argue with his logic. Crossing the room, he handed it right to her. She stared at it for a few seconds before looking up at me.

"Can you unzip it?"

I did as she asked, and then we started going through the bag together. There was no sign of anything from Izzy. The main section of the bag was full of diapers, wipes, three pink outfits and a few pacifiers. Keely's face fell as we pulled everything out and found nothing.

"I must've dreamt it," she whispered sadly.

"It's okay," I assured her. "We'll get to the bottom of—"

I stopped talking when I got to the changing pad tucked into the front of the bag. As I pulled it out, a fairly thick envelope came with it. Keely's name was scrawled in black marker across the front.

She let out a gasp as she grabbed the envelope, lifting it up to inspect it.

"It's Izzy's writing!" Reaching out, she handed it off to me. "Please open it," she said.

I looked to Chuck first to make sure it was okay. When he nodded his approval, I opened it carefully. Inside I found a letter written to Keely in Izzy's handwriting. There were also thirty-one money orders, each made out to Keely for five hundred dollars.

The money orders got set aside the moment Keely gasped as

she began reading the letter.

She let out an, "Oh my God," as she kept on reading.

The suspense damn near killed me. The few minutes it took her to read the entire thing seemed to stretch out for an eternity. I could tell when she finished because the hand holding the letter dropped down onto her lap.

"What's it say?"

"It… she—"

She stopped speaking and closed her eyes for a second. Her eyes opened after she inhaled and exhaled slowly.

Finally she said, "It was all a lie."

Lifting her arm, she held the paper out to me. "I can't even explain—you need to read this to believe it."

Chuck had been standing next to me, so he and I were able to read it at the same time.

> *Kiki,*
>
> *I'm thinking by now you've already figured out the truth. I lied. If my plan goes off as it should, you'll be reading this in the hotel room I'm taking you to so we can 'meet the parents' after we leave the hospital. I have a feeling you won't be surprised to know you were right to be suspicious this whole time. I'm not a surrogate.*
>
> *This baby wasn't planned—my birth control failed. I was set to terminate. I thought I could end the pregnancy without any problem. I was wrong. I tried three times, and each time I couldn't go through with it.*
>
> *I can't keep this little girl. I'm a lot of things, but I'm not a mother. I've never wanted children. Being a mom isn't my dream. It's always been*

yours, though. The amount of begging I did to get Will to allow me to do this was almost unbearable. Even now, he's not happy with me. You don't like him, so you don't see what I do. Will is my world and my entire life. I can't live without him, nor do I want to. He's the only person who's every truly loved me—every single broken piece. I know you want to argue and say Dad loved all of me, but you're wrong. Dad loved Kassidy. Everything else was just pretend. Anytime he had a chance to really be a father, he always showed me how little he thought of me.

Once I made the decision to have the baby, it meant I needed to figure out what it meant long term. Will is mad I won't just give her up for adoption. He doesn't understand why I've been so stubborn about it. I know you'll get it. The reason I can't do it is because of Will's brother. How'd adoption work out for Ronan? Not good. I don't want the same fate for my daughter.

The more I tried to plan for what to do after I give birth, the clearer the answer became. There's only one person I can rely on to do the right thing for this job. Of course, it's you. You've always been a bleeding heart, but you're also tough as hell. I know you, Kiki. You'll love this baby with all of your heart, and you'll give her a life I can't even imagine. No one else would do even half as good a job as you will.

Will's already signed off and terminated his rights. By the time you read this, I'll have signed mine away as well. I'll have our lawyer contact you within a day or so to wrap everything up. You'll need to stay in town for a few days while the paperwork is filed and finalized. Once everything is taken care of, I need you to rent a U-Haul, pack your life up, take her and get out of this town. Do not look back and don't you ever try to tell me where you are.

All along I've been buying all the baby stuff for you so you'd have everything you need for quite a while. I've also been getting money orders whenever I've been able. I know it's not much in the grand scheme of things, but you should be able to set yourself up for a little while.

I know raising a baby alone won't be easy, but I know you've got this. We've never been close—in all honesty, we both know we don't even like each other. For all of that, somehow, I'm positive you're this child's forever mother. I'm counting on your soft heart to do the right thing.

Please don't try to call me after you read this. Keeping Will calm about what's happening has been getting harder by the day. He needs a break from anything to do with the baby, and I need to spend some time loving him back to our normal.

I know I'm asking for a lot, but I need to ask for more.

It would mean more to me than I can say if you would email me photos of her life each year on her birthday. The photos can never include landmarks. When you go, you stay gone. I've set up an email account Will doesn't know about—please be sure to email me there. I've told him you're taking the baby and leaving and we won't ever have to see or hear anything about her. He can never know I'm asking for updates.

Take care of yourself and love our girl. Whatever story you tell her about me and her birth, I hope you'll let her know I loved her enough to do the right thing for her by letting her go.

Wherever the road takes you, never forget you're carrying a piece of my heart—the best piece—with you. Keep her safe. You're the only person I trust to do that.

Be strong,

Izzy

My mind was blown. I looked up at Keely, only to find her just as stunned. In that moment, I couldn't even form words.

"This is the most selfless thing Izzy ever did," she said softly. "I didn't know it was in her to think of anyone other than herself or Will."

"Sometimes people surprise you," Chuck said. "But at least you've got your answer and, for what it's worth, I think you were the right choice. It's good for you to know even before she lost her life, Izzy knew who she would choose to take care of the baby."

I was immediately annoyed at Chuck for putting pressure on Keely. At nineteen she was far too young to have to take on a parental role.

"Don't make her feel obligated," I snapped. "She's damn lucky to be alive. It was selfish of Izzy to expect Keely to raise Emma. It's a huge responsibility and I don't think—"

"Of course I'm going to do it," Keely interrupted. She said it firmly, not a lick of hesitation about it.

I absolutely did not want Keely to raise the baby by herself. The baby needed two parents. The thought of Keely one day marrying some asshole who Emma would call Daddy made my stomach roil. I refused to think too much about *why* I felt so strongly.

"Think about what you're saying," I implored her. "You're nineteen—"

Her eyes flashed angrily as she gave me a look that could have frozen a small country. "I'm well aware of how old I am," she snipped. "Age doesn't have a damn thing to do with the kind of mother I'll be. A number doesn't decide whether a person will be a good parent. It only matters what's in a person's heart—and mine is committed to Emma."

"Like I said, Izzy chose right."

I looked back at Chuck in annoyance. Crossing his arms over his chest, he gave me a pointed look.

Not willing to ask why he was looking at me like that, I looked down at Keely.

"I wasn't insulting you," I assured her. "I just want you to think about it before you commit—"

She held up her hand to interrupt me. "I'm already committed, Ronan."

"Give yourself a little time. Maybe you'll see it differently in a day or so. It's a big decision."

She shrugged her shoulder as she let out a breath. "The enormity of the choice isn't lost on me. Sometimes the best thing you can do is dive into the water with faith you'll ride the wave. I felt it the second I saw her little face. Emma is my daughter. I choose her, and I know to the depths of my being I'll never regret it."

It was obvious she wasn't going to change her mind. I knew she was right. Emma belonged with her—but something wasn't sitting right which had me panicking.

I stared into Keely's eyes, searching for any sign of hesitation on her part. There was none. I gripped at the back of my neck as I turned to Chuck. "What needs to happen now?"

"I'll get in touch with child services and get the ball rolling. With the letter from Izzy detailing that she'd always intended to give custody to Keely, along with paperwork she had started with her lawyer terminating Will's rights, it won't be hard to get this pushed through as an intra-family adoption. All things considered, I can't imagine any social worker or judge holding it up."

That was a relief. I was an anxious mess, but I damn sure didn't want Keely being upset. She needed things to run smoothly.

"Before I go, we need to discuss what you want to do with William and Isabelle's bodies," Chuck continued.

It was the last thing either of us wanted to hear. I could tell Keely was upset and I sure as hell hadn't wanted to think about it.

My hands curled up into fists at my sides as I tried to control my anger. What the fuck was I supposed to do with Will's remains?

"You can throw Will's carcass into a fucking dumpster," I spat out angrily.

Chuck crossed his arms over his chest and let out a harsh breath. "I don't disagree, but it wouldn't be legal."

I thought it over for a few seconds before I made a decision. "Send him to whatever funeral home you'd recommend and have him cremated. I'll pay for it, but I don't want the remains."

I turned to Keely so we could discuss Izzy. "What do you want to do?"

She thought it over silently before answering.

"I'd like her cremated as well. I'll think about a permanent spot for her later."

"Sounds good," Chuck replied. "I'm going to get out of your hair now, but I'm sure I'll see you around. Before Ronan leaves, he'll be coming to dinner out at the house whether he wants to or not. You and Emma will come too."

I fucking hated the reminder that I'd be leaving Keely—and Emma—behind.

Chapter Eleven

Keely

Ⅰ KNEW IT WAS WISHFUL THINKING, BUT I SWORE EMMA recognized Ronan and me as soon as she saw us. Like the previous evening, Ronan held her and brought her to me. I'd gotten a bit more mobility with my arm, but Dr. Smith warned I would need to take it easy for a few weeks.

There were so many other things going on when she said it, I hadn't realized what it meant for the future. It didn't hit until about forty minutes after Ronan and I got to the nursery when the doctor in charge came and introduced herself to me. Everything was going along just fine until she asked who was going to help me take care of Emma after I got her home.

There was no one I could ask. My two closest high school friends were off at college—one in Denver, the other in Rhode Island, leaving them off the list of possible helpers. I hadn't heard from them much at all since they left, either. I got it—that jump from high school to college was about making new friends and starting a new life. However, it left me out of luck as far as having a support system. My other friends worked at the grocery store with me, and, like myself, they all needed a paycheck. No one could afford to take time off, and it wasn't as though I could afford to pay someone to do it.

I had never felt so alone. I couldn't believe I was so cut off, there weren't even people I could beg for help. Near tears I choked out, "I don't have anyone."

"We can't allow you to take her by yourself with the way your arm is," the doctor said firmly. "For at least ten days, you'll need help. If something were to happen, you could rip the stitches open."

I felt myself losing control—all of the control I worked tirelessly at maintaining was fast slipping away and it was all catching up to me. My parents were dead. My sister was dead. I'd almost died, and Emma came within moments of never being born. I'd held all of my emotion in, but right then it was threatening to boil over like hot lava.

My voice wobbled as I made a plea for help. "Isn't there a visiting nurse, or—"

"I'll do it," Ronan announced.

I turned and gaped at him in shock. It was so unexpected; I half expected to see Emma's jaw hanging open, too. Of course it wasn't—she'd been busy enjoying her snuggle time with him. I swear she ate it up when he held her.

"I can't ask you to—"

"You didn't," he pointed out matter-of-factly. "I volunteered myself."

I won't lie and say I wasn't thrilled with his offer. Having Ronan around made me feel secure.

"But your job…"

"Linc's got it. Trust me, he owes me. We've got a new manager in place too. I'm leaving him a lot better off than what I dealt with when he had to leave town."

"Are you sure?" I questioned anxiously.

"One hundred percent positive," he replied. "You girls need me here, so here's where I'll be until you don't."

I knew such a time was never going to come.

I was a nervous wreck during the interview process with the social worker that came to work out the details of the adoption. Gaining custody of Emma was imperative, and I'd been terrified something would go wrong. In the end, the adoption had been approved based on my sister's wishes and my ability to raise Emma in a safe and loving home. I was, once again, left feeling gratitude toward Izzy. Where Will's body had tested positive for alcohol and drugs, Izzy had been clean. If there had been any trace of those things in her system, it would've set the adoption back in a big way.

Through it all, Ronan was at my side. He left late each night to sleep at Canter's but he returned first thing every morning. Every day I felt closer to him. He focused on me and on Emma like we were the two most important people on earth.

For the first time in my life, I felt like part of a team. Ronan and I talked about everything and as I dealt with all the details of the adoption, he supported me every step of the way.

When I was handed Emma's birth certificate, Ronan held me as I cried. Emma Isabelle Carmichael, it read. As happy as I was to have the adoption finalized, her last name being Carmichael felt wrong. The way Ronan loved her—even if he didn't know it—was paternal. I wished Emma had his last name.

If only wishes came true.

When we finally got the all clear to leave the hospital, it was a huge relief. By then I was anxious to take my daughter home so we could start living a normal life. Ronan was all over that, and I couldn't believe what lengths he went to in order to be helpful. He'd rented a car—a sedan for safety, he emphasized—then went and bought a car seat. Izzy had purchased one that was sitting in my apartment, but Ronan declined to get it. When I pushed and asked why, he told me he "needed to do the research himself" to find the best and safest car seat.

I was nervous but excited to get Emma home. Ronan was mostly anxious. I would swear he convinced himself any exposure to the outside world was bad for her. He'd gone and gotten my prescriptions before arriving to pick us up to go home because he didn't want Emma out any longer than she needed to be. It was very sweet, the way he worried.

Kristi scheduled her break so she could take photos of us getting Emma into the car for her first ride. I appreciated the gesture so much I almost couldn't talk past the lump in my throat. She'd been such a huge help. The night before Emma and I were discharged, Kristi bought a pair of yoga pants and a sweatshirt for me to wear home. Two days before, she'd gone to Target and gotten me several pairs of underwear and some socks. I don't know what I would've done without her assistance.

It took upwards of ten minutes to get Emma in the car since Ronan panicked and swore he'd bought the one car seat in the world that wouldn't buckle in right. Kristi snapped pictures and took videos the entire time. She also chided him for being so over the top. When he was finished, she handed the phone back to him.

"Alright, Ronan—you've got this. Take care of your girls."

He looked pensive as he took the phone back and gave her a quick hug, and he said nothing about her calling us his girls. I wished we were his. Even as a young girl, I'd always felt so safe with him. I'd swear he'd been born in full protector mode. It just came naturally to him.

When he got into the car and buckled up, I'd been feeling good. Everything was fine, until the car started moving when he pulled away from the curb. Suddenly I was dizzy, and my heart was slamming against my chest. I closed my eyes as I gasped for air and tried not to cry. I was scared shitless and completely overwhelmed by an onslaught of memories from the accident. I must've been making a fair amount of noise because Ronan immediately stopped the car and put it in park.

"Shit, Keely! Talk to me, honey. What's wrong?"

Through clenched teeth I answered, "I feel like I'm back in the car with Will. I'm having a panic attack."

He unhooked his seatbelt and pulled me into his arms. Holding me tight, he stroked my hair.

"It's going to be okay," he promised. "I've got you. I won't let anything bad happen, I promise."

I clutched the front of his shirt and held on tight.

"Let's take some slow, deep breaths," he instructed. "You need to open your eyes, look at me and focus on what you can see in the here and now. You're not in Will's car, sweetheart."

I soaked up his warmth like a sponge, basking in the strength he offered. My heart skipped a few happy beats when he called me sweetheart. Opening my eyes, I did as he instructed and focused on what was happening in the moment as opposed to thinking about the accident.

When I could speak, I thanked him for helping me through my panic attack. He gently pushed my hair back from my face and looked me over. Once he found whatever it was he was looking for, he pulled away. I came within seconds of asking him not to let me go.

"You don't ever need to thank me," he said gruffly. "I want to take care of you."

After he buckled his seatbelt, he pulled away from the curb again. I didn't freak out again. The drive to my apartment, which should've taken less than ten minutes, wound up taking closer to fifteen. The posted speed limit was forty-five, but Ronan did thirty.

Cars blew past us. A few people honked their horns and one angry lady pulled up next to us at a red light and yelled, "Put your foot on the goddamn gas, Grandma!"

Ronan pressed the control button for the window, so it went down. Looking over at the lady he said, "Sorry ma'am. Brand new baby on board."

I just about died holding my laughter in. I wasn't even upset when the lady swooned at Ronan.

The woman looked horrified and immediately changed her tune. "You're so sweet," she hollered. "I'm sorry I yelled. Being a dad is hard. My husband almost lost his mind with our first. Good luck to you both!"

Ronan sucked in a breath when she said the word *dad*. He seemed lost for a second before he shook it off, gave her a smile and rolled the window up.

He was silent as he started driving again. I wondered if the woman assuming he was Emma's dad bothered him. Granted, it bothered me too—but purely because I wished it were true.

A minute or so passed before he broke the silence.

"I hope I didn't give Emma a chill by opening the window."

I was positive she wasn't cold. He'd gotten a fleece liner for her car seat, and she was wearing a warm outfit, a knit cap, socks, and there was also a blanket tucked around her legs. If anything, she was probably too toasty.

"The window was open for less than a minute," I reassured him. "She's fine."

"We'll have to keep an eye on her. Any sneezing or sniffles, I'll have Kristi check her over."

Right then, I felt sorry for Kristi. I knew if I didn't stay on top of him, Ronan would call her every time he thought anything could be wrong with Emma. Knowing he took her safety as seriously as he clearly did touched me. I wished he could be her dad. She deserved someone who cared as much as he did. I'd turned to look out the car window so he wouldn't see the sheen of tears in my eyes.

Once we got to my apartment building, he helped me out of the car before grabbing Emma's seat.

"I'll come back for the rest of what I got at the store after I get you both settled."

I hadn't been home since the night of the accident. My apartment was generally clean, but with all the baby stuff Izzy amassed, it was going to be a tight squeeze just getting the three of us in there.

"What did you buy?"

"Just some stuff," he said vaguely. "Don't worry."

Figuring he'd realize getting anything else into my apartment would only happen with an industrial sized smasher, I shrugged it off and let it go.

When we got to my door, Ronan opened it and let me in first. He brought up the rear with Emma's seat safely clutched in his hand.

The apartment was where I'd set my head down since graduating high school, but it didn't feel very welcoming. As a rule, I kept things tidy, so it wasn't crapped up or anything—it was just kind of blank. Even all of the baby stuff piled high did nothing to give it personality. I'd refused to set down roots in Fort Collins so keeping my apartment sterile and basic was a way for me to keep my focus on getting out. It had been fine for me, but I wasn't thrilled to be bringing Emma home from the hospital to a place which screamed temporary.

"Looks like I've got some stuff to put together," Ronan chuckled from behind me.

He wasn't wrong—there was a ton. Setting Emma's carrier on the table, he unbuckled her and lifted her out to cradle her against his chest before he looked around at all the boxes.

"Damn. The car seat I just bought? Izzy got the same one. Guess I should've listened to you before I went to Babies 'R' Us," he admitted.

My apartment was small, so there wasn't a lot to show him. I gave him the grand tour in less than ninety seconds. There was a dinette set for two in the galley kitchen, which was the first place you walked into upon entering. Through the kitchen, we entered the living room/bedroom. My only splurge was a king-sized bed. It was crappy quality, but I couldn't sleep in anything smaller. The bedding was ugly, a twenty-dollar set I'd found in the clearance section at the local Walmart. It was black with neon yellow daisies that were hideously ugly. The saving grace was its softness. It could best be described as comfortable yet butt ugly chic.

A few inches from my bed was a gray recliner with a small side table next to it. Both of those were Craigslist curb alert pieces. They were free—and looked it—so they were showing their age. On the other side of the room there was a small console table with an old nineteen-inch television on top of it. All the available wall and floor space around the television was taken up with more of Izzy's purchases.

The apartment tour was over when I gestured toward the bathroom, which was also home to a stackable washer and dryer. "So," I told him, "I'm going to go through the two boxes of newborn clothes, pull the tags on everything and wash it.

"It's a shame I didn't get all this stuff yesterday," he mused. "I could've done this at the Laundromat when I did all the clothes I bought."

I was completely stunned. We'd brought Emma home in one of the outfits Izzy packed in the diaper bag. There hadn't been worry about washing it because it was already done. I'd been relieved to find Izzy thought it through.

"What clothes?"

"I picked up a few outfits," he admitted.

I asked for clarification. "What's a few?"

He avoided my gaze by staring down at Emma. "I don't know… five? Maybe ten?"

I could tell by the tone of his voice and the way his eyes darted away there were more than *a few* outfits. I couldn't believe Ronan Sharpe voluntarily shopped. My dad used to call him Johnny Cash because, like the singer, Ronan wore a lot of black. He was really mixing things up when he went with grays or whites. He didn't add color because he didn't have the inclination to shop often. It was a well-known fact.

I couldn't believe he'd gone out and bought things for a baby girl.

"Seriously?"

He shrugged. "She should have the best."

"So you just raided a rack at Babies 'R' Us?"

"Well… no. After I was finished there, I went to Gymboree and Carter's."

All signs pointed to my being correct in assuming there were more than five or ten outfits.

"Okayyy," I said softly.

It was clear talking about his crazy shopping habits was making him uncomfortable, so I decided to let it go.

"It's great you took the time to wash it all," I said. "I don't want to upset you, but I did some research and babies need to have their clothes washed in scent and dye free detergent—"

"I talked to Kristi and a nice grandmother at Babies 'R' Us. I got a case of Dreft detergent," he replied. "Everything is washed just the way it should be."

I couldn't believe just how amazing he was. He'd gone out of his way to buy Emma a car seat and clothes (even though he hadn't needed to, which was another story) and then took the time to launder everything. I'm pretty sure I must've started looking at him like he was an angel.

He shuffled back and forth a few times before blurting, "How about you sit down and hold Emma? I'll run down to the car and get the bags. Afterward, I'll get on putting some of this stuff together."

I didn't have to be asked twice. Because I was still sore, my range of motion was diminished. I'd been assured it would get better day-by-day. I'd been really upset about it since I desperately wanted to hold my baby. Ronan came up with the solution. We tried it several different ways before figuring out if he set Emma on my left shoulder, I was able to hold her without having to move my right arm very much at all.

Being able to have her so close to me was the highlight of each day. Striding the few feet to the gray recliner, I sat down and got comfortable. As soon as I was situated, I nodded at him. Inevitably, I'd come to love how close he needed to get to me to place her in my arms. Close enough to feel the stubble on his cheeks and smell his body wash. I longed to trace my fingers over his tattoos.

After making certain Emma was secure, he stepped back. Smiling down at the two of us, he reached into his pocket and pulled out his phone.

He smiled as he said, "Babies' first few minutes at home gets a picture."

I appreciated the way he'd taken to snapping photos regularly. I didn't want to miss documenting Emma's life each and every day. Between the two of us, pictures were covered. I'd taken dozens of photos of her, many of them when she was in Ronan's arms. When he would leave the hospital at night to go to Canter's, more often than not, I'd find myself scrolling through the photos while I tried not to cry. I was so happy to have him there. Still, a part of me felt as though fate was very cruel in showing me what I'd always wanted so desperately but would never truly have.

In addition to buying the clothes, he'd also bought a few pink gingham lined wicker laundry baskets. Each one was piled high with folded baby clothes. I knew between what Izzy purchased and what Ronan added on, it was unlikely Emma would be wearing the same outfit twice for at least two months.

The expression on his face as he brought it all inside got me laughing. If I didn't know better, I'd have thought Ronan had a shopping addiction. It touched me to know he'd spent so much time doing something he disliked in order to be certain Emma had everything she would need.

By the time he got it all in the house, Emma was out cold. We had the perfect window to get some stuff put together, so I asked Ronan to help me put her down. Since nothing for her was together yet, we ended up strapping her back into the car seat, which he put in the middle of my bed, surrounded by pillows. I laughed as I told him he didn't need to worry she'd try to make a run for it. He was over the top in his need to protect, but I wasn't about to complain.

Chapter Twelve

Ronan

WHEN I SAID I WOULD STAY AND TAKE CARE OF KEELY and Emma, I hadn't realized I'd be doing so in an apartment so small it made my eight hundred square foot house seem like a mansion.

The size of her apartment wasn't a problem just because it was tight. The issue was Keely being close enough to touch pretty much all of the time—and I wanted to touch.

We were busy for the first couple of hours putting together Emma's bassinet and changing table. It seemed innocuous enough, but it was a fucking nightmare. She insisted on helping—even when I argued she needed to relax. Thus, we wound up sitting across from each other on the floor while putting the furniture together. I assembled and she handed me the different parts and tools. This meant we were continuously touching which got me so hard I could've used my dick as a hammer.

Once the torture of putting the furniture together was over, I insisted on putting together some small things by myself, citing that they would be easy. After putting together a diaper genie thing, I started work on some whacked-as-fuck chair. The damn thing vibrated, went up and down and rocked. It was called a Mamaroo, or some shit. I'd never seen anything like it, and I thought it was stupid.

I'd wanted to toss it into a donate pile but Keely stopped me. She insisted Izzy had wanted Emma to have it, so I agreed we would at least try it. The damn thing was nuts and crazy high tech. By the time I finished putting it together, my hard on was under control. I was in the clear until we started reading the directions and realized we could install an app on our phones to allow us to control the chair. It didn't make sense to me seeing as how her apartment was so small I could probably sneeze and hit the controller, but Keely was excited which meant I did it with a smile.

My hard on came back with a fucking vengeance when she sat next to me at the kitchen table. The goddamn thing was about as big as a plate and the two seats were side by side. This meant our thighs were touching, and when she leaned in to touch my phone and show me something on the app, her cheek was against my shoulder. Everywhere she touched me felt hot and I wanted nothing more than to grab her and kiss the fuck out of her. I reigned in the impulse, barely.

After we got the chair figured out, Keely got down on the floor and started going through the baskets of clothing I'd brought in. I did my best to avoid looking at her while she went through everything since I'd lowballed the estimate of what I'd bought for Emma by more than a little bit. I'd said five to ten outfits—it was a bit more than two dozen. I knew it was overkill—Emma weighed just over seven pounds, and as far as I knew there wasn't a baby fashion show each day, but still. Logic didn't matter to me because I wanted her to have everything. In all honesty, I forced myself to stop shopping. I'd have gotten more.

After she finished with the clothes, we set up the diaper-changing table together. Once again, we kept brushing up against or flat out running into each other. It was a nightmare. After that exercise in torture concluded, we tackled the boxes stacked in the galley kitchen. We found Izzy had divided clothing for the baby into said boxes by size for the first year.

When it was all said and done, the apartment was so tight the two of us could barely move. I called Canter and asked if we could store what wasn't immediately needed in his garage for a while. There were cases of diapers Emma wouldn't need until she grew into them along with five extra cases of wipes. The cases of formula Izzy bought weren't what Emma had been drinking in the hospital, so they needed to be donated as well.

I'd like to say I did this as a matter of practicality, but the truth is I was desperate for a break. Not because I was overwhelmed by the baby, far from it. I loved spending time with and holding her.

The reason behind my anxiety was simple, with every passing hour I was struggling more and more with my desire for Keely. Being with her around the clock wasn't going to make things any easier, clearly. Every time we touched, I got closer to the edge. On top of that, the yoga pants she was wearing hugged her legs and showcased her gorgeous ass, which didn't help one bit either. I was damn near drooling, which wasn't a good thing.

Canter had been on his way home from whatever case he was working when I'd called, so he came right away. Emma was just finished being changed, having her bottle and being burped, which meant Keely wouldn't have to move her arm around too much to take care of her. Still, I had the receiver to the baby monitor I'd bought clipped to the pocket of my jeans. Keely laughed at me and said a monitor was overkill considering the size of her place, but the grandmother at Babies 'R' Us said I needed one. So in the cart it went.

When I swung the door open for Canter, Emma was cradled

in my left arm. For whatever reason, I found I liked holding her as much as possible. Knowing I wouldn't be around forever, I'd decided I should suck it up while I could.

Canter gave me a knowing look when he looked at me holding Emma.

"Holy shit," he exclaimed. "You really are Mr. Fucking Mom."

I shut him down with a glare. "Don't curse around the baby, idiot."

"All right, all right. I mean holy poop. You're like the baby whisperer now. I thought maybe it was just a hospital thing but you're taking this all the way. If I didn't see this with my own two eyes, I'd never believe it."

I shrugged his comment off. "Yeah, yeah. Let me put her in this crazy chair thing and then we can lug this all down to your car."

Following me into the living area, Canter walked over to where Keely was sitting reading some baby book on her phone. I didn't know how she was reading off such a tiny screen, but she said she was used to it.

While his attention was on Keely, I surreptitiously smelled Emma's head a few times before giving her chubby little cheek a kiss. Once I got her strapped into the Mamaroo, I put it on a rock-a-bye setting. I watched for a minute or so, making sure the damn thing was steady. Surprisingly, it was, and since Emma looked happy, I was good with it.

Walking the few steps to where Canter was standing next to Keely's chair, I felt my blood pressure rising when he made her laugh. I didn't like it one little bit. I'd trust Canter with my life, but it didn't matter right then because I was feeling territorial. Stepping close to her, so her attention was on me and not him, I pointed at the monitor clipped to me.

"Don't panic if she gets upset while we're taking all this stuff out," I instructed. "If I hear her crying, I'll stop and get her right away."

"I'll be fine," she assured me. "The doctor said I couldn't take care of her all the time by myself, mostly because I wouldn't be able to bathe her or carry her for long periods of time. I'm not totally useless, though. You worry too much."

Someone needed to worry about them. "I don't want you hurting yourself. Just let me do this for you, okay?"

Her expression softened as she smiled and then nodded. "Okay."

Canter and I made quick work of getting the first round of shit down to his car. The second we got to the car, he started with his commentary.

"Guess you were wrong about not being father material," he remarked.

I grunted as I heaved a box of baby clothes into the back of his Durango. "I'm not her father."

He gave me a wry look as he rearranged what I'd put into the SUV.

"Keep right on bullshitting yourself," he chided. "Pretty sure if Emma had words, she'd be calling you Dada right about now."

Through gritted teeth, I snapped, "She's Keely's. Not mine."

"Yeah? It doesn't come across that way. Looked to me like she belongs to both of you."

I threw a box in hard enough that some of the contents scattered.

"Then you need glasses."

Canter chuckled as he gathered the clothes that had popped out of the box when I tossed it inside the SUV. "I didn't need glasses to see you were ready to go fucking caveman because I was talking to Keely."

He was pissing me off. What the fuck did he think he was doing? Trying to drop logic on me? I wasn't feeling it.

"She's fucking nineteen," I growled.

He laughed in my face. "Really? That's the rope you're going to swing on? Keely Carmichael might be nineteen, but she's more mature than both of us put together. You're using her age as an excuse not to make your move."

"I'm doing no such thing," I asserted. "I'm not even attracted to her."

He smiled like a Cheshire cat. "Why didn't you say so? I like babies, so dating a woman with a child isn't a problem for me. Keely's beautiful. You mind if I ask her out?"

There was barely a second between him saying it and me getting furiously angry. I grabbed his collar, twisting it in my fist as leverage as I yanked him toward me.

"You so much as open your mouth to ask her out and I'll goddamn kneecap you. She's off limits!"

The bastard laughed in my face as he shoved me away.

He stared at me knowingly as he adjusted his shirt. "You were saying something about not being attracted to her?"

I ignored him as I put another box in the back of the SUV. After a prolonged silence where Canter stared at me smugly, I threw my hands in the air.

"Fine. I may be a little attracted," I conceded grudgingly.

"That's like saying you're a little bit of an asshole. You just went nuts. I've never seen you so obviously into someone. Especially not with—"

I stopped him from going further. "Don't bring her up. It's in the past, and it needs to stay there."

Canter crossed his arms over his chest and stared at me thoughtfully.

"It is, and it does, but it's never going to happen since you're the one holding onto it. It's time to let it go."

I exhaled slowly before nodding my agreement. "I thought I was over it until I got here, and it all came back to me."

He made a thoughtful sound. "I didn't think you were over it," he said. "You've avoided commitment like it was a plague. You took that shit on like you had some fault in it, but you didn't. What she did wasn't a reflection on you. She fucked up. Not you. You're letting something you had no control over keep you from having a real relationship."

There are some things in life that can't help but shape how you see things going forward. My world hadn't just crashed down in one afternoon—it imploded.

"You didn't see what I did."

"You're right, I didn't. But here's what I think, you look at it like finding out what was going down is the worst thing ever to happen to you. I disagree one hundred percent. I think you got fucking lucky, and you should be thankful."

I couldn't believe what I was hearing. "You think seeing that sick shit was good?"

He didn't back down even a little.

"Yeah, I do. If you hadn't seen it, you'd have married the bitch, maybe had a kid or two with a lying whore. You dodged a fucking bullet. She was garbage. You felt fucking sorry for her because she snowed you with bullshit lines about wanting a better life. She was an asshole."

I wasn't stupid—he made a fucking point. I stared at him silently as I tried to process his words.

"When you put it that way, I guess I did," I conceded.

Canter gave me a self-satisfied smile— his go-to expression whenever he was right.

"I've known you for a long fucking time," he said. "The way you look at her is different. Don't fuck around and let this go. Keely's gorgeous and being a mom at nineteen won't keep guys away from her. Just think about it, man. Don't miss out on something great because you're holding on to the past," he said, leaning up against the back of the Durango.

"Fuck me, you're a bitch," I chided in an effort to diffuse the seriousness of the conversation. "I'll get right on living my 'best life,' Oprah. Don't worry."

He extended his middle finger in my direction. "You just hate me being more enlightened than you," he chuckled.

"Yeah, yeah, yeah. Hey," I said condescendingly, "How long ago was your last relationship?"

He puffed up as he gave me a shit-eating grin.

"Last night. Her name was Joni, and she had amazing oral skills."

I threw back my head and laughed. "You're calling your one-night stands relationships now?"

"Hey, we related," he chuckled. "All night long and again this morning."

I'd missed hanging out one on one with Canter. He was a great best friend.

"I can't believe I'm even considering taking relationship advice from someone who got hives both times you tried to ask Nikki Cole out. Without Benadryl, the elephantitis of the face and neck would've been permanent."

One of his hands went right to his throat as he shuddered with the memory. "Dude, it was scary as hell. I don't know why she made me so fucking nervous."

"'Cause she didn't like you, dumbass."

He punched me in the shoulder as he chuckled.

"She liked me fine," he argued.

"Yeah, when you were doing her chores. Otherwise, she had no use for you."

"Her loss," he laughed.

"Right. Hard to believe she passed on thirteen-year-old you. I bet she's still crying about it."

"Oh Canter," I said in a girlish voice as I batted my eyelashes at him. "Tell me again about the time you farted in study hall and the teacher dry heaved and ran from the room."

He doubled over from laughing so hard. "You're such an asshole," he wheezed out in between fits of laughter.

We were both laughing when I heard Emma making noise on the monitor. I then heard Keely talking to her softly. Immediately, my priority was getting back to them.

"Duty calls. Let's get the rest of the shit loaded up."

We made quick work of getting everything else into the Durango. After I thanked Canter for all his help, he took one last shot.

"Get back to Keely and your baby, Daddy."

If I'd been in less of a hurry, I'd have snapped at him for calling me Daddy. Instead, I gave him the finger before running up the stairs to the apartment. Nothing mattered more to me than being there when my girls needed me.

It didn't occur to me that I needed them just as much.

Chapter Thirteen

Keely

I T WAS GREAT TO BE HOME INSTEAD OF THE HOSPITAL. AFTER days of eating bland and unappealing food, I was starving. Emma had woken up but was easy to settle, so I moved her high-tech chair about four feet so I could see her while I was in the kitchen. I knew there were a few boxes of macaroni and cheese in my pantry, and I was planning to make two of them. I was in the process of filling up a pot with water when Ronan came back in after taking the last load of boxes to Canter's car. The second he saw me in the kitchen, he immediately shooed me away from the stove.

"Are you nuts? You can't be cooking!"

"Putting water into a pot is hardly cooking," I laughed.

"It's my duty to take care of you. I'm not doing a very good job if you're in the kitchen," he answered dryly.

I couldn't contain the goofy grin as it spread across my face. I tried to reassure him I was fine. "You were doing a lot of work. I can handle mac and cheese."

"Not while I'm here," he said. "You go sit and watch some TV and I'll make the mac 'n' cheese. You got any protein to go with it?"

I nodded as I gestured to the freezer. "It's not ideal, but there are hotdogs."

I half expected him to tell me he'd long since moved on from eating boiled hot dogs and mac 'n' cheese. I'd learned to make mac 'n' cheese with hotdogs when I was eight, so it had been a staple in my house. Since he'd been around a lot, he'd eaten plenty of it.

Instead of turning up his nose, his eyes lit up with excitement.

"That's awesome! I haven't eaten it in forever. Time for me to perform culinary magic," he joked.

I laughed as I leaned against the counter and watched him work.

"You're really going to light the world on fire with this one," I teased. "Bet you'll be adding this to the bar menu the second you get back to Montana."

The smile he'd been wearing faded as he sliced open the package of frozen hot dogs. "Yeah," he agreed half-heartedly.

I wanted to question the abrupt change in mood, but Emma let out a cry. I hurried to her, unlatching the restraints keeping her in the seat. Before I could lift her out, Ronan was there to do it for me.

"Don't want you hurting yourself," he mumbled.

The shift in mood from just a minute or so before was puzzling. I wondered if I'd offended him by teasing he should serve crap food at the bar. Fortunately I didn't have to worry about it for long. As soon as Emma was in his arms, he was smiling down at her.

"Hey pretty girl. Were you feeling left out in your crazy chair?"

Her little lips pursed together as she made several grunting noises. After a minute or so of those noises, she let out an angry cry. I knew right away what it was, but Ronan didn't.

"Her face is getting red and she's really squirming. She's mad," he said. "Forget that chair—we pissed her off putting her in it. Never again."

"I won't put you back in there, baby girl. I'll just carry you around all the time," he promised her.

She didn't stop crying. As he was making his case against the chair, she was getting more and more worked up.

"I'll throw it out on the street right now. Please don't cry," he pleaded.

When she kept on hollering, he looked over at me with a frantic expression. "Should I call Kristi?"

I'd been doing a good job of holding in my laugh, but I lost the battle. I giggled so hard, it hurt.

His expression indicated he was questioning my sanity.

"She was pooping," I told him between peals of laughter. "It wasn't the chair or you putting her down. She just wants a fresh diaper."

The relief he felt was written all over his face. It was so sweet the way he worried about her.

"Bring her to the changing table so we can take care of it," I instructed.

I was a few steps ahead of him so I got a diaper and opened the wipes. He un-swaddled her and we worked together to get her out of her little outfit. We'd both changed her during the previous days, but we hadn't yet changed anything but pee. When we saw the destruction she'd left in the diaper she'd been wearing, we let out simultaneous groans.

It was a nightmare. When Ronan lifted Emma up to take the dirty diaper away, she started crying even louder. Her cries made him start moving faster which in turn meant he was not as coordinated. I was trying to help but both of us were all thumbs. The next thing I knew there was poop on her legs and the diaper had dropped down onto the floor. Fortunately, it landed poop side up.

Things went from bad to worse when the diaper wipe made

contact with her skin. She went from crying to outright screaming, and her little face was beet-red.

"I'm sorry, baby girl," he told her as he wiped her down as quickly as possible.

As he took care of diapering, I was wiping her legs down. The diaper wipes were pissing her off, big time. The longer it went on, the harder she cried. Ronan was damn near apoplectic by the time he got a fresh diaper on her. I saw his hands weren't as steady as they normally were as he worked on dressing her.

Once I was finished wiping her legs and Ronan was able to put her outfit back on, she stopped crying. She watched us both silently as he swaddled her back up before lifting her off the table. He was a wreck and I wasn't much better. The way she'd been crying, I'd started to think something was really wrong.

"That was insane," he said shakily. "What did I do wrong?"

My nerves were as fried as his.

"I have no idea," I admitted. "She normally cries a little when we first get the diaper off, but this was beyond. I thought she was going to scream the house down when I wiped her."

He glared over his shoulder at the wipes. "Those damn things must be all wrong. You sit down so I can hand her off to you. I need to wash my hands and then call Kristi and find out what brand we should buy."

After he settled us in place on the recliner, he ran the few feet across the room and grabbed the wipe container. He stopped next to me, picking two of them out so he could wipe down the hand I'd used to help change her. After he went and washed his, he got on calling Kristi.

He paced the room like a caged animal as he told her what happened. "Never saw her cry like this before," he told her. "She scared the hell out of me."

He listened intently as Kristi spoke. After a few seconds, he looked down at the wipes and nodded. "Yeah, they're hypoaller-genic."

More listening, followed by the arching of his eyebrows. "Why did no one tell us that? I didn't even realize. I'll get right on it and let you know if it works. Thanks."

As he hung up, he breathed out a deep breath and set the wipes down. "She says there's nothing to worry about. Sometimes babies get pissed if the wipes are too cold. After dinner, I'm going back to the store to pick up a wipe warmer."

"So the chair can stay then," I joked.

He looked over at it as though he was conducting a threat assessment. After a few seconds, he turned and looked back at me.

"All right," he agreed. "But it's on probation as far as I'm concerned. If she gets upset after getting out of the chair again, it's getting drop kicked out the damn door."

"You won't," I chuckled. "She loved it in there."

"The chair can stay for now," he conceded grudgingly. "But I'll be monitoring."

He was a soft touch where she was concerned, no doubt about it. I looked down at Emma, who was by then staring at me content-ly. Her mini freak out hadn't phased her one bit.

"You almost gave da—Uncle Ronan a heart attack. You're go-ing to keep Mommy on her toes aren't you, Emma?"

I came within half a second of calling Ronan Daddy. As freaked out as I was by that, the feeling I got when I said mommy was massive. I was a mom and there was nothing I wouldn't do for that pint-sized beauty.

As my finger traced over her cheeks in wonder, she turned her face and opened her mouth. I was delighted I knew what the look meant. I looked up and found Ronan watching me intently with a look on his face I couldn't quite decipher.

"Could you make her a bottle? She's hungry."

He startled slightly when I spoke. After a few seconds, he nodded and then went into the kitchen. He came back after a few minutes with a bottle for Emma and then went back to the kitchen. I could smell the hotdogs and mac and cheese cooking while Emma sucked down her bottle, and my stomach started growling big time.

Because I didn't have a full range of motion with my arm yet, Ronan took Emma from me for burping after she finished her bottle. I loved the way he held her and talked to her the entire time.

"No more cold wipes for you, little princess. I'm going to get the best warmer there is. Your wipes will be so warm, you won't even notice they're on your skin."

Her answer was a series of burps. He was always happy when she burped, and I could tell he got a feeling of accomplishment about getting her to do it. Changed, fed, burped and snuggled on Ronan, Emma didn't stay awake long.

Once he was certain she was out, he stood up and headed for her bassinet. He settled her in and then stood over her for about a minute to make sure she was okay. After he was satisfied she was comfortable and secure, the two of us sat down and ate dinner. Our legs brushed together as we ate side by side. I loved it, but Ronan seemed edgy. He ate so fast, I couldn't help getting the impression he wanted to get out of the house.

"I'm going to run down to Walmart to get the warmer," he told me as he put the plates in the sink to soak.

"I'll be as quick as I can. Do not even think about doing the dishes," he admonished.

"It's okay," I assured him. "I've got this. You really do worry too much."

As he dried his hands on a kitchen towel, he glanced over at me. "It's my job to worry," he said. "I don't want your stitches opening. Dr. Smith said you could still fuck your arm up if you aren't cautious."

"He didn't say it in those words," I chided.

"Well," he said gruffly, "that's what I heard."

After my mother passed, I'd never been taken care of a day in my life. Knowing Ronan cared enough to disrupt his life so he could stay in Fort Collins and help me with Emma meant everything. If he needed me to reassure him then I knew I needed to do it.

"I'll be careful," I promised.

"I'm turning the volume on my phone all the way up. If you need anything, call me immediately."

I saluted him with my left hand. "Roger that, Captain."

He laughed, but I sensed something was off with him. All I was able to do was hope like hell he wasn't regretting agreeing to take care of us.

Chapter Fourteen

Ronan

I'D ALL BUT SPRINTED OUT OF KEELY'S APARTMENT. YEAH, I'D been in a hurry to get a baby wipe warmer for Emma, but that wasn't the reason I needed out.

My mood took a turn for the worse when Keely commented about my eventual departure back to Montana. I loved where I lived and I didn't want to stay in Fort Collins. Period. However, the very idea of leaving Keely and Emma behind nauseated me.

I'd been actively avoiding thinking about Emma's future. I was so obsessed with her having the best it made it easy to pretend there wasn't a bigger issue. In the hospital, when Keely said she intended to keep Emma, I'd been against it because I didn't want her doing it alone.

And then, when she was talking to Emma, she'd referred to herself as Mommy.

It hit me like a thousand pound weight right to the gut. Keely was Emma's mom. It was a fact. I'd known—as far back as the first night in the NICU, if I was being honest—Keely wanted to be in that role. I just hadn't been willing to consider it as a possibility.

Not because I thought she couldn't do it. Being around her for a few days showed me without a shadow of a doubt, Keely had her shit together. She was more than up to the challenge of being Emma's mother.

The problem was realizing that when I went back to Montana, I'd be leaving them both behind. Alone.

What was almost worse than thinking about leaving was my sudden obsession with wondering who would take care of them. Canter was right—Keely was a fucking prize. Honestly, I was shocked to shit she didn't already have a guy glued to her side. It would only be a matter of time before she was in a relationship.

The very thought of someone touching her made me feel things I never had before. Jealousy, anger—and worst of all, fear.

So, yeah, all of it was fucked up.

But that wasn't why I ran either.

I ran because when Keely called me Uncle Ronan, it felt wrong. I didn't feel like Emma's uncle.

I felt like her dad.

I'd been fucked by the feeling in a big way, hence the whole running from the apartment thing. As I wheeled a cart through Walmart, I thought about the situation rationally. I was not father material. I knew this. I lived in a small house, all alone except for my dog. I went to work, I hung out with my friends, I went to the gym, and, on a regular basis, I fucked. That was all it ever was to me. Sport fucking. In the five years that passed since I left Colorado, I'd never considered trying to have another relationship. I was undoubtedly attracted to Keely in a way I'd never been toward any other woman. But how the fuck could anything ever happen between us when we lived in different states?

Keely was a mom and I was clueless when it came to babies. I had zero exposure to children until Emma came along, and as far as I was concerned, I wasn't doing a bang up job with her. If I'd been prepared like a father would be, I would've read some damn books and known to have a damn baby wipe warmer.

I was back at Keely's about an hour later, warmer in tow. I'd also picked up a few things, some of which I left in the car to deal with the following day. Nothing about her place was homey, and I'd decided to fix what I could.

I fucking hated it on sight and it only went downhill as the hours passed. The recliner was a decrepit piece of crap and the television was, at my best guess, a relic from the late nineties. Everything in the place felt run down and second hand. The only newish thing seemed to be her bedding, and it was fucking hideous. Her apartment wasn't a home.

It worried me to realize she didn't make enough to live comfortably. How was she going to support herself with a baby? The store she worked for was being decent and signed off on her taking family leave, but it was unpaid. Granted, Izzy left behind a little cushion, but it wasn't going to last forever. I agonized wondering how Keely would pay her rent and her bills. I knew fuck all about kids but the one thing I was certain of was that they weren't cheap.

When I wasn't consumed mentally about her apartment and her bills, I was freaking out about her non-running car. One look in the parking lot of her building and I knew exactly which car it was, too. The teal-colored Toyota—at least, I was fairly certain it had once been teal—was at least twenty years old. It was a fucking disgrace and wasn't, in my opinion, road worthy. How the fuck could I let her out on the road with Emma in the damn thing? The answer was that I couldn't. Something would need to be done.

On top of all of the other things causing me anxiety, her cabinets had been pretty damn barren of food. Everything she did have was low cost crap. Ramen noodles, hot dogs, macaroni and cheese, soup and popcorn. The healthiest thing in the whole house was a carton of eggs. She worked in a goddamn grocery store so it sure as hell wasn't like she wasn't able to get to the market.

As I'd wheeled the cart through Walmart obsessing about how fucked up my emotions were, I decided to take care of the things I could. That was how I wound up bringing eight grocery bags back to the apartment with me. Under the guise of needing a blanket and pillows to sleep with while I stayed there, I'd also bought the nicest and most expensive bedding they carried. It wasn't much, but it was better than the neon nightmare she'd been using.

When I let myself into the apartment, I heard soothing tones of classical music. After putting the groceries down, I walked into the living room and stopped short. Keely was seated on the end of the bed with her face resting on the side of Emma's bassinet. They were both sound asleep, and I couldn't resist taking a few photos of the sweet sight.

I'd been as quiet as possible while I'd put the groceries away, plugged in the warmer for the wipes and put the new sheets I'd purchased in the wash. Through it all, she stayed asleep. Knowing she couldn't sleep there the entire night, I lifted her up and arranged her in a better position on the bed. She was so tired she didn't even stir. I ran my fingers through her hair softly while I stared down at her. Her perfect lips were slightly parted and I had an impulse to wake her with a kiss. I barely managed to hold that need in check.

Eventually I had to walk away because I knew I needed to sleep, too. After grabbing the new comforter I'd bought, I got as comfortable in the shitty recliner as I could. For the next two hours, I slept in spits and spurts. Ten or fifteen minutes of sleep, tops, and then I'd be up and out of the chair. I hadn't been able to go down for the count knowing Emma was in the room. At the hospital she'd gone down to the nursery each night, so I hadn't realized she made noise in her sleep. Nothing loud, but it was enough that each time she did anything at all, I jumped up to check. Then I psyched myself out so much worrying, even when she wasn't making sounds I was still getting up to check on her. If I felt she was too still or too quiet, I'd set my finger under her nose to feel her breath. I'm pretty sure I got my first round of gray hair right then.

Keely woke up like a shot when Emma let out a cry. We worked together to feed and change her, and then I walked around the apartment with her on my shoulder as I burped her. After Emma went back down, I thought Keely would go right back to sleep.

Instead, she wound up doing what I'd been doing, which meant both of us were obsessively checking on Emma. Around two in the morning, Keely looked over at me and let out a soft sigh.

"I had no idea letting her sleep would be so scary," she whispered. "I'm afraid when she makes noises and afraid when she's silent. This is terrifying. How do people do this?"

"I'd love to tell you I'm not scared," I murmured. "But if I said it, I'd be lying. I never realized someone so tiny could cause so much anxiety. I'm too keyed up to relax," I admitted.

Twirling a strand of her hair absently she said, "I wonder if it ever gets easier. I've never felt such terror. It's making me nuts."

I nodded my head at the same time Emma made a noise in her sleep. Even though Keely was right over the top of her, we both jumped in alarm. The same way we'd been jumping for hours.

I decided to throw a Hail Mary suggestion up.

"Maybe if I hold her instead of letting her sleep in the bassinet, it'll be less scary. I'd feel more secure if she was in my arms," I admitted.

Keely bit her lip as she stared into the bassinet. "I know I should say no—the Internet is full of people saying you shouldn't let your baby sleep with you because then they never want to sleep in their crib. But—maybe just this once? You can sit on the bed and

I'll put pillows around you."

I was lifting Emma out of the bassinet before Keely even finished the sentence. As I did, I felt a weight lifting off of my shoulders. When Emma was close like that, I could feel her breathing, which meant I knew she was okay. I climbed onto the bed carefully so as not to wake the little angel. Keely put pillows on my left side once I got myself as comfortable as I could propped up against a wall.

I didn't realize my mistake until she climbed onto the bed next to me and mimicked my position. We were shoulder to shoulder and she was close enough for me to be able to smell her shampoo. She wanted to be closer to Emma though, so I'd lifted my arm so she could tuck right under it. With one arm holding the baby tight and the other wrapped around Keely, I relaxed.

I couldn't keep the smile off my face when I realized they were both asleep. It felt so right having them both right up against me, safe and protected. Emma was warm over my heart and Keely was snuggled against my side, so I allowed myself to enjoy the moment. Before I knew it, I was asleep, too.

We slept like that for almost three solid hours.

We were lucky Emma didn't wind up needing to be held constantly in order to sleep. She was such a little angel. As I set her in her bassinet the following night, she kept right on sleeping soundly. I'd been worried she'd wake up and start screaming.

I still watched her for a few minutes, just to be sure. Keely took a seat on the bed next to me and stared down at her.

She trailed her finger over the top of Emma's head and let out a sigh.

"She's so beautiful," she whispered. "I never knew anyone

could be so perfect."

I nodded my agreement as I watched the gentle rise and fall of Emma's belly. Before Emma, I'd never have guessed how incredible watching an infant could be. The cute baby noises, the little sighs and that perfect baby smell. She couldn't walk or talk but she was one of the most fascinating people I'd ever known. She and Keely made my days better just by being in them.

Leaning into me, Keely murmured, "I see a resemblance to Izzy but not to Will."

I'd spent a lot of time searching Emma's features for signs of my brother and hadn't really found anything specific. I hadn't been looking because I still believed she might turn out like him. She was perfect, and I knew she would never ever be anything like Will or Izzy. Keely was too good of a mother for it to go any other way. What I'd been looking for was some part of Will that would've been passed on genetically.

"It's like Izzy's genes knew better than to let his get too involved," I said gruffly.

Keely nodded as she ran her hand along the side of the bassinet and stared at me.

"Can I ask you a question?"

"Of course."

She gestured down to Emma. "All babies start out innocent. Will was raised by the same parents you were. I know they sucked, but Will was a thousand times worse than either of them. Do you know where they went so wrong with him?"

I rubbed at my jaw as I gathered my thoughts. Of course I had a working theory about what had made my brother such an insufferable prick.

"Will was always spoiled," I explained. "Mom had a terrible pregnancy with him. Delivery was so bad it left her unable to have any more children. My dad always wanted a large family so he wasn't happy. Mom felt like a failure, I guess. She wasn't in a good space. I think she had postpartum depression, but she never called it that. Things got so bad that she checked into a clinic for depression when Will was about a month old."

I remembered finding the admission and discharge papers in a folder after my father died and I'd been going through his stuff. A lot of the pieces of the puzzle had fallen into place for me then. I looked up at Keely, only to find her still listening intently.

"I found all this out after going through Dad's papers," I continued. "When I talked to my mom about it, she was drunk which meant she was talkative. I guess my dad was pissed that she needed help and he started shit with her saying she wasn't a real woman. She felt guilty about being away for almost two months to begin with, but his shit made it worse. He preyed on her insecurities and told her she was a shit mother. She decided she would give Will everything to make up for her absence. Not to be outdone, my dad gave him even more. It was nothing but a tug of war between two fucked up people. In the end, Mom felt she had won because she proved my father wrong by loving Will to the moon and back."

I huffed out a sound of disgust. "Those were her words. *Loved him to the moon and back.* Never once did I hear her say anything so touching about me. Surprise, surprise, right?"

Keely surprised me when she reached out and cupped my cheek. My pulse skyrocketed as she stared at me intently.

"Your mother wasn't a good parent—to either one of you. I'm so very sorry you had to go through that. You of all people deserved so much more."

Like I said before, Keely always listened and cared. It was part of the very fabric of her being. Unlike so many other people I'd met throughout the course of my life, Keely was genuine and good down to her bones. I was scared of how connected I felt with her.

"No matter what your parents did or didn't say to you, they

were both wrong to spoil Will the way they did. It didn't do him any favors."

She lifted her hand off my cheek when she finished speaking, and I instantly missed her touch. It wasn't as if I could ask for her to bring her hand back though.

"That's one way to put it," I agreed. "Their bullshit sure as hell didn't help him. There's no way to know what he would have been like with real parents."

Keely's jaw clenched as she made a sound of annoyance.

"I just can't envision him as anything other than what he was."

Neither could I. All over again, I felt relief knowing he was gone. The idea of him being near Emma made me sick. His death meant it would never be an issue. The other silver lining in the entire situation was the certainty that Emma having Keely as her mother meant she would turn out nothing like either of her biological parents.

Eager to steer the conversation away from Will and Izzy, I announced that we could watch some TV. I loved Keely for letting me completely drop the subject. Of course when I suggested watching, I hadn't factored in how we wouldn't be able to raise the volume. We wound up watching *Seinfeld* reruns with the volume set so low it was practically inaudible.

At the end of the first episode Keely went to take a shower. Since the first morning in the hospital, I'd come to love and hate the time after she showered. Each time she opened the bathroom door afterward, the soft scent of her shampoos and soaps would waft out and crash into my senses. I looked forward to and dreaded it with equal measure.

When she came out, she smiled at me shyly. "Can you dry my hair?"

I'd learned her having such long hair meant there was shit she did to keep it healthy. She told me she only washed it every other day. This meant I'd been drying it every other day while we were in the hospital. When she went in to take her shower, I'd been wondering if I would be drying it for her since she was home. I'm a sick son-of-a-bitch because when she asked, I was happy to be called up again.

My happiness lasted until I got into the postage stamp. I mean bathroom. I held in a groan as I looked around the space and realized what I was working with. Compared to the bathroom in her apartment, the tiny bathroom at the hospital was practically triple the size. If I thought I'd been in tight quarters with her there, it had nothing on the apartment.

The good news was I had a better hairbrush and hairdryer to work with. Even though it was a form of torture to have her so close to me while I tended to her, I still drew it out. By the time her hair was dry, I'd easily brushed it five hundred times.

When I met her eyes in the mirror and told her I was all finished, I was struggling to remember how to breathe. My mind scrambled to find words. Just my luck, the words I found made the situation even tougher on my already fragile commitment to keeping things purely platonic.

My throat was dry and my dick was throbbing as I croaked, "Where's the antibiotic ointment?"

I lost my view of her in the mirror as she opened the medicine cabinet and pulled out the tube of Neosporin.

"I've got it right here," she said in a breathless sounding voice as she closed the cabinet.

I took it from her with shaky hands as I carefully avoided meeting her gaze in the mirror.

"Need to keep on top of this," I said gruffly. "I'm going to roll your sleeve up and apply some."

She nodded her head as I rolled her tee shirt sleeve up over her shoulder. Moving to her side, I lifted her arm and began applying a thin layer of the ointment over her stitches. The thunderous pounding of my heart was so loud I wondered if she could hear it. I hoped she couldn't.

Her stitches looked good—or as good as they could, given the fact she should never have been in a situation that required them. The doctors and nurses had told me what to watch out for and I wasn't finding any issues. There would be some scarring, but Keely was emphatic in pointing out how little a few scars mattered in the big picture.

By the time we came out of the bathroom, I was so hard it hurt. I watched as she climbed into her big bed while I tried to get comfortable on the recliner. It was, for lack of a better word, fucking torture. Sleeping in an upright position the night before was akin to sleeping on a cloud by comparison.

I would doze off for five or ten minutes only to wake up when a spring would jab me in the ass or the fucking chair would creak. Two hours later, I was ready to light it on fire. Meanwhile, Keely and I each got up to check on Emma every thirty minutes or so. Clearly, neither of us was really sleeping. I wondered how people with multiple children did it.

Each time I went back to the recliner after checking on Emma, it was a fucking nightmare trying to find any kind of comfortable position. I'm not a short guy, so I hung off at the top and the bottom. The last time I got into the recliner, I'd thought I was being quiet, but apparently not.

I'd startled like a frightened cat at the sound of Keely's voice.

"Just sleep in the bed with me."

When I looked over, she was on her side staring at me tiredly. Did I want to sleep in the bed? Duh. Of course.

I wasn't a fool, which meant I knew damn well getting into bed with her wasn't going to make it easier to fight the attraction.

"I'm good," I assured her quietly. "Go to sleep."

"I've been trying for two hours. Obviously I can't go to sleep knowing you're uncomfortable. It's a king-sized bed so there's more than enough room. We both need to sleep when the baby sleeps. Everyone says that. You're not sleeping. Either get on the bed, or let me sleep in the chair," she said firmly.

God, I was tempted. I was exhausted and I wanted to be on something soft. But I couldn't give in.

"I like the chair," I lied.

I was proud of myself for saying it with such conviction. Too bad she didn't buy it.

Sitting up, she crossed her arms over her chest and glared at me.

"You're so full of it. No one likes that chair. I'm not asking you to sleep in the bed with me—I'm telling you. We're adults, Ronan. Exhausted adults, I might add. We're perfectly capable of sleeping near each other. Get. In. The. Bed."

I realized she wasn't going to back down. Seeing no alternative, I gave in. I silently gave myself a high five for having bought a new set of bedding. Talk about perfect timing. Having to share a comforter with her would've been torture, I thought. Since I bought my own, it would be easier to stay separate. I climbed into the bed beside her carefully, making sure not to touch her at all. I positioned myself on the edge, hugging it like a virgin on prom night. *There*, I thought. *There isn't a problem. We aren't even close together.*

I woke up an hour later when Emma started crying. The comforter I'd been so glad to have? The damn thing lay in a heap on the floor. Somehow I'd wound up under the comforter with Keely. She was wrapped around me and her head was on my shoulder. No sooner were my eyes opening than hers were, too. We stared at each other for a second or two before we each jumped into action. I got Emma out of the bassinet and Keely ran to the kitchen to prepare her bottle.

That set a precedent for the following nights. We'd go to sleep separated only to wake up together. Each night it seemed like we got closer, too. First it was her head on my shoulder, then her arm over my stomach. By the third night, I had her pulled up against me and my face was buried in her neck. I'd been inching closer and closer to the line by the second. I knew it, yet I did nothing to stop it. I wanted her. Plain and simple. Not just her body— although of course I wanted that desperately. The bottom line was I wanted all of her, inside and out.

If I was asleep long enough to get to a dream state, I dreamt of Keely. Touching, kissing, eating, tasting, fucking—I dreamt it all. I'd come to love the dreams—almost all of the fun but none of the guilt I would have felt if I were touching her in real life. The only downside was that I always knew it was just a dream as it was happening.

I smiled to myself as the dream started. We were spooned together, her back against my front. The silken feel of her skin beneath my hand was too tempting. I trailed my fingers up her leg, lifting the hem of her sleep shirt when I reached it. My fingers continued their journey up, traveling past her navel and onward to her breasts. She made a keening sound as she shifted her bottom against me. If she did it just a few more times, I'd come. My dick was like a livewire where she was concerned. I'd been jerking it in the shower every night before bed but it didn't matter. With Keely, I was always either rock solid or on my way there.

I pressed my palm against her to hold her in place.

"Stay," I growled.

She nodded her head once in understanding. My hand moved again, this time gliding up to cup the weight of her left breast in my hand. She was a perfect handful.

I buried my face against her neck, tracing my tongue against her skin. Beneath my hand I could feel her racing heartbeat, and under my tongue I felt her pulse pounding. I opened my mouth and bit down gently, sucking on her soft skin. She tasted as good as she smelled. She gasped softly, but didn't move. I was impressed with her self-control, because I could almost taste how desperate she was to move.

As I licked and suckled at her neck, I traced my thumb over her nipple. That got a desperate sounding groan out of her, and I smiled against her skin. Without a doubt, I knew she was wet. Desperate to see just how wet, I let go of her breast and ran my hand back down her torso. When I got to her panties, I gently trailed my fingers just above the elastic.

I teased her, sliding part of a finger beneath the fabric only to retreat. She reached her arm back and slid her hand into my hair.

"Ronan," she whimpered.

I growled against her skin as I gave in and slid my hand beneath the elastic. I stopped breathing when I felt her wetness against my fingers. She wasn't just a little turned on—she was drenched.

When my middle finger traced over her clit, she gasped and arched back against me. It took every single ounce of my self-control not to pull my cock out. I wanted to shove those panties to the side and shove my cock in deep. I barely contained myself from doing just that. Instead, I ground myself against her ass as I slid my finger lower. I circled her opening twice before I started sliding my finger inside.

She was so fucking wet and tight around my finger, I almost came right then. She tightened around my finger as I slid deeper. The sound of our rough breathing filled the room as I began fingering her slowly. When I felt she was ready, I pulled out and added a second finger.

Her pussy squeezed hard as she struggled to adjust. I gave her that time, keeping the in and out motion slow and steady. When she started letting out little moans, I knew she was close. I started stroking her clit with my thumb as I picked up speed. She ground her ass against my cock desperately as I fucked her with my fingers. Unable to resist, I ground into her harder and harder.

I knew she was close to coming because her pussy was soaking my hand and she was trembling. I bit down on her neck harder, sucking at the skin as I ground against her.

Her body went stiff as a board and her pussy squeezed my fingers like a vice and I felt her wetness coating my hand. She let out a soft cry as she came.

I thrust harder, desperate to pull my sweats down so I could pull my dick out and get it inside of her.

"Fuck, Keely," I whispered.

She made a sound that I felt in my goddamn soul as she ground back on me.

And then Emma let out a wail.

My eyes flew open as I jumped up off the bed in a panic.

Two things hit me all at once.

My dick was hard.

And my fingers were wet.

I lifted them up and stared at them dumbly before looking back to the bed. Keely was in the process of sitting up. She grabbed at the hem of her shirt to pull it down but before she did, I saw the telltale sign of a wet spot on her hot pink panties.

When she looked up at me, I saw the scruff of my beard on her neck.

I hadn't fucking been dreaming. I'd really fucked her with my fingers and, if Emma hadn't woken up, my dick would've been buried hard and deep inside of Keely's tight pussy.

Emma cried again, bringing me back to reality. I was in no

condition to tend to her right then. Looking over at Keely guiltily I said, "I have to use the bathroom."

She nodded without actually looking at me. Getting up from the bed, she walked over to Emma's bassinet and picked her up.

I turned tail and locked myself in the bathroom. I tried to think about baseball and food facts in order to make my dick soften, but it didn't work. I had no choice but to get into the shower to jerk off. Bracing an arm against the wall, I shuttled my fist up and down my cock. Memories of Keely's tight pussy squeezing my fingers had my dick going off in no time flat. It didn't matter—even having come, I still wanted inside of her so bad it fucking hurt.

I stayed in the shower for another five minutes letting the ice-cold water pound at my skin in an attempt to get my shit together. Eventually I realized it wasn't going to happen. When I came out, Keely was in the glider with Emma and they were both sound asleep. I breathed a sigh of relief that I'd been granted a reprieve. It wasn't as if there was a protocol for how to proceed.

The only thing I was certain of was that, "*Sorry I finger fucked you and made you come while I was in a dreamlike state,*" definitely wasn't the way to go.

The next morning when we woke up, nothing was said about the night before.

It was almost like it never happened—except for the fact that one of the bites I'd given her had turned into a hickey. It was very faint, but enough to be visible to me.

Instead of talking about it, we just went on. She said nothing about continuously waking up with me wrapped around her like a goddamn octopus. It probably would've been awkward if we both hadn't been so fucking exhausted. Babies were no joke and anyone who thought taking care of one was a cakewalk hadn't done it. Emma was up every few hours during the night, so there were no long stretches of time to sleep.

I wanted to blame lack of sleep on my rising stress level, but that wasn't it. The truth was with every passing day, I was painfully aware it was only a matter of time before the girls didn't need me anymore.

There had never been anything that terrified and upset me more.

Chapter Fifteen

Keely

I WAS EXHAUSTED IN A WAY I'D NEVER BEEN BEFORE IN MY life, but also fulfilled in a completely new way. For as long as I could remember, I'd wanted to be a mom. It didn't take a rocket scientist to figure out it probably had root in the loss of my own. I'm sure the fact my family was completely nuts and non-supportive helped the yearning to grow.

Since *Mom* didn't seem like enough of a life goal to write down on any of the "what's your dream job" all students are subjected to in high school, I never put two and two together. With Emma in my life I found out the truth fast—what I wanted to do was raise her. My passion wasn't going to be found in a classroom working toward a degree. I still wanted to be able to work, but I didn't want it to define my life. My most important job, I knew, was Emma.

The last baby I'd had real contact with prior to Emma belonged to a former co-worker. In other words, I had no experience with infants. I felt I was learning on the job with Emma every single day and I loved it. I'd had no idea what to expect, but each day I noticed some new thing about her.

For example, I'd been ready—as ready as one can be when they're in the midst of a panic attack—for Emma to hate bath time. Considering how pissed off she got about the wipe situation, I'd figured we were in for it when it came time to give her a real bath. Instead, she'd loved it. Ronan held her securely while I washed her hair, and she'd been in heaven.

Waking up every morning and realizing all over again that I was a mom was a gift. There was some fear, of course there was, but the bigger feeling was always joy. I knew I'd been blessed with Emma, and I gave silent thanks again and again to Izzy for giving my baby life.

I wasn't a fool—I knew the other reason I was greeting every day with a smile was because of Ronan. The only time I ever frowned when he was around was if I started thinking about him leaving. Inevitably the thought made me sick to my stomach. I ignored it as much as I could—which wasn't hard since he never talked about it. Other than laughing whenever his neighbor sent a new photo of his dog Snuggles, he didn't mention his home life at all. I'd finally caved in and asked if he had a girlfriend. When he said he didn't, I was beyond relieved. My feelings for him weren't just back—they were stronger than ever.

The way he threw himself into helping with Emma and taking care of both of us was remarkable. Declaring my old recliner to be a safety hazard, he'd replaced it with a glider with a matching ottoman. He'd also stocked my cabinets and my refrigerator to bursting. He did the wash, made bottles, changed Emma and held her as much as possible. So much, in fact, that I sometimes had to pressure him to put her down. Any part of me that hadn't already been in love with him would've fallen after watching him with her.

I knew I was setting myself up for heartbreak, it was all but guaranteed from the moment he arrived. Forcing him to sleep in the bed with me was an insanely selfish move on my part, yet I did it anyway. I'd wanted to be closer to him—but once I was, I couldn't see how I'd ever be able to let him go.

The way he celebrated every one of Emma's tiny milestones and new developments was everything. The fourth day we were home from the hospital, Ronan was with Emma at the changing table while I'd been in the kitchen putting a bottle together for her. I jumped about a mile when he called for me excitedly.

"Kee! You have to see this. Get in here quick!"

I'd left the bottle on the table as I ran into the living room. I'd been able to tell just by the tone of his voice nothing was wrong, but I figured it had to be something.

"Grab your cell phone," he called out.

I knew then it was something photo worthy. Picking up my cell phone from the bed, I walked over to the table. The smile on his face was huge and infectious, and he was staring at Emma like she'd just reinvented the wheel.

"What is it?"

"Look!"

Following his gaze, I gasped when I saw her little thumb tucked in her mouth. It was, without a doubt, one of the sweetest things I've ever seen. The hospital sent us home with a pacifier for her, but she wasn't as taken with it as what I'd been expecting. I'd figured she just wasn't a sucker, but the way she was going to town on her thumb said otherwise.

I took a quick video and then started snapping photos. Emma was as happy as could be, staring up at the two of us contently as she kicked her legs and sucked her thumb.

"I can't believe she figured out how to get it into her mouth. When I changed her, she was touching her face, sucking on her fingers each time they got near her mouth and then, bam! She mastered the thumb. She's very advanced," he declared proudly.

Every parent believes the same. Their child is the most advanced, the most special, the most amazing. I knew I felt that way about everything Emma did—whether it was turning her head or staring at me as though she knew who I was. Everything she did was masterful, in my opinion. That Ronan felt the same melted my heart and scared me at the same time.

It was so clear that Emma adored him. I loved him. How would we handle being without him?

And why weren't we enough for him to want to stay?

I loved waking up and finding myself in his arms. We hadn't discussed it at all—it was almost like we were both thinking it could go on as long as the other didn't say anything—but each night, we slept closer together. I'd wake up in various positions, each and every one a dream which had become reality. Sometimes I'd be spooned against him, my back to his front, while other times I'd be snuggled on top of him.

I'd been dying to know if he was attracted to me. Every day I swore I saw or felt some interest from him. A flash of heat in his eyes, his arms wrapped around me in the night and the way he treated me all got me wondering. I was trying to figure it out, but short of asking, I didn't think I'd ever get an answer. Not unless he made a move—and I didn't think he would—at least not while he was awake. When he slept, he was a lot more tactile. Twice I'd woken to find one or both of us rubbing against the other. I wondered if he was as turned on as I was, but it wasn't like I could ask.

Each night we got closer together, until the night he fingered me to an explosive orgasm. I thought he was awake, but the shock on his face when he'd jumped off the bed said otherwise. I was so mortified, that I didn't say a damn thing. I was relieved he didn't either. It was like the giant elephant in the room, and we both did our best to ignore it.

⁓

One morning I woke up with my head on his chest just over his heart… and my hand under his shirt. The tautness and heat of his stomach beneath my fingers was the ultimate temptation. I'd half-heartedly tried to restrain myself before I threw caution to the wind and trailed my fingers over his abs.

His harsh inhalation was followed by the sound of his heartbeat thundering beneath my ear. He was awake. I'm blaming my sleep-deprivation for what happened next.

Without any real thought, almost as if I'd done it a hundred times, I maneuvered myself so my knees were resting on the bed at either side of his waist. When I sat down on him, I felt his erection straining against me at the same time I heard his low groan. He'd made me come, but we'd never kissed. I wanted to, badly. Our gazes locked as I bent forward and ever so softly touched my lips to his.

I hesitated, unsure of what to do next. Reaching up, he settled a hand at my waist and then slid the other hand into my hair. Cupping the back of my head, he brought me in closer so our lips would meet again.

For a split second, I worried about morning breath. But when his tongue touched my lips, I didn't give it another thought.

The way he kissed me was electrifying. It felt wild yet somehow sweet all at once. I threw myself into it head first, completely enthralled with the experience. My body lit up as I experienced sensations I never had before. Almost of its own volition, my body began rocking on top of his. My core clenched and my clit throbbed as I rubbed against his erection. I knew how he could make me come, and I wanted him to do it again.

More than that, I wanted to make him come, too. Feeling him

through his sweatpants was driving me mad with lust. I didn't think it through when I reached down and ran my fingers over his hardness.

He pulled away fast, his breaths coming in loud pants as he stared at me.

"Fuck, Keely," he groaned. "It would be so damn wrong."

It was both humiliating and devastating to be shot down. I mumbled an apology as I tried to scramble over him in order to get off the bed. Lightning fast, he'd jackknifed up into a sitting position to wrap an arm around me to hold me still. He kept me there, my back to his front.

"Please don't be upset," he pleaded huskily.

"I'm so sorry… I shouldn't have touched you. I'm an idiot and I'm embarrassed," I mumbled.

Embarrassed wasn't even really the right word. I was mortified. I'd finally gotten the courage up to make a full on play for him while he was awake—and he'd rebuffed me. I wanted to crawl into a hole somewhere and hide.

I trembled as he set the palm of his hand against my rib cage, just under my breast.

"Don't be embarrassed, baby. What happened just now—what happened the other night—wouldn't have started if I didn't want you. I know you felt me rubbing my dick against you as you came on my fingers," he said huskily.

The memory of his hardness pressing against me caused ripples of pleasure to pass through me. "I thought maybe it was a morning thing," I blurted.

"It wasn't a morning thing, sweetheart. It was a Keely thing."

My heart beat against my chest frantically as happiness flooded my system. Ronan was attracted to me! My suspicions were proven correct.

"Then why did you just say it would be wrong?"

I'd wanted to turn and look directly at him, but he kept me from doing so by holding me to him tighter.

"You're nineteen."

I waited for him to say something else. After a few seconds, I realized he had nothing more to add. I was affronted. Of all the reasons he could have given me, my age was definitely not an acceptable response.

"That's *it*? I'm nineteen?"

"Isn't that enough?"

I wanted to strangle him. "First I wasn't mother material and now I'm untouchable. I guess I missed the memo decreeing nineteen as the new twelve," I snapped.

"You know I don't mean it that way—"

I elbowed him in the ribs to shut him up. Not hard but it was enough for him to know I was annoyed.

"Really? Because you could have fooled me with the way you throw my age around. I'm an adult, Ronan. I can vote. If I put a pillow over your face and smother you in the next two seconds because you're acting like a jerk, I'll go to jail with other adults. I pay my taxes, I've got my own apartment, I pay for health insurance, and I'm a parent. I'm about as adult as a person can get," I declared.

"I'm sorry," he murmured. "I didn't mean it that way. I just mean you're still young and fresh and I'm—"

"About two seconds from being shoved onto the floor," I snapped. "First of all, you're not old, so don't even go there. And second, I'd like to remind you of how old my mother was when she married my dad. She was eighteen—and a fresh eighteen to boot. When I was born, she wasn't nineteen yet. They seemed pretty happy. I think if she'd lived, they'd have been together until he died."

He was silent for almost a minute before he responded.

"I'm not staying here," he said so quietly, I had to strain to hear him. "This is only short-term."

His reminder effectively took the wind out of my sails. No matter how I tried to pretend I would be okay if we did something and he left, I wouldn't be. As things stood, without getting sexual, I'd already been feeling down about him going. I sagged against him as I accepted defeat.

"Okay."

He held on for a few more seconds.

"I'm not saying I won't visit—"

I shimmied away, huddling into myself as he stood and looked down at me with an expression of concern.

"You're not obligated to do so," I said stiffly.

His head reared back and his eyes went wide. "I didn't mean it like that at all. Don't put words in my mouth. "

I was over talking about it. "Let it go," I pleaded. "We'll put what just happened down to temporary insanity and move on."

"I'm sorry, Keely. I never want to hurt you."

I shut down the conversation without another word. Any response I made would've continued the conversation and I was all out of things to say. After a few seconds, he seemed to realize I wasn't going to speak, so he turned and went to the bathroom.

When the door closed behind him, I went and picked Emma up out of her bassinet. I knew the rule about never waking a sleeping baby, but I desperately needed her right then. She stirred, but didn't wake. Taking a seat in the glider, I snuggled her to me and began rocking back and forth.

Having her in my arms was a reminder of what my priority was. I was emotional and upset knowing Ronan would be leaving, but I held myself together. For my daughter.

When he came out of the bathroom, I could see him gauging my mood. I plastered a soft smile on my face to show him I was okay. I wasn't, but for Emma, I would be. There was no other choice.

Chapter Sixteen

Ronan

I'D SUSPECTED SHE WAS ATTRACTED TO ME—FUCK, SHE CAME on my goddamn fingers, so that was a pretty big indicator. Having it in my face was a whole different thing. It made things so much harder. Her hand touching my dick for even a few seconds just made my hunger for her grow.

I'd been so eager to get rid of the shitty recliner in her living room and then suddenly, I wanted it back. Without it, there was nowhere else to sleep. I'd left myself with no choice but to continue sleeping in the bed with her. We were forced to continue to sleep in the same bed, but we stayed apart, which I hated. I wanted her back and wrapped around me, but I knew it wasn't right. I warred internally with my desire to try and my certainty that anything I did would be doomed to failure.

We continued to live together and take care of Emma as a team. No matter what had happened, we worked together and had become a well-oiled machine. Even though we were learning on the fly, I was proud of how we both adapted and went with the flow.

As the days passed and Keely's arm continued to heal perfectly, I knew my time in Fort Collins was coming to an end. I'd stopped sleeping almost entirely by then. Instead, I lay in the bed each night and stared at the ceiling as I tried desperately to get a handle on my anxiety.

❧

"You're sure I look okay?"

There was a fucking desert in my mouth and my dick was throbbing. She looked better than okay. I'd gotten used to seeing her in yoga pants and tee shirts. We were headed to Canter's parents' for dinner, so she was wearing a cream color sweater dress and a pair of knee high brown boots. The only way to describe what I saw is to say she was stunning. Also, I wanted to lift the dress, bend her over and fuck her on every available surface.

The only thing saving me from absolute insanity was her nervousness of possibly making a bad impression. She'd needed my support, not my lust, so I stayed calm and kept it all to myself.

In any event, there was nothing for her to worry about. I knew it would be an impossibility for her to make a bad impression. Keely was a genuinely good person, which meant the Wests would love her.

"You look perfect," I answered honestly.

"I want them to like me. People in this town, they normally don't see me at all," she admitted. "I'm just the girl who runs a register at the supermarket. For Emma's sake, I need to put myself out there more. I need to work on making a good impression and this is my first shot. If I look like a dork—"

I'd never seen Keely so uncertain about anything. I knew I needed to do a better job of reassuring her.

"You're beautiful, Keely. Nothing about you is less than perfection."

She bit her lip nervously as her face flushed.

"I'll tell you who looks beautiful," she said as she bent down and touched Emma's cheek. "This little angel. Mommy is so excited to show you off," she laughed.

Again, I felt the fucking pang in my heart when she referred to herself as Mommy. Every time she said it, it did something to me. Shaking it off, I grabbed the diaper bag and lifted Emma's car seat as I headed for the door.

"I'm going to put the princess in the car. Take your time," I called over my shoulder.

"I just need to put my jacket on, lock the door and then I'll be down," she replied.

I'd take it. Even one minute of breathing room was welcome right then. I'd just finished making certain Emma was secure when Keely appeared.

"Do we still have enough time to stop and pick up a selection from Mary's Mountain Cookies?"

The cookies at Mary's were so good I'd have made time even if we didn't have it.

"We do," I assured her.

Once we got to the bakery, I carried Emma's seat inside so we could make our selections. After we'd agreed, Keely got on ordering. She was busy chatting with the woman behind the counter when I heard a voice that made my blood run cold.

"Ronan."

The hand I was gripping Emma's car seat with tightened so painfully I'm surprised I didn't shatter the handle. Gnashing my teeth together, I turned to face the most unwelcome blast from the past. I was surprised to find the years hadn't been kind to her. We were the same age, but she looked a decade older. Her once natural blonde hair was a fried looking platinum mess and her makeup looked as if she'd been fucking around in a crayon box. She also had the look of someone who did drugs—and a lot of them. Tiffany was, without a doubt, fresh off the hot mess express. I didn't have it in me to feel any sympathy for her. Anyone else, maybe. Her? Never.

"I have nothing to say to you," I said stiffly.

When I initially turned around, her expression had been pleasant. Once I said I wasn't interested in talking, she stopped the bullshit. She glared at me as she stepped closer.

"Look at Mr. High and Mighty," she chided. "I couldn't believe my fucking eyes when I saw you get out of the car. I thought you said you'd never set foot in this shithole again."

"Just walk away," I said shortly.

I hoped she would go, but deep down I knew there was no chance.

Her eyes were full of venom as she sneered at me. "Like you did?"

"Sure," I agreed. "Exactly like that."

"You act like your shit doesn't stink, you judgmental fucking cocksucker—"

Out of the corner of my eye, I saw Keely rear back, her eyes widened. "Shut your filthy mouth around my daughter," she said heatedly as she stepped next to me.

Tiffany's expression had gone from angry to murderous. "Are you fucking kidding me, you white trash bitch? You always thought you were so special," she snarled. "You aren't shit, you stupid cunt."

Before I could say a word—and trust me, I'd been about to—the woman standing behind the counter called out. "Excuse me," she huffed. "Your language is unacceptable for a place of business. Please leave."

As ever, Tiffany resisted being told what to do.

Lifting her arm, she raised her middle finger. "Fuck you, Grandma," she screeched. "People curse, you old bag!"

"That's enough!" I ground out. "Crawl back into the gutter you came from. I have nothing to say to you."

Taking Keely's elbow with my free hand, I began guiding her toward the door.

"I see you've got a baby," Tiffany called out from behind us. "Didn't see the high and mighty cunt with a baby bump, so I know that's Izzy's kid. Gotta say I'm surprised to see you with Izzy and Will's baby," she cackled. "You were so quick to judge them—and now you've got a miniature version of them both. The apple won't have fallen far from the tree, I'm sure."

That stopped me cold. Turning on my heel, I glared down at Tiffany.

"Go ahead and run your mouth about whatever bullshit you feel like, but you keep it shut about this child. She is *nothing* like those twisted fucks, nor will she ever be," I spat angrily.

"You're fucking garbage," she snapped back. "You'll get what you deserve if she starts working a pole."

Instead of making me angrier, her words and the attitude she'd been tossing out lifted a weight off of my shoulders. I couldn't believe I'd ever imagined myself to be in love with her. What kind of person talked shit about a baby? Tiffany fucking Transom was the answer. She was pathetic.

"I don't know how I ever found you even moderately interesting," I said honestly. "You're a complete waste of space and a God-awful human being. Go to hell, Tiffany."

Without another word, I spun on my heel and went back to Keely. I heard Tiffany screeching obscenities from behind me, but I ignored her.

Five years after I'd left Fort Collins, I was finally free of all the what-ifs where she was concerned. Canter hit the nail on the head when he said I'd gotten lucky. Dodging a life tied to her was a blessing.

Keely stayed silent until after I'd snapped Emma's car seat into place and gotten behind the wheel. As I pulled away from the curb, she spoke.

"You okay?"

I could hear the concern in her voice, and I was touched she cared enough to worry. She didn't need to, but it made me feel good to know she did.

"Believe it or not, I'm fine. If I never see her again it will be too soon, but I think I needed the reminder of what a nut she is. I can't believe I was dumb enough to have thought I should marry her crazy ass."

"I'm glad you didn't because I have *always* hated that girl," Keely said bitterly.

Thinking back I realized Tiffany never liked Keely. I'd put it down to her being jealous. Time and again Tiffany had sworn that she should've been Izzy's sister. The funniest thing was I'd never realized how weird her attachment to Izzy was until it was too late. In retrospect, it was clear as day. It was also clear when Tiffany was running her mouth in the bakery that it hadn't come as a surprise to Keely. I suspected it wasn't the first time she'd been rude to her.

"Was she always that nasty to you?"

Keely let out a harsh laugh as she turned and looked out the window. After a few moments, she turned back my way as she let out a sigh.

"Not when you were around," she said dryly. "But otherwise, yes. Most times it was much worse than what you just saw—and more often than not, it got physical. When I was younger and Izzy lived at home, I'd complain to my dad and beg him to stop letting Tiffany spend the night. He never did a thing."

I fucking hated Tiffany more than ever. Izzy and Hollis Carmichael weren't far behind. What the fuck had Hollis been thinking? I'd known he could never have won father of the year, but allowing his daughter to be bullied was beyond the pale.

"You should've told me. I would have put a stop to it."

Out of the corner of my eye, I saw her shaking her head.

"She was your girlfriend and you lived together. I was just a pain in the ass neighborhood kid. I was lucky you tolerated me shadowing you. No one else ever paid me any attention—I couldn't risk losing you, too."

My hands clenched around the steering wheel and I had to remind myself to breathe. I'd let her down and I'd never even known it. I'd been a fool to let Tiffany lead me around by my goddamn dick. I'd always thought I was the only collateral damage. But based on what Keely told me in no uncertain terms, I was dead wrong.

"You wouldn't have lost me," I assured her. "It's too little too late now, I know. I also know without a doubt I would never have allowed her to treat you the way she did if I'd been aware of it. I'm sorry."

"Please don't feel as though you need to apologize. You did more than anyone else. I was grateful to you for being so kind. After my mother died, you were my one real outlet."

I felt like the world's biggest piece of shit. How had I not known how bad things were for her? If I'd realized, I would have done more.

"Don't thank me. Everything I did, I wanted to do. Now I'm realizing I could've done more."

A sound of annoyance was her response. I figured the subject of the past was closed, but then she dropped a bomb on me.

"Why did you leave? I'm assuming it had something to do with Tiffany."

Even thinking about what happened before I left made me ill. I owed Keely a real response, but I didn't have it in me to tell her what happened.

"You don't want to know," I responded. "Just trust me when I say what happened was a fucking nightmare. I don't want that shit in your head. It's bad enough it's in mine."

She nodded as she picked at a piece of lint on her sweater. As we were turning onto the Wests' street, she turned and looked at me.

"Whatever it was, I hate knowing she hurt you. You deserved better than to have to deal with her craziness."

We were pulling into the Wests' driveway then, so there wasn't anything more to say other than thank you. My head was jacked to shit. Seeing Tiffany and having her go off the way she did sucked. What was worse was finding out years too late to make a difference that she'd tortured Keely. I fucking hated knowing it had gone down.

With monumental effort I pushed it as far to the back of my mind as I could. I knew if I walked into the Wests' house upset, Canter would be on me like a flea on a dog. After shaking it off, I got out to get Emma while Keely got out and grabbed the box of cookies we'd gotten at Mary's Mountain Cookies. When I noticed her fidgeting with her dress, I spoke up.

"You're perfect," I reassured her. "Stop stressing. You know Chuck and Canter are great, you love Kristi and I promise, Nancy is just as awesome as the rest of the family."

She smiled at me shyly as we began walking to the front door. We didn't even have to knock—the second we stepped up onto the porch, Canter's mom threw open the door and came out.

"Ronan Sharpe! You're a sight for sore eyes," she laughed. Leaning in, she gave me a hug and a quick kiss on the cheek. Bending down, she looked at Emma who was all snug in her car seat. Placing a hand over her heart, she gasped. "Oh my Lord, she's beautiful. I can't believe she's got her little thumb in her mouth!"

I was about to introduce Keely, but Nancy rendered an introduction unnecessary. Standing up straight, she turned to Keely and set her hands on her shoulders.

"Hi honey. I'm Chuck's wife and Canter and Kristi's mom—but you can call me Nancy," she chuckled. "I'm so excited you're here tonight. I've been dying to get my hands on your little angel. My kids have both let me down in the grandchild department—"

"Ma! Stop making it sound like Kristi and I are cruelly keeping grandchildren from you and let your guests come inside," Canter teased as he walked onto the porch.

"Good gravy Ma," Kristi called out from the house. "Are you starting that up already? They just got here."

When we got into the house, I set about taking the baby out of her car seat. As I did that, Nancy took Keely's coat. The second I got Emma up and out of the seat, Nancy was asking Keely for permission to hold her.

"May I? I've just washed my hands," she assured Keely.

"Of course," Keely smiled.

I loved Mrs. West, but I admit I was a little put out when she took Emma from me. I liked holding her. Keely jokingly referred to me as a baby hog, and she wasn't wrong. I just felt better if Emma and Keely were both close to me.

"Aren't you a beautiful baby," Nancy crooned as she ran her finger over Emma's chubby cheek. "Have you been keeping your mommy and Uncle Ronan on their toes? I bet you have," she laughed.

I cringed inwardly when she referred to me as Uncle Ronan. It bothered me even though I knew damn well it shouldn't.

Looking over at Keely, Nancy smiled. "I remember when my husband and I brought Kristi home from the hospital like it was yesterday. Each little sound out of her mouth had us both jumping out of our skin. As stressful as it was, I loved every second of it. We both did. That's how we ended up with Canter," she chuckled.

"The first few nights were really rough," Keely admitted. "I was terrified to be more than eight feet from her at any given time."

Nancy nodded knowingly. "It's not easy, but it's worth it. I'd give anything to shrink them down for a few days, so I could hold my babies again," she said. "They got big so fast. In the blink of an eye Chuck was walking Kristi down the aisle and Canter was building his own house. It boggles the mind why he'd build a house with more than two bedrooms considering he's probably never going to give me grandchildren."

"Oh my god, Ma! He's never going to have kids if you keep pressuring him the way you do," Kristi laughed as she walked into the room holding hands with a man I assumed was her husband.

"Ronan and Keely, this is Bryce," she said as she gestured to the man at her side. "We've been married for five seconds and my mother is already acting as if we should have fourteen kids."

Keely and I both laughed as we each shook Bryce's hand.

"Nancy's not impatient or anything. No pressure, right?" I quipped.

"Oh, none at all," he answered through a laugh. "Saying Nancy is a little impatient for grandchildren is like saying the Pope has a little bit of faith. Kristi and I got married in May—and two weeks later, on Father's Day, Nancy gave me a World's Greatest Dad mug. She told me I'd better get to work if I ever wanted to see it again."

Just then Chuck walked into the room wearing a chef's apron. After saying hello to Keely and me, he dropped down onto the sofa next to his wife.

"Now honey, I keep telling you, we're just too young to be grandparents."

"You just turned fifty," she retorted dryly. "Besides—just think of how great it will be to have a baby around again. Look at this little angel. Remember when Kristi and Canter were this small?"

His gaze softened as he looked down at Emma. Chuck had always been a softie where children were concerned.

"Yeah, I do, and they grew up too damn fast," he grumbled as he ran a thumb over Nancy's cheek. "Seems like five minutes ago you were walking down the aisle toward me in your wedding gown. Can't believe almost thirty years have passed and now you're talking about grandchildren."

I'd forgotten how funny and affectionate the Wests were. Growing up, I'd always been surprised by how close they all were because it was exactly opposite to my own family situation. Chuck and Nancy loved their kids and each other, which made them solid in the best of ways. Canter and Kristi had always enjoyed the un-conditional support of their parents, something I'd often envied.

As I was watching the Wests talk, Emma started to fuss. Glad for the excuse to be able to have her with me, I went and got her from Nancy. The moment I picked her up, she stopped fussing. Smiling down at her, I traced her face with my finger.

I started talking to her softly. "Look at you, little lady. Pretty in purple and out for dinner. You like meeting new people, don't you baby girl?"

As I talked, I realized the room had gone silent. Looking up, I found everyone watching me talk to Emma.

"What?"

Kristi was the one who answered.

"You're really good with her. You've come a long way since the first night in the NICU. I'll never forget how when I first handed her to you it looked as if you were going to faint."

I laughed at the memory. "I was scared to death," I admitted. "I was just lucky she didn't hate me."

"Not a chance—from the very first second, that girl has loved you. I think Emma is the lucky one," Kristi said softly. "Having you and Keely there to pick up the pieces is the best thing that could have happened. You're both doing a great job with her. She's a very happy and content baby."

It was a compliment, but it made my palms start to sweat and my stomach started to churn. How content and happy was Emma going to be when I left? With each passing minute I was one step closer to having to go. Lincoln had been great about covering me, but there was a limit.

For the first time since I'd left Fort Collins behind five years before, I cursed the distance between Colorado and Montana.

Dinner was good. Chuck served his signature barbeque ribs and homemade macaroni and cheese. Rather than put Emma down, I kept her with me and ate one handed. It wasn't the easiest thing to do seeing as how I'd been eating ribs, but I really hadn't wanted to let her go. Deep down I knew it was because I was trying to hold her as much as humanly possible before I needed to go back home. I was afraid she would forget me as soon as I left.

I didn't have much to say as we ate. Keely was right by my side, something that got a raised brow out of Canter. I wanted to tell him to fuck off, but there had been other people in the room.

My mind was spinning out at a million miles an hour and I was having trouble staying focused. Fortunately the attention wasn't really on me since Nancy got busy peppering Keely with questions about Emma. I was relieved to see Keely smiling and having a good time. She genuinely enjoyed being at the Wests', and I was glad for it.

After dinner, I was given no option but to give Emma up again. Nancy demanded baby time and Kristi wanted to hold her, too. The second I handed the baby off, Canter tapped me on the shoulder.

"Porch. Now."

I wasn't surprised, considering he'd watched me like a hawk

during dinner.

When we got out onto the porch and sat down, he didn't waste any time.

"Something's up. Talk to me."

"Ran into Tiffany at the fucking bakery earlier," I shared.

His eyebrows shot up. "What the fuck? I haven't seen her in at least three years. Last I heard, she'd moved to Denver and was dating the owner of a strip club."

I rubbed at my temples as I shook my head in disgust. "Who knows why she's here. It's just my luck the bitch would come back to town at the same time I'm here."

"Did she talk to you?"

"Of fucking course she did," I grated. "The crazy bitch came into the bakery pretending to be nice, but once she got I wasn't having it, she went off like a bat out of hell. It would've been bad enough dealing with her bullshit myself, but she started her shit while I was holding Emma's carrier and she also got fucking mouthy with Keely. I wanted to strangle her."

He smacked his hand on the chair as he let out a harsh breath. "She fucking went off like that in front of the baby?"

"Yep."

"Jesus," he mumbled. "What a goddamn cunt."

"Yep," I agreed.

"You got anything on board aside from yep? 'Cause you sound like a dog right now."

"Don't give me shit," I said. "I'm having a fucking day."

"I see. I'm also getting the idea that other than her big fucking mouth, you're not affected about seeing Tiffany. Doesn't take a fucking brain surgeon to figure out what the issue is."

I turned and stared at him, but said nothing.

"You don't want to leave your girl and your baby," he said.

"I don't know what you're talking—"

He let out a tsk tsk noise as he held out his hand.

"Can I see your phone?"

I stared at him dumbly. "Huh?"

"Your phone, motherfucker. Give it to me."

Reaching into my back pocket, I pulled out my cell and handed it to him. He pressed the button to light up the screen and then let out a laugh.

"You say you don't know, but you do." Holding the cell phone up so I could see the screen, he gave a knowing look before he continued. "You see this?"

The this he referred to was my phone's background. It was a picture of Keely and Emma on the floor staring at each other during a tummy time.

"Yeah, I see it. What're you trying to say?"

He tossed the phone at me without warning, and I fumbled the hell out of it as I tried to keep it from dropping onto the patio.

"I guess Montana made you stupid. You know what I see when I go to Keely's apartment to visit or when I look at your phone?"

I glared at him as I bounced my leg nervously. "What?"

His answer was simple and straight to the point. "You've got a family."

I swallowed hard past a lump in my throat as I struggled to get my bearings. I didn't know what to say. I looked over his shoulder through the sliding glass door and stared at Keely. She was smiling at whatever Kristi was saying to her when suddenly she froze and looked out the sliding door directly at me, almost as though she'd felt my eyes on her. We stared at each other for a few suspended seconds before I broke the connection and looked away.

"I don't know what the fuck I'm doing," I confessed quietly. "All I really know is I can't stay here. My house and my business are both in Montana. I'm nowhere near financially able to just walk away from the bar. I make good money, but I'm no millionaire.

Plus," I rambled anxiously, "I fuckin' like Montana."

Canter cracked his knuckles and stared at me. "Did you eat a fucking moron sandwich? Because right now, I'm really thinking you've lost all brainpower. There's a solution to all of this. So simple—and yet you've never mentioned it once."

My head snapped up as I glared at him. "If you tell me to sell my house and the bar—"

"No, asshole, I'm not. You can't leave Montana—but what about asking Keely to go home with you? Take your girls and go build a life."

"I'd fucking kill to be able to take them," I admitted. "But she's stayed here for a reason. I don't know if she'd be open to leaving Fort Collins."

"You'll never know the answer if you don't ball up long enough to ask the damn question," he chided.

He wasn't wrong. I hated how fucked in the head I was. No one had ever chosen me, not really. I'd been given up for adoption, raised by assholes, tormented by my brother and mentally annihilated by Tiffany. The idea of putting myself out there to Keely and asking her to take a chance on a life with me—and having her say no— was terrifying. I knew she was physically attracted to me—but that didn't guarantee actual feelings.

What if she wouldn't even consider moving to Montana? I'd look like a damn fool for asking.

"Don't be a chicken shit," Canter said from beside me.

I turned and looked at him sharply.

"I can see the cogs turning in your head," he explained. "You're freaking the fuck out when there isn't a reason to. I've been to the apartment several times. I watched you both at dinner tonight. Stevie fuckin' Wonder could see you two have feelings for each other."

"Maybe," I conceded. "Definitely on my end, and I think

probably on hers but who knows if it's the kind of thing that would last. It's not like I'm going to ask her to ride off into the sunset with me. We'd need to date. For all I know, she'll find me annoying."

"Or maybe she won't. You won't know unless you try. I gotta think if she doesn't want to toss you out on your ass now after living with you for two weeks, you're good."

"I could hardly be annoying her right now," I argued.

"Dude—you fuckin' Bogart the baby like a motherfucker. You're also crazy overprotective and have been insanely paranoid ever since you guys brought her home. Keely's a saint for putting up with you," he laughed.

"I don't Bogart the baby."

The look he gave me was a clear indicator he disagreed. "You do, and you know you do. I thought you were going to gnaw my mom's arm off to get Emma back. You're all in and you need to make sure Keely knows it. Bottom line—if you don't make your play, your girl is going to wind up with another guy and your daughter won't remember you. You and I both know you're her dad. You ready to admit it?"

Canter pushed all of my buttons, but I knew he was giving it to me straight. In my heart, I wanted Keely as my girl and I wanted Emma to be my daughter. The question was, did Keely want me in that role?

"I'll try to feel her out," I answered.

He rolled his eyes as he stared at me. "That'd be a great start, Einstein."

"If she says no—"

He punched me in the arm before I could finish the sentence. "If she says no, I'll be your girlfriend."

Canter always could make me laugh. "No thanks, asshole. You're hairy and you've got some equipment I've got no interest in."

"Since she's not going to say no, you'll never have to worry about it," he assured me.

I hoped he was right about Keely being willing to move.

Chapter Seventeen

Keely

BEFORE WE SAW TIFFANY IN THE BAKERY, I'D BEEN RIDING a pretty big high over Ronan's reaction to my outfit. I didn't wonder anymore if he was interested in me—his eyes told a story I'd have been stupid to discount. He wanted me but was too stubborn to do anything about it. I spent a lot of time trying to formulate some kind of a plan, but had yet to come up with anything solid. In the meantime, I enjoyed all of the time we got to spend together. Going to dinner at the Wests' felt a lot like a date, which was another reason I'd been so anxious about my appearance.

Ronan was right. I'd had nothing to worry about. The Wests were friendly and welcoming, and I felt as though I fit right in. Their house was inviting and it screamed family. It was exactly what I wanted to give Emma—a home base she could always return to, no matter how old she was. I'd never had anything like it, which made me want it for her all the more. My daughter would have the life I'd never had.

The one downside to dinner was Ronan's behavior. He said

and did the right things, but he was robotic. When he held Emma during dinner, I'd suspected he was using her as a shield. I was certain he was having a delayed reaction to seeing Tiffany. How could he not? She'd popped up from out of nowhere like a demented maniac. As uncomfortable as her presence made me, I knew it had to have been infinitely worse for him.

By the time we were getting ready to leave the Wests', Ronan was more on edge than ever. After all of the goodbyes were said and Emma was securely in her seat enjoying an after bottle nap, Chuck stopped us at the front door.

"I wanted to talk to you both real quick, and I didn't want to bring this up over dinner and ruin your night," Chuck explained.

My pulse spiked, and I noted Ronan was looking at him warily. "What's up?" he asked.

"It's nothing to worry about, but I did want to talk to you about going through William and Isabelle's house. You'll need to put it on the market or rent it out."

I could see Ronan's agitation growing.

"You've got to be kidding me. Why the hell would we be responsible for that?"

"Next of kin—"

"Don't remind me," Ronan responded. "If I never had to set foot in that house again, it would be too soon. I just don't see the point. If we leave it be at some point the bank will foreclose or something, right?"

Arms crossed over his chest, Chuck looked between Ronan and me.

"You're not thinking straight," he announced. "I know you don't want to deal with it, but I also know if you sell it and make any money, it will help Emma. Maybe you could put it into a college account, or—"

"I hadn't thought of it that way," he admitted. "I'll get on it right away."

Just saying Emma's name erased Ronan's annoyance immediately.

Chuck nodded approvingly. "You're good with her—with both of them," he said.

Clearly uncomfortable, Ronan shrugged his shoulders.

"Thanks," he said quietly.

"All right, all right," Chuck laughed. "You've never been able to take a compliment if it wasn't food related. Take your girls and get them home. Let me know if you want Nancy and I to watch Emma sometime while you two deal with the house."

"Sounds good."

After we'd both thanked Chuck for thinking of Emma, we left. During the car ride, we discussed how to handle Will and Izzy's house. Both of us were loathe to go in there, but we knew it needed to be done.

"It's the last damn place on earth I want to go," he told me. "But for Emma, it'll have to be done. I'll hire a locksmith tomorrow."

"You don't need to," I sighed. "Chuck gave me Izzy's purse before I left the hospital, and the keys were inside."

"All right, one problem solved. Might as well get it over with then. We can take a quick look around and decide what needs to be done. Anything requiring real work or moving crap around, I'll hire some helpers. I don't want you jacking your arm up, and I sure as hell don't want Emma in that house for any real length of time."

I didn't want her there either. Will and Izzy's house was my own personal hell.

"I agree. A few minutes is one thing—but anything more is a no go."

He glanced over at me quickly. "You don't have to go," he assured me. "I'll take care of it."

I knew he would. I also knew I had a responsibility to my dead sister to find one or two things of hers to keep for Emma. I felt strongly that I needed to do it myself instead of passing it off on Ronan. It would be easier—Lord knew I didn't want to go anywhere near the house—but I was committed. As long as I stayed out of the basement, I figured I would be fine. At least, I hoped I would.

"I need to do this once. Someday Emma will have questions and I want to give her a few things of Izzy's," I explained. "After I get whatever I can pass on to Emma, I don't ever want to go back."

Ronan surprised me when he reached out and squeezed my hand.

"I support whatever you want to do," he assured me. "I'll be right by your side."

I knew he would be—but I also knew he wouldn't be there forever.

I squeezed his hand back to let him know I was grateful as I turned my head and stared out the window. I knew I should have said something, but the lump in my throat left me unable to speak.

When we got back to my place—being at the Wests' had proven once and for all my apartment was not a home—Ronan took Emma out of her car seat while I went to take a quick shower.

Since I'd gotten back from the hospital, I'd essentially started wearing a uniform of sorts. Yoga pants and a tee shirt or a sweatshirt. I'd considered trying to spice it up a bit to appeal to Ronan, but it just wasn't practical with a baby. After getting out of the shower, I changed the routine a bit and put on a tee shirt and a pair of Victoria's Secret *Pink* sleep shorts. It was a small attempt to break up the monotony of my day-to-day wardrobe, but it made me feel sexier. I'd thrown my hair up into a messy bun before getting into the shower. After deciding it looked good, I left my hair up that way and left the bathroom.

Emma was awake and down on the floor with Ronan. After he started reading books on infant development, he'd insisted on implementing tummy time. He would put a few toys around her, but she never really looked at them. Instead, she'd lift up and look at one of us. Particularly him. More and more I'd started to worry about how she would react once he left. I knew it wasn't going to be good.

Dropping down on the floor on the other side of Emma, I mirrored Ronan and got comfortable on my side with my head propped up on my hand.

"Look at her," he said proudly. "She went up to eight minutes yesterday. When she goes to the pediatrician for her one-month check up, I'm betting they'll be blown away by her. I know I am."

I smiled as I watched Emma hold herself up so she could look at Ronan.

"Such a strong girl," I crooned.

She looked over at me and made one of her sweet baby noises. I stuck my tongue out and blew a raspberry at her, laughing when she started kicking her legs excitedly. I did it again, and then Ronan did it as well. Her head whipped back to look at him. He did it a few times and then stopped as he reached into his jeans and pulled his phone up.

"She's trying to do it back! Quick, get on this side and try to get her to mimic you. I'll take a video."

Going to the other side meant I was right next to him, darn near cheek to cheek. Emma stared up at us as though we were the most fascinating people ever. Sticking out my tongue, I blew a few more raspberries. By the fifth time I did it and got no response from her other than a happy look, I figured Ronan was imagining things. When she stuck her little tongue out and focused intently on what I was doing with my own, I got choked up, overwhelmed with emotion.

Before Emma and Ronan, I'd just been going through the motions. Essentially my life was in a permanent hold pattern as I planned for my some day. I'd been merely existing as opposed to living. I'd reassured myself again and again that once I left Fort Collins real life would start. Ronan and Emma changed everything and I never wanted to let either of them go.

Ronan cheered her on as she lolled her tongue around and made her silly baby noises.

"Yay Emma! That's my girl!"

Everything faded away as I had a vision of him cheering her on when she learned to ride without training wheels, played at soccer games and graduated from high school. It hit me like an anvil to the head. I'd fantasized about Ronan being her father—but it wasn't just some obscure dream. It was a reality.

Ronan was, without a shred of doubt, Emma's daddy. Not because of proximity or time spent with her. No. If it were just that, he'd have been fulfilling his role as her uncle.

What he did was so much more. He wasn't an uncle—he was a dad. Everything he did for her and the way he showed how he felt for her was parental. He adored her, plain and simple. An idiot would've been able to see it. He doted on her and celebrated all of her achievements, took pride in her, cheered her on and hated to be away from her. He was everything a father was supposed to be.

There was only one thing to do. For Emma's sake, I was going to have to put it all on the line. I made up my mind then and there to do whatever I needed to do in order for him to see the reality.

After twelve minutes of tummy time (I thought Ronan was going to explode with pride) and some time in her high-tech chair, Emma nodded off. I could tell going out for her first excursion and being fawned over by the Wests had tuckered her out. I'd never seen her yawn so much. It was absolutely adorable.

I was riding a high, which meant I wasn't tired. Dinner had been a success and I was busy formulating my plan of attack to help Ronan realize what he needed. Ronan was in the shower when I climbed into bed. Grabbing the remote to the new TV, I chuckled. My old one suddenly "stopped working" one day while I was in the shower. He'd replaced it with a thirty-two inch flat screen, claiming he needed to be able to watch the Food Network.

It was cute how he believed he'd gotten one over on me. When I'd gotten out of the shower and walked into the living room, he made big production of showing me how the TV wouldn't go on. When I saw the severed power cord and the scissors sitting next to it, I knew what he'd done. I wasn't dumb—my entire apartment bore signs of Ronan's presence. New TV, new bedding, new gliding rocker, new pots and pans (so he could cook great meals, he assured me) and my kitchen was stocked with enough food to get me through in case of an outbreak of zombies. He was taking care of us and I ate it up.

As I flipped through the channels in search of something to watch, Ronan climbed into bed next to me. This was unusual. After "the kiss," he'd started getting into bed after I'd rolled over to go to sleep. Him breaking his normal routine was unexpected. I broke out in goose bumps as he lifted the covers and got in next to me.

"What're we watching?"

I watched his lips moving, but didn't process his words for several seconds after he finished voicing the question. I popped back to reality when I lifted my eyes and realized he was staring at me expectantly.

"Huh? Oh! Watching… right! The TV."

Lifting the remote, I handed it to him. "Whatever you want," I answered.

His eyes drooped down to my lips, causing me to lick them nervously. I saw the flare of heat in his eyes as he looked back up at me.

"*Whatever* I want? So this means I can I request something special, yes?"

My heart was battering against my chest at a frantic pace as I nodded my head dumbly.

"How about…"

The pause killed me. *What was he going to suggest? Holy crap,* I thought. *Was he going to kiss me? Were we going to have sex?*

My mind raced frantically as I tried to prepare myself for what his question would be. Meanwhile all I could focus on was trying to remember what kind of underwear I was wearing. The harder I tried to remember the answer, the more I panicked. Was I wearing period underwear? What the hell had I taken into the bathroom with me to change into when I showered? I started sweating as I imagined the worst. What if it was an ugly pair of enormous granny panties that had seen better days? I mean really. Who replaces their period underwear on the regular? You wear it until it's practically see through. Was I wearing see through underwear?

Please, God, I prayed silently. *Don't let me be wearing period underwear.*

"WillyoumovetoMontanatolivewithme?"

I got none of it since he'd said it all in one giant jumbled rush. I did, however, remember what underwear I was wearing. The universe hadn't thrown up that particular roadblock—my period underwear was safely tucked away for another day. I wasn't even on my period so I'm not sure how I let myself get so off track and freaked out for no reason. I stared at Ronan as he stared at me, waiting for me to respond to whatever gibberish he'd blurted out.

"I don't know what you just—"

"What'll it take for you to know? What can I do?"

Clearly, he didn't understand what I was trying to ask. It was mutual because I didn't know what he was saying, either.

"No, I'm saying I don't—"

He reached out and took my hand in his.

"Don't shoot it down, Kee. Think about it," he implored. "There are a dozen reasons why it's a great move and—"

The aggravating man wouldn't let me get a word in edgewise.

"Ronan! Stop. What I'm trying to tell you is that I didn't hear what you asked me. Ask me again, slower. So I can actually comprehend your words."

His shoulders sagged and his cheeks flushed.

"That's a fucking relief," he said as he exhaled a whoosh of breath. "I really thought you were saying no."

"No to *what*?"

He swallowed, I thought nervously, before taking a deep breath.

"I'd like you to come to Montana and move in with me."

Holy. Shit.

When, I wondered, did God decide to start granting my wishes? I grinned at Ronan like a flipping lovesick idiot.

"Really?"

He nodded emphatically. "Yeah, really. I know I'm asking a lot, expecting you to leave Fort Collins but I really think you'll love Montana."

I blinked rapidly as I cocked my head to the side in confusion. How the heck had he jumped to the conclusion I wanted to stay in Fort Collins long term?

"I hate it here, Ronan. I've been saving up to leave for almost two years. What made you think I wanted to stay?"

His eyebrows shot up in surprise. "You never said, so I just assumed…"

"Look around at my life," I said dryly. "I've been living on the cheap so I could get out. That's why my apartment is a dump. It's taken a while for me to build up my savings, but I figured I had about ninety days left before I could leave. My car blowing up probably set me back another eight months or so. I was never going to stay here forever."

The smile he gave me lit up his entire face. "So you'll come home with me?"

I was all but jumping out of my skin with excitement. My plan to break him down and get him to realize that he didn't want to be without us had just taken ninety-five enormous steps forward.

Moving to Montana with him was something I'd do regardless of how he answered my next question—but I needed to voice it, regardless.

"I have a question."

"Anything," he assured me.

I gestured between us. "What does this mean for you and me, old man? Are we going to pretend we're just friends, or are you ready to admit nineteen doesn't mean I'm jailbait?"

His jaw dropped right around the time I called him an old man. When I finished my questions, he smiled at me.

"We're a hell of a lot more than just friends," he said huskily.

I couldn't hold myself back, so I threw my arms around him and squeezed. "This day just keeps getting better and better," I squeaked.

He hugged me back tightly. It was our second real hug. This one was better than the first, because this hug meant when he left again, I'd be going with him.

We pulled back at the same time. I opened my mouth to say something—I have no idea what—but I never got the chance. Instead, he slid both hands into my hair and tilted my head back. My stomach got the most amazing butterfly feeling as our lips locked and our tongues met. I couldn't believe he'd asked me to move in with him and followed it up by kissing me like I was his entire world.

My arms wrapped around his shoulders as my fingers threaded together in his hair. We kissed like we were reuniting after being separated by war for years.

When we broke for air, I was surprised to find myself on my back. Nothing else existed when we kissed. I would have heard Emma, but she's the only thing I'd have stopped for. We were both breathing heavily as we stared at each other.

"I want you, Keely. I want everything. Not tonight, obviously, since I'm an idiot and I don't have any goddamn condoms, but—"

I put up my hands in a time out motion.

"Mirena."

He cocked his head and looked at me in confusion.

"I don't even know who that is."

My face was so hot, I was positive I was eggplant purple from embarrassment.

"Not a who, a *what*. It's birth control. I'm covered," I babbled. "If you're um… clean, I mean. If you're not clean we need to talk. Clean is very important."

His eyes damn near bugged right out of his head as I rambled on. I forced myself to stop talking before I dug a deeper shame hole for myself. I felt like I was giving him the Tourette's syndrome version of pre-sex conversation.

"Clean?"

"Disease free," I whispered.

He laughed so hard he needed to cover his mouth to keep from waking Emma.

"That was one hell of a way to ask, sweetness. But, to answer your question, I'm entirely disease free. I haven't had sex without a condom since—"

He stopped mid-sentence and grimaced.

"After *her*, I got tested every six months for two years. Since then, I've been tested at my yearly physicals," he continued.

I hated even thinking about the two of them together, but I tucked that piece of information away in my head. Without realizing it, he'd given me a pretty good indication of why he'd left town.

"Then we're good," I assured him. "I want you to touch me. Everywhere."

I saw his pupils dilate as he started to breathe heavier.

"Trust me, you can't want me to touch you more than I need to. During the five seconds of sleep I get a night, all I think about is touching you," he admitted.

My core clenched and I let out a whimper.

"Ronan…"

He kissed me then, and my pulse skyrocketed. I moaned into his mouth and bucked against him when he gripped my knee and pushed it back. I could feel him as he shifted against me, hot and hard.

I wrapped my other leg around him to anchor myself as I arched against him. He broke the kiss to let out a desperate sounding groan.

"I don't want this to be over before it begins," he said hoarsely.

I had no real idea what I was doing, but I knew he felt good and my body wanted more of everything. I was desperate to experience everything with him. Grasping the hem of his tee shirt, I wrenched it up his torso. Taking the hint, he let go of me and whipped the shirt over his head.

Him doing so gave me the opportunity to take off my own shirt. It was a forward move, particularly in light of my braless state, but I didn't care. I wanted to feel his skin on mine. He went stock still over me when I got my shirt off. The way he stared at my body made me feel like a goddess.

"Fuck," he hissed. "You're so fucking beautiful, Keely."

I felt myself blushing as I smiled shyly. He leaned forward and kissed me again, this time soft and slow. When he pulled back, he watched my face as he trailed a line from my collarbone to just below my belly button with his index finger.

He started to trail the same line in reverse, this time with both of his index fingers. I forgot to breathe when he got to my breasts and made swirls with his fingers around each of my erect nipples. They tingled as he continued gliding his fingers around my breasts, coming close to but never touching my nipples. I made a desperate sounding mew, which made him smile.

"You're so sensitive," he said softly.

I nodded my head as I whimpered, "Yes."

"You'll love this."

Before I could ask what he meant, he leaned in and licked around my left nipple. The feeling of his tongue against me was incredible. I bit my lip to keep myself from crying out and I arched my back to give him better access. He tortured me in the best way as he alternated from one breast to the other, but he still hadn't touched my nipples. I wanted so badly to feel his tongue on them I was trembling.

"Please Ronan," I whispered.

He growled low in his throat as he nodded his head. Cupping each of my breasts, he ran one of his thumbs over my nipples. The sensation was unbelievably good; so much so I didn't think it could get any better. I was, of course, wrong. When he licked my right nipple, then started flicking his tongue against it, I felt myself getting wetter.

I rubbed against his hard length when he sucked my nipple into his mouth and gave it a little bite. I wasn't just a little wet then, I was soaked. I wondered if he would feel anything like I did if

I gave his nipples some attention. Setting my hands on his abs, I trailed them up his chest. When I got to his nipples, I ran my thumbs over them. He groaned and thrust against me desperately as he sucked my nipple harder. I loved his reaction, so I kept working him. When he bit down gently on my left nipple, I pinched his.

Our lower bodies were continuously thrusting together, our motions becoming more and more frantic. When he pulled his mouth away from my nipple and raised his head to look at me, I clenched so hard I had a little orgasm.

I panicked when he got up from the bed, but realized he wasn't going anywhere when he pulled his sweatpants off. That left him in a pair of Calvin Klein briefs that did absolutely nothing to hide his erection.

He stared down at me wildly as he came to the edge of the bed. I shivered when he set his hands on either side of my sleep shorts. He didn't immediately take them off. It dawned on me that he was waiting for my permission. Instead of speaking, I lifted my hips off of the mattress. Going by the wolfish smile he gave me as he started pulling down my shorts and my panties—cream-colored lace, thank you very much—he approved of my response.

I'd been taking extra time in the shower for grooming purposes since he'd moved in —*just in case*. It had felt silly at first, seeing as how I wasn't sure he was attracted to me, but once I knew he was, I primped even more. Knowing I was prepped and ready took away a lot of anxiety.

I struggled to catch my breath as Ronan began running his fingers up the outer sides of my legs. Up, up he went, over my hips where he stopped and tickled gently, which caused me to giggle. Then his fingers started moving down, and I forgot to breathe at all.

He ran his fingers from just under my belly button down to my inner thighs. The fleeting feeling of his fingers as they skated across my mound made me gasp, which was a reminder to start breathing again. He chuckled as his fingers continued their journey downward until they stopped on my inner thighs. His hands stilled as he pressed his hands gently on either side.

"Spread your legs and set them on my shoulders," he murmured huskily as he stared up at me from between my legs.

I forced myself not to look away shyly as I complied. The warmth of his back radiated against my calves as he leaned in and inhaled. His eyes fluttered shut as he growled low in his throat. When he opened them to look at me, I let out a little moan. The expression on his face made it clear he was ravenous—for me.

"I knew it," he admitted with a groan. "You smell amazing everywhere."

I blushed furiously at his words, then threw my head back and held back a loud moan as he leaned in and swiped his tongue against me. I wasn't a virgin. A six-week relationship in tenth grade with Ben Stearns had taken care of that. My dad had just been diagnosed with cancer and I was looking for an outlet. I found it in Ben for a short time. It lasted until he moved on to the next girl. There were no hard feelings about it because I'd had no real feelings for him.

Since it had been short lived, I knew nothing about real sex. Ben and I had fumbled and pawed at each other. He went down on me twice and both times, I'd been embarrassed and uncertain, plagued with anxiety. Did I smell or taste bad? Was I really supposed to be turned on by the stabbing tongue motions he made against my clit?

Ronan between my legs was not even a little bit similar. It was clear he was a man who knew what he was doing. My clit throbbed as he used his tongue to amazing effect. I couldn't help myself from threading my fingers into his hair to use his head as leverage as I thrust against his tongue. Nothing had ever felt better and I felt myself getting closer and closer to the edge with each wiggle and dip of his tongue.

"Oh God," I whispered desperately. "I'm so close!"

He seemed to know I needed something more to get there. I threw my head back and let out a silent scream when he slid two fingers inside of me and started thrusting them in and out. I wanted it to last forever, it felt that good. On the other hand, I wanted to come. Badly. I knew how to get myself off, but I'd never even gotten close with Ben. Ronan got me there fast.

I thrashed against him desperately as he worked me. I could feel it coming and I knew it was going to be huge. I reached out blindly, grabbing a pillow to pull it against my mouth to stifle my moan as I came.

He continued to work my body, tonguing me faster as I rode out the best orgasm ever. When I finished coming, he was suddenly poised right over me. I felt the heat and weight of his arousal against me, and I reached out to grip his ass in my hands as I tried to pull him in.

"I love the noises you make when you come," he said. "I can't wait to hear them again."

He captured my mouth and slid his tongue inside, kissing me like I was his entire world. I moaned when I tasted myself on him—nothing even a little bit dirty about it.

His thick head rubbed against my clit as he kissed me. I felt myself getting wetter by the second, and I wanted him inside. My core clenched in anticipation as I shimmied against him.

I wrenched my mouth from his, breathing heavily as I let out a whimper. "I want you inside," I whispered.

He groaned as he held himself over me with one hand and fisted his cock with the other. I felt him right at my opening, and I gasped in wonder as he slowly started to enter me. Half an inch, then an entire inch, followed by a few more. When he settled all the way in, I clenched around him.

"Fuck, Keely," he murmured. "You feel so good on my dick, baby. Such a perfect pussy, so hot and wet against me."

I arched against him, which caused my nipples to rub against his chest. Our eyes stayed locked together as he pulled out slowly before thrusting back in. He repeated the motion again and again, and each time he bottomed out inside of me, we would both make a desperate sound.

I'd not expected to be so vocal, but the feeling of him pulling out each time drove me crazy. My fingernails dug into his ass as I tried to hold him inside of me.

"More," I begged softly. "Please."

He picked up the rhythm and my body somehow knew to go with it. The thrust and retreat was amazing, a perfect build up of sensation. We both breathed harder, gasping or panting into each other's mouths while we kissed. It felt so good, so damn right, having him inside of my body.

I tore my mouth from his and gasped when he started fingering my clit in time with his thrusts. Our motions became more frantic, taking on a desperate feel as he began pumping into me faster.

"God, fuck, Keely," he groaned as he thrust. "You're fucking amazing and you feel so goddamn good."

I clenched around him as I felt myself getting right to the edge.

"I... I... Oh God—Ronan!"

Throwing my head back, I arched my back and tried not to scream as I came. Behind my eyelids, I saw explosions of color and I felt myself shaking as he pounded into me.

"Oh, baby! Fuck, fuck so tight," he growled. "Fuck!"

My eyes flew open and I found him staring at me with a desperate look on his face, and then I felt the first heated burst of his come deep inside of me. We were both frantic then, thrusting desperately against each other as we both rode out our orgasms.

When we finished he didn't pull out. Instead, he rolled onto his back, keeping his arms around me. I enjoyed listening to his heartbeat as it thundered beneath my ear as we both tried to catch our breath. As our breathing started to return to normal, he began trailing his fingers across my shoulders in a soothing motion. Lifting my head, I smiled up at him.

"Wow," I said softly.

"Amazing," he agreed. "Beyond. That was—that was fucking epic."

I knew I was beaming at him like a nut, but he was smiling right back. It felt as though we were communicating something very important. When Ronan cupped the back of my head and kissed me softly, it felt like a promise.

The moment ended when Emma let out a hungry cry. Breaking the kiss, we both chuckled as we sprung into action. He lifted me off of him quickly but gently.

"Go get cleaned up. I'll throw my sweats back on, grab her up and make her a bottle," he said.

I laughed as I grabbed my pajamas from where they were piled on the floor. After I got into the bathroom, I started humming to myself happily as I went about cleaning up and putting my tee shirt and sleep shorts back on. Staring at my reflection in the mirror, I couldn't help but smile. I was flushed but I thought it looked a little sexy. I loved that it was because of Ronan.

When I came out of the bathroom, I found him sitting on the bed feeding Emma. Climbing up next to him, I traced my fingers over her face before dropping a kiss on her head and inhaling her perfect baby smell. She watched me do it while she continued to drink happily. I loved how she always seemed to be taking everything in. Once her bottle was drained, Ronan burped and changed her before handing her over to me. Throwing his arm over my shoulders, he rested his head against mine as we stared down at her. I couldn't have kept the smile off my face for any amount of money.

Emma was still tired from our earlier outing so she didn't stay awake long. I held her until she drifted off to sleep, and then Ronan put her back in the bassinet. When he got back into the bed, he wrapped his arms around me and held on tight. It was perfect.

I'd never been happier.

Chapter Eighteen

Ronan

BEING WITH KEELY WAS INCREDIBLE. I'D HAD SEX hundreds of times, but I'd never gotten emotional about it. Even when Tiffany and I were together, it wasn't like that for me. The only real difference was that while I was with her, I wasn't with anyone else. I'd been committed, even though she hadn't been.

With Keely, I wasn't being bamboozled by bullshit. She was authentic and genuine, always. I felt things for and with her I knew I'd never experience with anyone else. I didn't just care about her—I revered her. Not many girls would've stepped up to the plate the way she did. Keely didn't just accept the challenge—she embraced it and met it head on. Watching her interact with Emma warmed my soul. I was proud of her for being such an amazing person, but even more—I was in awe of her. She inspired me to be a better person, someone who was worthy of everything that she was.

We'd made love once more before bed, and it had been as mind blowing as the first time. Of course that meant we were exhausted when we woke up, seeing as how we'd been up and down a few times over the course of the night with Emma. You couldn't tell we were exhausted by the way we acted. Knowing looks, smiles, soft touches and kissing whenever we had the chance.

All would've been right with the world, had we not needed to go to Will and Izzy's house. It was obvious as we both got ready and then readied Emma that neither of us wanted to go. The drive there was awful. Keely was shakier than I'd ever seen her—which was quite a testament, all things considered. As I drove, I reached over with my free hand and linked our fingers together.

"We'll get in and out," I assured her. "Afterwards we can take Emma home, work on tummy time and give her a bath. We can lie in bed together while she naps and watch a movie. Keep your focus on the positive."

She squeezed my hand as she let out a pent up breath.

"I know you're right—I just can't wait to get it over with," she replied.

"Trust me," I assured her, "I can't either. The sooner we're in and out, the better."

I was trying to hold it together for her. Still, when I made the turn into Will and Izzy's driveway, my stomach churned. The last time I'd been at the house had not been a pleasant experience, to say the least.

It was set well back from the road and the nearest neighbor was quite removed. It was an older area, built long before houses became cookie cutters that were built ass to ass. From the outside, the house looked normal. There weren't devil horns coming out of the roof and the area didn't smell like sulfur. Nothing about it screamed out that a giant evil asshole had lived there. You could tell it was empty because there was a distinct lack of life about it.

Nothing about it was welcoming. I knew I was projecting, but something about it just felt wrong. I half expected Will to appear from out of nowhere in order to start one of his infamous scenes. It was a relief to find Emma had fallen asleep during the drive. Even knowing she wouldn't retain anything she might see, I still hated having her there. I'd come within seconds of asking Canter's mom to babysit for the few minutes we'd be at Will and Izzy's, but I panicked at the idea of leaving Emma anywhere Keely and I weren't. I knew I would need to work on that, but it wouldn't be solved in a day.

We walked up to the front door with Emma's car seat in my hand and Keely tucked under my arm. My fingers were stiff and uncooperative, making me clumsy as I worked the lock. After a few tries, the door finally swung open.

The house was silent and there was a stale quality to the air. The first thing my eyes settled on was the coffee table. An array of empty beer cans and two half full bottles of liquor were strewn across the table. I wasn't surprised to see the apple hadn't fallen far from the tree—both of the liquor bottles were our mother's old favorite, Jack Daniels. Will developed a taste for it early and going by its front and center presence in his home, he'd never lost it. By the time he was fifteen, Mom had been allowing him to take one bottle out with him each weekend night.

The sound of the door shutting behind me pulled me back to the present. I turned to Keely and apologized for leaving it open.

"Don't worry about it," she murmured. "I'm going to run into the bedroom and look through Izzy's stuff. You can stay out here with Emma—"

"Hell no," I said emphatically. "We go together."

She looked relieved. Reaching out, I clasped her hand and walked to the bedroom with her. Like the living room, it was stale and had an abandoned feeling. The biggest difference between the two rooms was the lack of alcohol on the tables. It was fairly tidy and the bed was made. I swallowed past what felt like a mountain of bile in my throat when I noted the eyehooks screwed into each end of the bed. I had to forcibly shake off the memory of the restraint system I knew went with the hooks. I'd seen one just like it before.

Keely went directly to the dresser and the jewelry box sitting on the back corner. I looked away when Emma shifted around in her seat, but my eyes went right back to Keely when I heard her gasp. Seeing the expression on her face had me rushing to her side.

"What's wrong?"

My heart felt as though it were in a vice when she looked up at me and I saw tears in her eyes.

"My mother's wedding and engagement rings," she whimpered. "Will or Izzy stole them after my dad's funeral. She told me Will pawned it, but they're both here. She lied. Why would she do that?"

What I'd wanted to say hadn't been appropriate, so I bit my tongue. Telling her that her sister had been a selfish, lying cunt wasn't going to help her any. The best thing I could do was be there for her while she processed another one of Izzy's lies. I wrapped my arms around her shoulders and pulled her against my chest.

"I'm sorry, sweetheart. We should go—"

She dashed away her tears with her right hand as she shook her head against my chest. After a few seconds, she took a deep breath and then moved out of my arms.

"If it was just me I'd take my mom's jewelry and leave, but it's not. Emma is the most important part of this," she reminded me. "Let me gather what I need and we can go."

It was impossible not to admire her strength. Whenever life threw up a hurdle, she kept going. Looking down at Emma sleeping in her seat, I thought about how fortunate she was to have Keely as her mother. It was a good thing Izzy had known she wasn't fit to raise her.

After picking out the rest of her mother's jewelry and a few of Izzy's pieces Keely closed the lid on the box. She slid it all into the reusable shopping bag she'd brought with her before setting it down on the bed and walking over to the closet. It was apparent she knew just where to find what she was looking for. Going right for the top shelf of the closet system, she pulled down two photo albums.

After putting the albums into the bag, she turned to me and nodded. "Now we can go."

It was a good thing. The longer I stood in the devil's bedroom, the harder it was to block out the memories. I wanted Keely and Emma as far away from all of it as humanly possibly, and fast.

I swung the front door open, prepared to leave everything about my brother's fucked up life behind me. Our exit was blocked by the unwelcome presence of Izzy's mom, Ettie—and right next to her was Tiffany. They stood shoulder-to-shoulder, arms crossed in a clear attempt to keep us from leaving.

"Get the fuck out of our way," I commanded.

The sound Ettie made was more witch cackle than human laugh. It was as unpleasant as nails on a chalkboard, and my blood ran cold.

"Is that any way to speak to that child's grandmother?"

"You are *not* her grandmother," Keely hissed.

Ettie smirked while she looked Keely up and down. "You look just like that husband stealing whore you called a mother. Listen up, shit for brains. I've got a hell of a lot more claim to her than you do. My daughter is dead and I'm here to collect the last piece of her. There's no way I'm letting my granddaughter live with you," she crowed gleefully.

"You'll take Emma over my dead body," I interjected forcefully. "You don't get shit, Ettie. I don't know why you're here now, but no court anywhere would grant you custody. You were a shit parent who abandoned her daughter. How dare you show up here pretending to give a fuck? You're a joke."

Looking to Tiffany, I glared down at her. "And you. What kind of low life bitch are you that you wasted time unearthing this troll?"

As I spoke, something dawned on me. We'd seen Tiffany for the first time the evening before. When did she have time to find Ettie? And how did they know we were at Will and Izzy's?

I was about to ask when Keely did it for me. "Did you follow us here?"

"Puh-lease," Ettie mocked dramatically. "You are one self-important little bitch, aren't you? No—we didn't follow you. We're here for business reasons. Your being here just saved me a trip to your apartment to pick the baby up."

She gestured back over her shoulder to a box truck parked at the end of the driveway. In my anger, I'd missed it.

"Like I said, business. And after I get what I need, I will be taking that baby. You couldn't be more wrong about my not being able to get her," she sneered. "I've seen my daughter plenty. Once a month like clockwork, I'm right here."

From the corner of my eye, I saw Keely's head rear back in shock. I was certain she hadn't known Ettie and Izzy were in contact. My eyes widened as one by one, the dominoes began to fall into place.

Ettie's assertion that she saw Izzy once a month, the truck in the driveway, the sudden reappearance of Tiffany in town and Izzy's letter to Keely all made sense.

Take the baby and get out of Fort Collins, she'd written. When I'd read the letter, I assumed she'd demanded that to save herself from having to see Keely being a mother to the child she'd carried. Maybe it *had* been part of the reason, but the bigger picture sent off a flashing neon sign. Keely had been right the whole time—Izzy had finally done something selfless for someone else.

She'd planned to send Emma away from Fort Collins so she'd

never run the risk of being exposed to Izzy and Will's business. The family business, she'd told me once. I thought she meant herself and Will, along with her 'sister of the heart,' Tiffany. I'd not realized it was so much bigger than that. When she said family, she'd been including her mother in the description.

I had absolutely no doubt I was looking at the person who was responsible for what Izzy had become.

Chapter Nineteen

Ronan

Five Years Ago

"H EY SHARPE!"

Burned out after a busy lunch service and looking forward to two hours off before I went to my next job, I had to hold back a groan when I heard my boss bellowing my name. Glancing up at the clock, I confirmed what I already knew—I had less than ten minutes left on my shift. If he asked me to work overtime, I was going to have to say no. Setting down the knife I'd been using to chop the herbs at my station, I lifted my head.

"What's up, Dennis?"

He came to a halt next to my station and spoke in a low voice. "Got a call up in the main office—your brother says he needs you to get over to his house pronto. Seems Tiffany was out with Izzy for lunch and she had a few drinks. He says she's covered in puke and you've got twenty minutes to get her yourself before he kicks her ass out the door. You've only got a few minutes left—go ahead and take off."

My eyes flew back up to the clock to double-check the time. It was just a few minutes before two o'clock in the afternoon. What was Tiffany thinking getting hammered in the middle of the day? And why would she never realize that things always went wrong every time she went out with Izzy? Izzy held her back, whether she realized it or not.

I was also annoyed because, earlier that morning, Tiffany had been packed and ready for her trip. Every six weeks, she made the two-hour trek to Colorado Springs to visit her grandmother. Mrs. Transom had Alzheimer's, which was really hard on the family. The way Tiffany stepped up and helped her grandmother's caregivers whenever she could was unbelievable. It sucked being without her for four or five days every six weeks, but my pride in her actions made up for it. Not many people would be so devoted to a grand-mother they'd never really had a relationship with.

It bothered me how Canter never softened toward her. Over and over again he insisted there was something 'shady as fuck' about her, but he didn't know her the way I did. Tiffany was beauti-ful but she was also tough. I saw beneath the tough exterior—Can-ter didn't. I knew one day he would. I'd thought she was a night-mare for a long time, until she let me in. I felt shame in myself for having once believed she was a bitch.

The idea of going to my brother's house held no appeal. We didn't get along because he was a smarmy asshole. With both of our parents having died, neither of us saw any reason to stay in touch. I hadn't heard from him in months, not that I minded. I wasn't happy he called my work to issue threats about kicking my shitfaced girlfriend out of his house, either. I had a full head of steam as I thanked Dennis for being cool and headed off to Will's.

I didn't get why Will insisted on living in butt-fucked nowhere, and I was annoyed I had to speed to get there before the twenty-minute timeframe was up. It was fucking cold out, and I was panicked imagining Tiffany passed out drunk outside the house if I didn't get there in time.

The door of the Mustang slammed behind me as I ran up the front porch. I was grumbling about Will being a fucking asshole as I raised my hand to knock on the door when I heard the sound of a thud. My pulse skyrocketed and my head started to pound as I imagined Tiffany had likely just fallen over. I knocked once and was surprised when the door swung open. I had not noticed it wasn't fully latched.

After closing the door behind me I headed toward the bathroom, assuming Tiffany was in there. I was almost at the end of the hall to the bathroom when the sound of a muffled scream stopped me dead in my tracks.

Spinning on my heel, I walked down the hall toward the kitchen where the sound seemed to have emanated from. When I stepped into the kitchen, I heard another scream, this one followed by Will bellowing the words, "Shut the fuck up, you filthy cunt, or I'll make it hurt more."

My heart felt like it was going to explode as the terror seized me. I spun in a circle and then stopped dead when I saw it.

The basement door was open a quarter of the way.

The basement door was never open. There had always been an enormous padlock on the door and Will never allowed anyone to go down there. I assumed a long time ago he was probably dealing drugs. He sure as hell didn't have a nine to five job but somehow always managed to have money. It didn't take a brain surgeon to figure out shit didn't add up.

I sprang into action when another scream pierced my ears. Flinging the door open, I raced down the stairs. What I found when I got there was the stuff of nightmares.

In the middle of the room, there was a large bed on a wooden platform. My eyes bugged out of my head when they landed on the figure in the middle of the bed. Tiffany was face down and restrained with red rope. Her ankles and hands were bound and there were ropes running from one side of the bed to the other, over her throat and her back to hold her down. Her face was turned toward the basement stairs but she couldn't see me because there was a blindfold over her eyes. Her mouth was covered with duct tape and there was a man in a black rubber suit on top of her, thrusting into her ass.

"Fighting only makes it better," the voice behind the mask ground out as he continued to pound into her angrily.

I recognized the voice and understood exactly who was violating my girlfriend. I couldn't believe my fucking eyes. Without hesitation, I rushed to the bed and lifted him off. I threw him toward the wall, then jumped toward him and started punching. My fists pummeled him relentlessly as I yelled obscenities. He was about to be a fucking dead man, I was that angry. He punched back almost as hard, the two of us slamming from one thing into another, breaking shit or knocking things over as we went.

"You rapist motherfucker! I'm going to kill you!"

From behind me, I heard Izzy screaming at me to stop. I hadn't seen her when I entered the room, but she could fuck right off if she thought I was going to let Will take another breath. We continued pummeling each other, but I was getting the upper hand. Rage and shock meant I couldn't feel shit, and I was angrier than he was. I slammed my fists against the disgusting rubber mask covering his face again and again as I got closer and closer to putting him down. He'd started to stagger, and I knew it was only a matter of time before I got the knockout punch.

I was damn near out of my fucking mind when Tiffany and Izzy grabbed me from behind.

"Ronan," Tiffany screamed into my ear. "Stop!"

Will got his best shot in then, slamming his fist into my stomach. I doubled over and dropped to my knees as I struggled to breathe. He tore the rubber mask off with a harsh laugh, dropping it to the floor next to me.

"You're tougher than I thought," he huffed as he wiped at the blood dripping from his obviously broken nose.

"Fuck you," I spat out between gasps for air. "You're going to jail, rapist."

The fucker shook his head as he smiled. His teeth were covered in blood, but he still looked at me like he was victorious.

"I'm not a rapist, you pathetic little fuck. I'm just doing my job."

It dawned on me that Tiffany and Izzy each had one of my hands behind my back. Turning to Tiffany I was stunned to see she didn't look upset in the least.

"What are you doing? You're free—go call the police!"

Later on I would put all of the pieces together and see all of the flashing neon signs. Like how she was no longer restrained but chose to help Izzy keep me from moving. That was probably the biggest red flag of all. The reality was right there, but I didn't see it—instead, I'd believed my girlfriend had just been raped by my brother.

She looked over my shoulder at Will and gave him a dirty look. "You did this on purpose, didn't you?"

He snickered as he crossed his arms over his chest. "Give the lady a prize. He's fucking annoying," he said as he gestured to me. "You know how much more money we'd be pulling in if you didn't spend weeks at a time pretending to be a loving girlfriend."

"We agreed—"

He cut her off with a flick of his wrist. "And now I don't agree," he snapped. "It's about the bottom line."

"But I like him a whole lot," she whined.

Having finally caught my breath, I wrenched my arms away from Tiffany and Izzy. I spun on my heel to face a still naked Tiffany. She liked me? She fucking *liked me*? We lived together. She told me she loved me all the time. Now, suddenly, she merely liked me?

My eyes darted around the room as I tried to make sense of what was going on. As I looked around, I saw several things I hadn't noticed before. Like the professional looking video cameras sitting on tripods set up on either side of the bed. It was then it started to dawn on me what was happening. I lost my breath all over again as the reality set in, and it hurt a fuck load more than Will's sucker punch to my gut.

I looked back to my girlfriend—the one I fucking lived with and assumed I would marry—in horror.

"Tiffany? He's lying—right?"

She stepped closer to me as she twisted her hands together.

"Don't freak out," she whined. "Nothing was happening here I didn't consent to. Will is telling the truth—this is a job."

My eyes darted between her and one of the cameras.

"A job?"

"Yes," she said in an exasperated tone of voice. "A job. Now that it's out in the open, you're going to have to deal with it."

Her attitude was like a punch to the face. She wasn't at all who I'd thought she was.

"What job, Tiffany?"

"Dude," Will laughed from behind me. "You're not blind. Look at the cameras, you fucking idiot. She means porn."

A wave of dizziness hit me hard. I reached out to steady myself, but Tiffany jumped away so there was nothing to hold onto. My arms flailed out wildly in an attempt to gain my balance. My desperation caused Will to laugh as I wobbled on my feet in the struggle to stay upright. Only sheer force of will kept me standing.

"Ronan," Tiffany said in a babydoll type voice. "You're blowing this out of proportion. It's a job—nothing more. This changes nothing."

It changed everything.

It took me a few extra seconds to get myself under control. When I could speak again I said, "I've seen porn. It doesn't look anything like this."

"You watch boring porn then," Izzy laughed. "We make fetish porn. It's a huge market and it gets bigger every day."

She may as well have told me they bred unicorns.

"What the fuck is fetish porn?"

Will came into my line of sight as he peeled off the rubber suit. Making no attempt to cover himself once he was naked, he sat down on the bed. I could see the triumph lurking behind his bored façade.

"Pseudo-rape, dubious consent, bloodletting, piss, choking, fisting, fireplay—it's a big fucking list. You want me to go on?"

"You're fucking disgusting," I exclaimed. "Acting like you're a big man because you upload shitty porn to the fucking Internet like a loser—"

He threw back his head and laughed before gesturing to the area on the other side of the basement stairs. I hadn't looked at it since coming down, but once he pointed it out, I saw hundreds of DVD cases lined up on labeled shelves. Over the shelves there was a sign taped to the wall that read Monthly Shipment. Along the back wall, I saw a set up of dozens—maybe as many as fifty—recording machines hooked up. A sign on the wall advised not to touch while burning was in progress. I knew what DVD burning was because one of the guys at the restaurant where I worked constantly brought in burned movies.

Swinging my head back toward the side of the basement where Will was still sitting on the bed, I shook my head.

"You sell illegal porn out of your fucking basement and you're proud of that?"

I'd scored a direct hit with my words. I knew because his nostrils flared as he glared at me.

"Don't talk to Will that way. We don't sell it from the basement and it's in no way illegal," Izzy announced. "We have a distributor. This is a real business," she said proudly. "Some day Will and I will get married and make it a real family business."

The walls in the basement were closing in on me. At some point while my attention was diverted, Tiffany had put on a robe. I recognized it as being one that our mother had given to Will on her last Christmas. That was it for me—I was done. D.O.N.E. I made my decision to leave right then and there. I promised myself I would never look at my brother, Izzy or Tiffany again. It was over.

I gestured to Will angrily. "You're a twisted piece of shit and a fucking loser. I'm fucking out of here and I'm never coming back. We're done, Will. You aren't my brother. Don't call, don't text, don't look for me. I'm gone. You're all welcome to each other. You make me fucking sick."

I turned on my heel and ran up the stairs, gritting my teeth when I heard Will calling out.

"I hope you meant that!"

The sound of Izzy and Tiffany giggling added fuel to the fire. I raced to my car as if there was a rocket strapped to my ass. Peeling out of his driveway, I headed to the apartment I'd been sharing with Tiffany so I could pack my shit.

I'd just finished tossing my crap into two duffel bags when she came home and tried to talk me out of going. I couldn't fucking believe she thought there was a chance in hell I'd stay with her. The vision of her strapped down to my brother's basement bed while he fucked her up the ass was playing on a goddamn loop in my head, but the crazy bitch thought it could all be written off. Over and over again I saw Will on top of her—without a condom. I wasn't just angry—I was also terrified she'd given me a disease. My entire world was in a million pieces. Writing it off wasn't fucking happening. I stayed silent as I zipped up my bags and stalked out of the bedroom to leave.

She raced ahead of me and threw herself dramatically against the door.

"How can you even consider leaving me? We're going to get married," she cried. "You said you would always be there for me!"

I looked at her in horror.

"This whole relationship was a lie," I bellowed. "I don't even fucking know you! Get the fuck out of my way before I do something I'll regret almost as much as I regret ever touching you."

She crossed her arms over her chest as she glared up at me. "You don't get to leave me," she said shrilly. "I'm the one in control."

It made me fucking sick to know she wasn't wrong. She had been the one in control for our entire relationship, and I'd ignored all of the signs.

I knew the answer to my question before I asked, but I needed to know just how fucking many chances I'd missed to figure out the truth.

"Have you ever gone to see your grandmother even once?"

She giggled like a vapid idiot. "No. Don't be mad about that.. I lied, but it takes a few days to recover after some of our shoots, so—"

"You're a fucking whore," I said quietly.

She shrieked angrily, but I didn't care. I grabbed her and lifted her up, depositing her away from the door so I could leave. I slammed the door behind me and raced down the stairs to the parking lot. I heard her from behind me, yelling like a fucking lunatic in a way I was sure all the neighbors heard.

"I know you'll be back," she shouted. "We're going to get married!"

She was fucking nuts. Period. I'd been completely snowed and I felt shame for having been so goddamn wrong about her. I peeled out of the apartment complex and floored it to Canter's. He knew something was wrong the second he opened the door. Once we got inside, I dumped the whole shitty story on him. His status as my best friend was cemented forever when he never once uttered the phrase *I told you so*. Because he had—so many times.

After I left his house, I got on the road to anywhere but fucking Fort Collins. I was almost out of town when it dawned on me there was one more person I should talk to. I took a sharp U-Turn and headed for the Carmichael house. Hollis had enabled Izzy to the point of insanity. If he didn't tough love her into changing, she was going to destruct. I didn't give a shit about Izzy, but I knew if something happened to her, Hollis would lose it. And, if he lost it, Keely would have no one. She was a great kid, and I believed taking the time to set Hollis straight might save her a lot of future heartache.

It never occurred to me to think Hollis already knew. He told me in no uncertain terms he would never turn his back on Izzy. She was, he voiced emotionally, his *baby*.

When I pointed out he had another daughter, he waved me off.

"She doesn't know what her sister does and she never will. This doesn't affect her. There's only one Izzy," he said firmly. "She's my priority."

I'd been half a second away from going over the table at him when Keely came down the stairs. When she realized I was there her face lit up—until she came closer and realized I'd clearly been in a fight. When she did, she panicked. I was pissed at Hollis and disgusted with everything. I wanted to punch him—badly—but I would never do that in front of Keely. I knew then I needed to leave before the entire house of cards fell down.

Under no circumstances could Keely ever know what her sister had become.

Chapter Twenty

Keely

RONAN STARED AT ETTIE WITH A LOOK OF ABSOLUTE disgust.

"You're the distributor," he said.

The way he said it indicated she should be ashamed. There was not an ounce of it on her face, though, when she shrugged.

"What's it to you?"

"You encouraged your daughter to allow herself to be violated—"

My stomach fell and fell and fell. *Anyone but Izzy's own mother*, I prayed silently.

"It was consensual! You act like she needed to be forced. All I did was tell her it was an option," she snapped. "This is a legal business. There are contracts and we pay taxes. No one has ever been violated."

I struggled to breathe through the pain as my heart shattered into smithereens. My sister had been a mess—it was a fact—but what chance had she ever really had? Our dad was an enabler and her mother had gotten her into porn. It was too late for me to help

Izzy—but I'd die before I broke the one promise I ever made to her. Emma was mine, and Ettie would never get her twisted hands on her.

My temper flared when I took note of the smug expression on Ettie's face. Her daughter was dead, and she was partially responsible for her demise. I'd always disliked Ettie, but right then, I turned the corner into hatred. My hand flew into the air lightning quick, connecting with the side of her face as I slapped her with all the force I had. She let out a shocked gasp as she covered her cheek and glared at me.

"What the—"

I cut her off angrily. "How could you persuade my sister—*your daughter*—to allow herself to be defiled the way she was? You ruined her life!"

When I heard Ronan's sharp inhale I realized he was surprised I knew. The feeling was mutual—I was just as stunned to find out he'd known.

"It's not like I asked her to do anything I haven't done myself. You can judge all you want but you know nothing. It's a becoming a lucrative business—"

I gaped at her sickly. She was talking about her daughter as if she had been nothing more than a co-worker.

"You're a disgrace! You ruined her life with your filth," I yelled. "How do you live with yourself?"

I'd have slapped her again if Emma hadn't started wailing. Later on Ronan would tell me that the second I raised my voice Emma woke up.

I bent down and rubbed my finger over her cheek to calm her. "It's okay, pretty girl. Mommy's sorry, baby. We're leaving."

As I stood, I saw Tiffany trying to come at me with a raised fist. I was ready for whatever she wanted to dole out, but it didn't come to that. Ronan put his free hand out and set her back like she was nothing more than a fly.

"Don't even try it, bitch," he snapped. "You do not want to test me, Tiffany. Unless you feel like going to jail, back the fuck off."

She scoffed angrily. "Jail for what?"

He let out a snort of disgust. "For the drugs you're on. You think it's not fuckin' obvious you're high as a goddamn kite? You aren't that good of an actress. You're tweaked to hell and you look like shit. One call to Chief West and you're toast. Step. The. Fuck. Off."

She tried to hold her ground and act as if she wasn't scared, but she did a piss poor job. Her hand was shaking when she raised it up and gave him the finger.

"I'm fucking out of here, asshole."

Tiffany stomped away and slammed the front door on her way out. Naturally, Emma's wails grew louder from the noise. Hearing her frantic cry did not improve Ronan's frame of mind at all. I was a little afraid for Ettie, to be honest. He stepped closer as he raised his finger and pointed at her.

"I'm gonna tell you straight up, you're fucking with the wrong people. You will not, ever, be this close to our child again. You want to take this to court? Bring it. We will destroy you. You have no legal right to her—"

"Excuse me," Ettie huffed. "I don't know who you think you are threatening me but you couldn't be more wrong. I'm her grand-mother and *any* judge would side with me."

I could see her use of the word grandmother in relation to Emma infuriated him. He stepped closer, crowding Ettie against the entry wall. I grabbed Emma's car seat from his hand, lifting it up so Emma could see my face. It broke my heart to see her crying so hard and the little tears sliding down her chubby cheeks made me want to cry too. I wanted to run outside but there was no way I was taking on Tiffany without Ronan. If she swung at me while I had Emma's seat in my hands, things would not end well.

"We need to go," I interjected. "I can't have her crying like this."

He looked over his shoulder at me and gestured for me to come closer. I walked the few steps until I was almost at his side and then stopped. Ettie was calling out obscenities, but Ronan put a stop to it fast.

"You keep fucking upsetting my baby and you're not going to like what happens. Shut the fuck up, now."

Ettie's mouth opened and closed like a goldfish, but she didn't say anything else. She did, however, watch angrily as Ronan set about comforting the baby. Reaching into Emma's seat, he traced her face softly.

"Mommy and I are right here, baby. I promise everything is going to be fine."

She didn't stop crying entirely, but the screaming stopped. It was as though knowing we were both there and focused on her took some of the fear away. She looked back and forth between the two of us as she fidgeted and fussed. When Ronan was satisfied she was okay, he leaned in and kissed her before backing away. I held the seat in both hands and rocked side to side as he turned his attention back to Ettie.

"One—you're *not* her grandmother. You don't fucking look at our baby, you don't talk about our baby, and you sure as shit don't make threats about our baby. Go ahead and get an attorney and try for custody. No judge will grant you any access to her, ever. You're a fucking disgrace who turned her only child into a porn queen."

"Fuck you and the 'our baby' bullshit," she snapped back. "She's not your anything, Ronan Sharpe."

I was surprised when he looked to me. "I'm her father," he said.

I had to swallow past the lump in my throat at his words. My lips trembled as I nodded my agreement.

Turning back to Ettie he continued, "I'll fight you in this life and the next before I ever let you anywhere near her. Don't test us. You won't like what happens."

She pointed at him angrily. "You think you can scare me but you can't. My daughter would've wanted me to take this child and that's exactly what I'm going to do."

He laughed in her face. Not a *ha ha* laugh—a laugh that said she had just gone too far.

"You think so, do you?"

"I *know* so," she hissed. "She hated this stupid bitch," she said as she gestured in my direction.

"It often seemed as if she did," he agreed.

Ettie smiled victoriously, but Ronan kept right on talking. As he did, her smile dimmed until it was gone entirely.

"And yet—Izzy still took the time to leave a handwritten letter giving custody of the baby to Keely. Even before she died, she'd always planned for Keely to take the baby. She even went as far as going to a lawyer to get the ball rolling. Emma's adoption is already official—Keely is her mother."

Ettie's eyes were saucer wide as she gaped at Ronan. He glared at her as he continued.

"I guess you didn't know Izzy as well as you thought you did. Get your lawyer and do what you want but know this—we've got proof she didn't want you anywhere near this child. The adoption has already gone through. No going back, Ettie. Keely and I will fight for what is ours until we've ruined you," he said coldly. "If you're fool enough to take us on, that's on you."

He stepped back from Ettie and then took the car seat from me after he finished, lifting it up so he could wipe away Emma's tears. He did this calmly, but the glacial look he gave Ettie as he did could've frozen the desert.

I could see the cogs turning in Ettie's head as she tried to figure out what exactly to do. Her face was practically purple while she

sputtered like an engine on its last leg. Still, underneath her brava-
do, I saw anxiety. No matter what she said, she didn't want to go to
court. Ronan was right—we would destroy her. If it cost me every
cent I ever made for the rest of my life, I would spend it gladly if it
meant Emma was never exposed to her.

"Take the kid if you want her so badly, but you do not get this
house," she said snidely.

And there it was. Proof she didn't care at all about Emma.
What she'd wanted the entire time was just the house.

Ronan yanked the front door open before reaching out and
taking Emma's seat from me. Once she was secure, he took my free
hand in his and linked our fingers together. Looking back at Ettie,
he gave her a look of disgust.

"What a parent you've been," he said snidely. "Your daughter
is *dead* and all you care about is the house. Have at it, Ettie. Have
fucking at it. Unlike you, we know what's really important, because
we have it. You can burn this piece of shit to the ground as far as
Keely and I are concerned. It's as toxic as you are. Fair warning. If I
see you again anywhere near me, or my girls, I will ruin you. That's
not a threat—it's a vow."

I held on tight to his hand as we stepped out onto the porch.
Tiffany was standing at the top of the stairs texting on her phone
and trying to look cool. She completely ignored us as we walked by
her, and we ignored her right back. Just as we got to the start of the
driveway, Ettie called out from behind me.

"Keely."

Instinct made me respond. I wished I hadn't. I paused to look
over my shoulder at her.

"What?"

The smug look on her face was a warning I wasn't going to like
what she had to say.

"You go ahead and think I was a shit parent, but know this.

Your father knew what she was doing. Not only that, he gave her money to help them get it off the ground. He supported my daughter because he loved her. I never heard one word about him supporting you. It doesn't take a genius to figure out why. Always the little outsider," she said haughtily. "You never even warranted a second glance. What kind of girl doesn't matter to her own father?"

She laughed as she finished, and of course Tiffany joined in. I forgot to breathe for a few seconds as her words replayed in my mind. I wanted so badly to believe Ettie was lying, but deep in my heart, I knew she wasn't.

If Ronan hadn't been holding my hand, I would've fallen to my knees. Only the strength of his hold on me kept me upright. I couldn't even come up with a response. I thought if I opened my mouth, I'd burst into tears. Ronan took care of it for me.

"The kind of girl who got fucking lucky," Ronan said angrily. "Between you and Hollis, you fucked Izzy up beyond repair. You destroyed her. When push came to shove and your daughter had to choose whom to rely on, instead of going with her drug addict best friend or her shitty mother, she chose the one good person she knew. You can spout all the bullshit you want, but it wont change the fact that your only child knew you were garbage."

Ronan squeezed my hand supportively as Ettie sputtered. Not giving her a chance to respond, he hurried us to the car as quickly as possible. Emma was no longer crying full force but she was fussy, so I climbed into the backseat to be next to her. We drove away quickly, but safely. I think if it had just been Ronan and I in the car, he would've peeled out. With Emma in the car he would never do anything of the sort.

As soon as we were on the road, he reached his hand back.

"Just hold onto me," he instructed. "I've got you."

I didn't have to be asked twice. I laid my face on the side of Emma's seat so she could see me. My left hand was on the other side of the seat to allow her to hold onto one of my fingers. My other hand, the right one, went right up onto the back of Ronan's seat. His right hand rested on top of mine, which completed our family chain. As devastated as I was by Ettie's revelation, I loved being connected to Ronan and the baby. As bad as the situation was, one thing stood out above all the rest. Ronan had claimed Emma as his own. Everything else paled in comparison.

Emma had stopped fussing almost the instant we started driving. After popping her thumb into her mouth, she settled down and alternated between watching me and happily sucking on her thumb. It was such a relief for me to watch her put it behind her. The toxic wasteland that had been part of my life since birth upset me, but I wouldn't let it hurt her. *We* wouldn't let it hurt her.

Entering my apartment with Ronan and Emma felt like coming home. Being at Izzy and Will's and seeing Ettie was a reminder that home wasn't a structure—it was the certainty that came when you were right where you were supposed to be.

Chapter Twenty-One

Keely

B Y UNSPOKEN AGREEMENT, WHILE EMMA WAS AWAKE, Ronan and I didn't talk about what had happened at Izzy and Will's house. It was definitely on our minds, but we didn't have the conversation we both knew was coming while Emma was alert. It just felt like the wrong thing to do.

Emma wanted to be held and loved for the ninety minutes or so after we got back. It was fine for Ronan and I to pass her back and forth to each other but she wasn't okay with being put down. It was probably better for both of us, her wanting the extra cuddles. It allowed us to connect with what mattered—our little family unit.

"She just wants Mommy and Daddy time," Ronan said huskily.

I loved that.

Running my hand up and down her back as she snuggled against her spot over Ronan's heart, I let it sink in fully. We were a family.

Later, after she'd been fed, changed, thoroughly loved and then put down for her nap, Ronan and I sat down on the bed to talk.

Before I could ask him how he knew about what Izzy and Will

had been doing, he asked me the same question.

"How did you find out what they were doing?"

I knew I was going to need to tell him, but it didn't make it any easier to talk about.

"It wasn't as if I'd ever liked Will to begin with," I began. "Even when I was a kid, he'd never tried to be even moderately polite to me. It only got worse when Dad got sick. Will wanted Izzy to get the bulk of the estate, so he went to work on Dad."

I swallowed past the lump in my throat and picked at a piece of lint on my yoga pants.

"The funniest thing is he didn't need to bother. When the will was read, the date on it was from two years *before* Dad died. The estate was already set up with a seventy/thirty split. Izzy got eighty percent of the house sale and all the money in the bank accounts. I got a life insurance policy, twenty percent of the house sale, my mom's jewelry, some of my grandmother's jewelry, my parents' wedding china and a bunch of pictures and odds and ends."

Ronan wrapped his arm around my shoulders and dropped a kiss on my head. "I'm sorry, baby."

I shook my head as I fought back tears. I'd cried enough in the months after my dad died to fill a river. I didn't want to cry anymore for someone who had let me down time and time again.

"Considering what you got after your parents died, I know I should be glad my father thought of me at all. I feel stupid for being upset—"

"Hey," he said softly. "Don't do that. You're allowed to be upset, Keely. My parents always sucked but your dad wasn't always such a pussy. When your mom was alive he was more of a dad to you."

I shrugged. "He pretended to be," I agreed. "Whatever the big show was he put on for my mom, once she was gone he was, too. It's taken me a long time to be able to put voice to my resentment over his actions. He left Izzy in charge of everything. Yeah, he left me things in the will, but with her in charge, I got nothing. I was a minor and she was my guardian. What little money I managed to argue out of her went to me buying my crappy car and paying rent after I left her house."

He sighed as he hugged me to him. "Your father wasn't very smart where she was concerned," he said diplomatically.

"No," I ground out. "He wasn't. Hearing Ettie say he knew what Izzy was doing was like a punch to the gut. I was certain there was no way he knew. Finding out he knew and was supportive kills me. He should've gotten Izzy help. At the very least, I can't believe..."

I trailed off as I held my tears in check. I could feel the tension in Ronan, so I knew he was as angry as I was.

"He could've made other arrangements for me," I whimpered. "He could have and he *should* have, but he didn't. Instead, I wound up having to move into that hellhole. At first, things were just uncomfortable. Looking at it differently, I see now that Izzy tried to keep the two of us away from each other as much as possible. She didn't want me to know what they did."

His hold on me tightened as I leaned into him for support.

"I was only there for a matter of weeks. It took no time at all for Will to blow shit up in such a way I couldn't be there anymore. He wanted no part of Izzy being my guardian for the year, so he took matters into his own hands and made sure the only thing I would do was run like hell right out of their lives."

Ronan stiffened as he pulled back. My eyes flew to his face, and I stopped breathing when I saw every ounce of color had leeched from his face. I opened my mouth to ask him what was wrong as he cupped my face in his hands. I could feel his hands trembling.

"How did I not see this? I knew he was the fucking devil but I never thought..." He swallowed hard, his breath nothing more than a series of gasps. "He fucking did something to you, didn't he? He fucking touched you!"

I reached up and covered both of his hands with mine. "No, he didn't. It's okay, Ronan. I'm okay. He never touched me. Ever."

He sagged against me in relief as he wrapped his arms around me to hold on tight. We hugged for several minutes, with him repeating a series of *Thank Gods* over and over again. When I felt he was ready to hear the rest of the story, I pulled back.

"He never touched me the way you were thinking," I reassured him. "But what he did do was cruel and obscene."

I could see Ronan's jaw ticking as he listened.

"The basement door was always locked," I explained. "Until the afternoon it wasn't, and he yelled up the stairs and ordered me to bring him a bottle of Jack Daniels. I rushed to do it, hoping to be in and out of the basement in a few seconds. Everything I did was wrong in his eyes, so I did my best to stay away from him. If I could change one thing in my life, I'd never have gone down those stairs."

As I continued, I began twisting a strand of my hair nervously.

"He was sitting on a bed in the middle of the room wearing only a pair of boxers," I said with a shudder. "I threw the bottle on the bed and ran up the stairs. Three steps from the top, I saw Tiffany. She was laughing when she slammed and locked it, trapping me down there with him."

I shut my eyes as I remembered what came next. "He and Tiffany had worked together to create a game of cat and mouse. After she shut the door, he was purposely doing things to scare me. Laughing in a demonic sounding voice, grabbing my ankle as I tried to turn on the stairs—I had no choice but to go back down into the basement. When I did he started trailing a whip across the floor as he herded me to the bed. After I sat down, he pointed to the movie playing on the TV across the room."

Ronan expelled a harsh breath. "It was your sister, wasn't it?"

I nodded as I licked my lips, remembering what came next. "It was Izzy and three other men. They were taking turns choking her as they smacked her around and violated her. I started to scream, which only made Will laugh. He grabbed the remote and started pulling up different movie clips, each worse than the one other. As bad as seeing all of that was, the worst part was the way he smiled when he told me he and my sister ran a fetish porn company. He said if I wanted to stay in the house, I was going to need to get into the family business."

Ronan's eyes went wide and he clenched his fists. "That motherfucker," he hissed.

Raising my hand, I covered his mouth.

"He wasn't serious," I explained. "He just wanted me to leave."

"When he let me out, I packed and ran. I stopped long enough to call Izzy and begged her to leave with me, but it just pissed her off. She screamed at me for being an 'uptight and judgmental little bitch.' I didn't see her again until she showed up at my door a few months ago."

His eyes were wide with anger as he clenched his jaw.

"That fucking basement," Ronan spat. "Someone should burn that house to the ground."

I cocked my head as I voiced my question.

"How did *you* know what they were doing down there?"

I said very little as he told me. After everything I'd experienced with Will, I wasn't surprised. When he finished, I jumped into his arms and held him. Regardless of the fact I hated Tiffany, I was heartbroken to hear how her actions blew up in his face on the day he left town. Once he explained it all, I completely understood why he chose to leave town. I would've done the same.

"I'm so sorry that happened to you," I said softly. "I know you were in love with—"

Setting his finger against my lips, he shushed me as he shook his head.

"No, I wasn't. I said the words because I thought I did. I see now how empty they were because I didn't feel them in here," he said as he tapped over his heart.

"I know how fake and stupid it all was now because for the first time in my life, love is real. It isn't forced shit I think I should feel. It's bone deep certainty that I love you, Keely. You're everything."

I grinned like an idiot as my heart melted into a puddle of goo in my chest.

"I love you, too," I said softly.

The smile that spread across his face was huge.

"I love that, baby."

I wrapped my arms around him tight. When I pulled back I dropped a series of soft kisses around his face—his eyelids, his forehead, his nose, both cheeks and finally his lips. I brushed my lips feather soft across his, intending to move on. Cupping the back of my head, Ronan held me in place as he covered my lips with his own.

I melted into him as his tongue slid against mine and we kissed passionately. The way my body lit up from a mere kiss was astounding. Our soft and slow kiss took on a life of its own around the time I climbed onto his lap and started grinding against him.

When he slid his hand into my yoga pants and touched me over my underwear, I let out an excited moan. Pushing my panties to the side, he slid his finger over my clit. I jolted like a live wire as he used his fingers on me.

Ripping his mouth from mine, he stared at me through hood-ed eyes. "You get so wet," he growled.

I blushed as I bit down on my lower lip. He was right—I could feel and hear how wet I was.

"I fucking love it," he said hoarsely. "Knowing you're this wet makes my dick so hard."

I whimpered as he slid one long finger inside of me and began thrusting it in and out. As he did, he used his thumb to rub my clit.

I rocked back and forth against him as he worked me over.

Several minutes later, he stopped what he was doing and took his hand away. I let out a needy sound as he traced my lips with the finger he'd just been fucking me with. Once he'd coated my lips with wetness, he teased me with his tongue as he licked it all away.

I moaned when he started kissing me again like he couldn't get enough. We started desperately pawing at each other's clothes as we tried to take them off quickly. When I got his shirt off, I felt a rush of pride. I trailed my tongue across his neck, leaving gentle bites as I worked my way from one side to the other.

He growled low in his throat as I nibbled and sucked. The next thing I knew, I was on my back as he peeled my yoga pants and panties off. I gasped when he spread my legs wide and dropped his mouth right where I needed him the most.

The stubble on his cheeks scraped against my inner thighs as he used his tongue on me. The dual sensations were sending me into orbit. I grabbed onto the back of his head just to keep myself tethered to him. In an embarrassingly short amount of time, I was thrusting against his tongue desperately as I came. I had to shove my fist against my lips to keep from yelling his name.

I was still coming when he rose up over me. I was trembling as he rubbed himself against me. When he thrust deep, I wrapped my legs around his waist and met him thrust for thrust.

He looked down so he could watch as he slid in and out of me.

"You feel so good on my dick, Keely."

I nodded frantically as he started going faster. "You feel amazing inside of me," I whimpered.

His eyes flared as he thrust harder. When he traced his thumb in a circle against my clit, I clawed at his back as I felt myself going.

"Harder," I begged. "Please!"

He thundered into me relentlessly as I lit up. I bit his shoulder as I started coming, and it only got better when he started to come, too. The hot warmth of his release prolonged my release and made me shiver all over as he pushed it deeper inside of me with each thrust.

"I love you so fucking much," he panted.

I squeezed him tightly with my arms and legs. "Love you too," I said breathlessly.

We stayed like that for quite a while—just holding on to each other and enjoying the afterglow. Once we were both able to breathe normally again, Ronan pulled out and went to the bathroom. I blushed as he wiped between my legs, but I appreciated the gesture. I loved the way he took care of me.

Instead of getting fully dressed, I picked up the tee I'd taken off of him and slipped it over my head. I snuggled into it as I enjoyed his scent wrapping itself around me. I smiled happily when he got onto the bed to lie next to me. Propping his head on his hand, he stared at me with a smile.

"I want to start our new lives," he said. "What do you say we blow this place in the next week or so?"

"I say let's do it," I said enthusiastically.

With everything out in the open and our commitment to each other guaranteed, I felt more optimistic about life than ever.

Chapter Twenty-Two

Ronan

CANTER STOOD AT MY SIDE AS I WENT THROUGH THE MOVING checklist for the final time. Because most of Keely's stuff had been junk, the majority of the things in the U-Haul trailer attached to my rental car were either clothes or baby stuff. All the stuff she hadn't wanted had been put out as Craigslist curb alerts. I'd been skeptical that any of it would be picked up. Surprisingly, it was all gone within an hour.

After we closed and locked the U-Haul trailer, Canter walked with me back into the empty apartment for a final walk through. Keely and Emma were at a hotel across town waiting for me. I'd planned everything so that we would leave late at night allowing Emma to be able to sleep as much as possible during the drive. Her main sleeping times tended to be between midnight and seven in the morning, so we hoped the drive wouldn't even be an issue for her. We'd gone back and forth about flying, but I wasn't feeling exposing her to other people's germs. Plus, the Internet was full of horror stories about colds and burst eardrums. No way was I exposing my girl to that.

The walk through took less than two minutes. As I'd expected, we'd gotten everything out. The apartment was now pristine and ready for the next tenant. I was surprised to realize I was a bit sad to close the door behind me for the final time. As ready as I was to take my girls home with me, it was emotional to leave the place we'd first brought Emma home to. There were a lot of memories in that small apartment.

The other thing that sucked was moving away from Canter again. It had been great to have my best friend back. When we got back down to my car, we bro hugged quickly, patting each other on the back.

"I'm real fuckin' glad you got your head out of your ass long enough to make your play," he chided. "If I hadn't been here to steer you straight, you'd probably never have done shit."

"I'd like to return the favor," I laughed. "But your reputation in this town proceeds you."

He lifted his middle finger in salute. "My reputation is just fine, fuck you very much."

"Uh-huh," I mocked. "The reputation of the town player is always solid."

"Dude, fuck off. I'm not a player," he argued.

I raised an eyebrow. "That's not what I heard…"

He rolled his eyes dramatically. "In between bottles, diaper changes and finding your woman, you had time to listen to the town gossip? You're fuckin' lame, man."

I burst out laughing. "It's not cool to call your sister the town gossip."

"Ugh, I should've fucking known. She says Mom is too much, but she's not any better. If I let those two have their way, I'll be married with five kids in about a minute."

"One can only hope," I said dryly.

"Oh sure," he chuckled. "Now that you're all settled down, you want everyone you know to do the same thing. Fuck that. I'll raise a toast to you tonight at the bar. I'm sure you'll be knee deep in dirty diapers or some shit while I'm having fun."

"Fucking asshole," I chuckled. "You always know how to make me laugh. Have fun at the bar but remember, you promised Keely and Emma you'd be visiting us in Montana sooner rather than later."

"Yeah, yeah," he laughed as he rolled his eyes. "I'm sure they'll really hold me to that."

"We all will," I assured him. "You promise my girls something, you fucking deliver. You're Emma's favorite uncle. She's going to miss having you around which means you will be coming to see her pronto."

He looked emotional for a second or two. Clearing his throat, he looked away. "I'm going to miss her, too. Never thought I'd like a baby so much. I promise I'll fly out next month for a visit."

Clapping him on the shoulder, I smirked. "My princess does not play," I laughed. "Once she gets into your heart, she sets up camp."

"You would know, Daddy."

I smiled big. "I fucking love being her dad," I said proudly.

❧

Keely had sent a text to let me know Emma had gone down to nap, so I was quiet when I let myself into the hotel room. Glancing around the room I saw Emma in her portable crib and Keely was sitting at the desk reading a magazine. My heart skipped a few beats when she turned and smiled at me softly. After securing the door, I covered the distance between us quickly and then pulled her into my arms for a kiss.

As she ran her hands up under my shirt, I pulled away with a laugh.

"I'm sweaty and gross from loading the U-Haul. How about you wash me off in the shower?"

Her eyes lit up as she took my hand and followed my lead into the bathroom. We worked as a team. I started the shower while she opened the toiletries on the hotel counter. I got naked before she did, which meant I got to enjoy the view as she peeled off her clothes.

When she was naked, I pulled her into the shower and shut the curtain behind us. After positioning her where she needed to be, I tilted her head back and got to washing her hair.

"You ready for the big move?"

She made a sound of approval as I massaged at her scalp.

"If I get this kind of shower treatment regularly, I'll follow you to the ends of the earth," she laughed.

"Just call me shower guy then," I quipped.

After I had all of the soap out of her hair and I'd applied conditioner, I turned her around and started lathering her up. She shivered when I started massaging her amazing tits. To say I was a fan of them would be a huge understatement.

"Feel good?"

"Mm."

Her eyes flew open when I pinched her left nipple. I grinned at her as I leaned in and gently bit her lower lip before kissing it softly. Then I covered her mouth with mine and let out a groan when our tongues touched. The kiss began soft but quickly became more aggressive. I made a desperate sound when she broke the kiss and pulled away.

"You almost made me forget why we got in here." Staring at me expectantly she held out her hand and wiggled her fingers. "Give me the soap."

The way she ran her hands over me as she soaped every inch

of my body got me painfully hard. My dick wept pre-come after she lathered her palm and began to shuttle her fist up and down my length. When she was satisfied, she turned me so I could rinse off my front while she washed my back. I turned back around at her command, letting out a growl when I found her on her knees. Seeing her at my feet was almost too much.

She started by trailing her tongue around my shaft. The visual alone almost made me come. I braced myself against the shower wall as Keely wiggled her tongue against my sensitive tip. She smirked up at me when I made a tortured sound low in my throat. Instead of letting up and allowing me to get my bearings, she opened her mouth and took me in.

One of her hands was busy sliding up and down my dick in time with her bobbing head. The other trailed up the inside of my thigh until it reached my balls. My eyes rolled back as I struggled to breathe. I knew the hot, wet heat of her mouth was going to make me come if I didn't take control. Her breathy protest when I bent down and pulled her up made me smile. Knowing she liked my dick in her mouth was a good thing. I absolutely planned to spend a lot of time there in the future. Right then, I was focused on my need to be inside of her.

I cut off her protest by capturing her mouth with mine. She kissed me desperately as I slid my hand down to her core to make sure she was ready. The wet heat of her arousal coating my fingers was my answer. I thrust two fingers inside while I worked her clit with my thumb. Her nails dug into my ass as she tried to grind herself against me.

I set my forehead against hers after ending the kiss and asked, "You want this?"

She nodded frantically. "Yes. Please!"

My hands cupped her ass as I lifted her up against the wall. "Guide me inside," I growled.

I could feel her hands trembling as she did. The first touch of her wetness against my dick made me crazy. I held on tight as I pulled her down onto my aching dick. I was in a Keely vice and I fucking loved it. Her legs squeezed around my waist, her arms were around my shoulders and her pussy was clenched around my cock when I started thrusting in and out. We couldn't have been more connected.

We kissed frantically as I picked up speed. I was forced to pull away when I started breathing heavily.

"You're so fucking hot," I ground out as I slammed inside of her.

She gripped me harder, biting the side of my neck as she pulsed around me.

"Ronan," she whimpered as I thrust. "God, Ronan!"

I could feel how close she was to coming and I knew what she needed to get there.

"Touch your clit, baby. I want you to come on my dick."

Her hand slid between us, going right to where she needed to be touched. Her pussy gripped me tighter than ever as she started chanting my name. I knew we were both about to come hard.

"Fuck, Keely. Come for me, baby."

She trembled in my arms, biting down on her lip before opening her mouth and yelping, "Now!"

The feeling of her coming sent me over the edge. I thrust hard and deep as I started pouring my release deep inside of her. When I finally came back to reality, I realized I felt completely at peace. I was right where I was supposed to be and I'd never felt better. Being with the most beautiful girl in the fucking world was everything I'd ever needed.

When I could breathe without sounding like I was mid marathon, I put my hand under her chin and tilted her head back so she was looking at me.

"I love you."

Her smile warmed me like it had the power of a thousand suns. "I love you, too. And just so you know, I'll never get tired of hearing you say that," she said softly.

I pulled out slowly, enjoying the shiver that racked her body as I did. By then we were both pruned up from being in the shower for so long. I made quick work of cleaning us both up all over again so we could get out of the water. After we were dry, I stood behind her and dried her hair. Her stitches were gone and she had full mobility again, but I still liked to do it. When I was finished, we climbed into the hotel bed for a short nap before we hit the road to start our new life.

Epilogue

Ronan

Seven Months Later

O N ONE OF THE HARDEST AND MOST STRESSFUL DAYS OF MY life, I fell in love. Twice. First there was Keely, and then came Emma. After that, I had everything, and the family I gained meant the world to me.

The sound of Keely's laughter was music to my ears as I entered the house after work. I smiled as I threw my keys into the bowl by the backdoor and hung my coat up on a hook. Coming home to my girls was everything I never knew I needed and could never again live without.

I'd been excited and nervous about taking Keely and Emma to Montana. Don't get me wrong—I wanted them with me all of the time. My nerves stemmed from fear that Keely might not care for Montana.

My worries were completely unnecessary. Within a week of moving in she was in love with the house, our neighbors and of course, Snuggles.

Stepping into the living room, I saw Tara and Dawn sitting on the floor with Keely. I held back a grin when I saw their Kindles—along with the one they'd given Keely as a welcome to the neighborhood gift the week of her moving in—sitting on the couch. Without a doubt I knew they'd been loading Keely up on what I called literary porn. I wasn't complaining considering the fact that my girl got a lot of great ideas from those books.

The grin I was holding back burst forth when I saw Emma happily kicking her legs and reaching up to touch things on her play gym. Snuggles was in position right at her side, watching intently as Emma played. From the instant Snuggles and Emma met, they'd been best friends. The dog damn near refused to leave her side, which delighted Keely and I to no end. Emma's very first giggle was because Snuggles was licking her face.

I dropped down onto the floor next to Keely, cupping her chin as I pulled her in for a quick kiss. If Tara and Dawn hadn't been in the living room, the kiss wouldn't have been so quick. Emma squawked excitedly when she saw me. Reaching out, I picked her up and brought her in for hugs and kisses before sitting her down in my lap so she was facing Snuggles. Keely leaned into my side as she looked up at me and smiled. Dropping another kiss on her perfect lips, I smiled back. Home with my family was my favorite place to be.

"It's here?" I questioned. "You have it?"

Keely nodded happily. "The official decree came today. Emma's officially a Sharpe."

I was so fucking proud I felt I could burst. Giving Emma my name meant the world to me. It wouldn't be long before Keely shared it with us. I kissed her again for good measure.

"Good God," Dawn sighed dramatically. "I still can't believe there was a real life book boyfriend living right next door to Tara all this time."

Tara and Dawn teased me relentlessly about the changes having Keely and Emma in my life had brought.

"Just goes to show there's hope for a lot of the guys you ladies call dogs," I joked.

"I'm taking credit for the whole thing," Tara announced. "If I hadn't forced Snuggles on him, he wouldn't have been housebroken and Keely would be ripping her hair out."

We all laughed. Tara's theory that Snuggles had trained me to be a good provider wasn't new. She said it all of the time. Mostly it was the wine talking, but I thought maybe she had a little bit of a point.

I couldn't argue with the fact that a lot had changed in a short amount of time. I'd gone back to Colorado with the weight of the world on my shoulders, expecting everything to be terrible. Instead, the place I'd avoided like the plague wound up changing my life for the better. Everyone I knew had been shocked when I came home with a girlfriend and a baby, but after seeing us together, people got it.

We'd left Colorado five days after the Ettie incident. I didn't know what to expect during those few days. Would Ettie show back up? Was it really over?

Fortunately it really was. We knew she had filed papers to get the house, and without us fighting it, she got it. That was the last we heard of her, which was exactly what we wanted. She could choke on the money as far as we were concerned. We had Emma, which meant we had the only thing that mattered.

The rest meant nothing.

Once Tara and Dawn left—to go talk about their porn books, I was certain—I took the girls into the kitchen. Our ritual was that

Emma would sit in the high chair with Snuggles at her feet. Keely and I stood at the counter and talked about our day while I prepared dinner. In between prep and talking, I stole kisses and found reasons to touch her. It had quickly become one of my favorite parts of the entire day.

We ate dinner together at the table as a family—something that delighted Keely to no end. Emma babbled happily as Keely and I took turns feeding her green beans and rice cereal. She was an incredibly happy baby, always entertaining us with her silly giggles and vivacious personality.

After dinner and clean up, we headed into the living room. I held Emma as I rained kisses on her cheeks, making her giggle when I would brush my beard stubble against her. She clapped her hands each time I did it, her way of saying again. I'd never have guessed how amazing having a child would be. Watching her grow was everything. I loved interacting with her and felt unbelievable pride in how smart she was.

"Emma, where's Mommy?"

She bounced excitedly as she pointed to Keely.

"Where's Snuggles?"

She babbled incoherently as she pointed down to her dog.

As was our routine, I asked her my favorite question last.

"Where's Daddy?"

She jabbed me on the cheek with her chubby finger and then started clapping her hands as she smiled at me.

"Can Daddy have a kiss?"

Emma's version of a kiss was slobbering all over my cheek, which of course I ate up with a big smile. Being her dad was an honor I wouldn't trade for the world.

I woke up when Keely tapped me on the arm and whispered my name. Opening my eyes, I smiled up at her before letting out a yawn. I wasn't surprised to find I'd fallen asleep while reading Emma her nighttime story, seeing as how I did so most nights. Something about rocking back and forth with my baby snuggled over my heart relaxed me. It didn't hurt that Snuggles was draped across my feet.

Emma was a little bit alert as Keely lifted her off of me and walked her to her crib in the nursery we'd spent a week getting just so when they first moved in. The walls were pale lavender and all of the accents were yellow or white. It was perfect for our little angel.

I stayed silent as Keely rocked her back and forth for a minute, dropping soft kisses on her face while she waited for me to join her. When I did, she put Emma down and then watched as I covered her. Letting out a quiet baby noise, Emma stuck her thumb in her mouth as her eyes fluttered closed.

We watched her for a few seconds to make sure she was really asleep before we moved. Once we were certain, I bent down and pulled the dog bed we kept under Emma's crib out so Snuggles could take her post. My pup didn't even consider sleeping in my room anymore. From the minute we brought Emma home, Snuggles chose to spend her nights watching over her baby.

Keely probably had five hundred pictures of dog and baby together. Many of them were displayed proudly in some of the photo displays Keely had throughout the house. My small house wasn't just a place to live anymore—it was a family home I couldn't wait to come back to every day.

When we got into our bedroom, I made quick work of getting my woman naked. The only thing I left on was the engagement ring I'd given her the month before. I'd agonized over picking the perfect ring. I'd considered updating her moms ring for half a second before scratching the idea. Keely and I were done with the past. Her mother had been a great woman, but Hollis hadn't been a good dad. Using anything Hollis had touched just wasn't an option.

The toughest part of choosing the ring was that Keely didn't favor diamonds. After I explained that to the jeweler, he pointed me in a different direction. What I wound up choosing was a ring with Emma's birthstone—a sapphire. Keely cried when I asked her to marry me, but she cried harder when she saw the ring and realized why I'd chosen that stone.

Snuggling against me, she kissed along my jawline and then stopped next to my ear.

"How would you feel about handcuffs?" she whispered.

I chuckled as I maneuvered her onto her back and got on top of her.

"For you or me?"

Winding her arms around my neck, she smiled. "How about both? We can start with me and then I can take control."

I kissed her deeply before giving her my answer.

"Anything you want, baby."

"Yeah?"

"Always," I promised.

Wrapping her legs around me, she hugged me tight.

"Every time I think I can't love you more, I'm wrong."

My pulse picked up speed as my heart melted. Being loved by Keely was more than I'd ever known I could possibly have.

"That's good," I answered. "Since I love you more every single day."

She kissed me softly before pulling away with a smile.

"I'm so glad I get to keep you," she said softly.

I was glad, too.

"I'm all yours. Forever"

Keely

Six months later

"You ready?"

Twirling this way and that as I looked in the mirror, I nodded back at Kristi.

"I've never been more ready," I answered happily.

"Okay—then it's final check time," she announced.

I turned from the mirror and gave her my full attention.

"First up, something old?"

"She's got a penny from the year Ronan was born tucked in her shoe," Dawn answered.

"Something new?"

I gestured down to my dress. "Everything I'm wearing."

"Borrowed?"

"Your moms' wedding earrings."

"That leaves us with something blue."

Tara snorted. "Do Ronan's balls count? Because I'm pretty sure he's ready to bust since Dawn and I have kept Keely from seeing him for twenty-seven whole hours."

"Tara," Kristi chastised with a laugh. "That was mean! Also, it doesn't count."

"It's okay," I chuckled. "My engagement ring is blue and I have blue lace panties on."

The three women applauded enthusiastically. I bobbed in a half curtsy as I laughed.

"It looks like everything is under control," Kristi laughed.

I had no nerves about marrying Ronan. Judging by the fact that he met me at the top of the aisle with Emma in his arms, I knew he wasn't nervous, either. Emma clapped when she saw me and then dove out of his arms into mine for a hug.

"Mom, Mom, Mom!"

I kissed her sweet cheeks and hugged her tight. She gave me two seconds of sweet before dropping a sloppy kiss on my cheek and reaching for her father.

"Dad! Dad! Dad!"

Ronan took her from me with a laugh and then took my hand in his. We walked down the aisle as a family, beaming the entire way. When we reached the altar, Emma dove out of Ronan's arms and into Canter's with a giggle.

"Can Can!"

Canter tried to act like a badass, but he adored our daughter. I loved him for that. She stayed in his arms, watching happily as Ronan and I got married. It was the best day of my life and I enjoyed every minute of it.

Later that night after our wedding reception, I gave my husband his wedding gift. Looking from the box in his hand to me, his eyes went wide.

"For real?"

I smiled as I climbed onto his lap and straddled him. Linking my fingers behind his neck, I dropped a kiss on his lips.

"For real," I confirmed. "Hope you're ready to do middle of the night feedings all over again," I laughed.

He wrapped his arms around me and hugged me tight. "I'm more than ready," he assured me.

I melted against him happily.

"I love you," I said softly.

"Forever," he said.

I smiled as I responded, "And always."

Special Note:

If you enjoyed *All That's Left to Hold Onto*, please consider leaving an honest review where you purchased this or Goodreads. Without reviews, books die on the vine. YOUR WORDS make the difference between fading into oblivion and being seen. Please review- it means the world.

Acknowledgements

Special shout out to the girls in Ella Fox's Book Babes. You are all amazing!

Thank you to Nancy Miller, Dena Marie, Joni Leonard, Nikki Cole, Dawn Cipressi & Sian Davies for always being there when I need them. Taco kicks for everyone!

Thank you to Tara Lynn and Dawn Lynn of Two Unruly Girls with a Romance Book Buzz for being so damn cool. I love you hookers.

Thank you to Bibi Arocho, Lara Ross Petterson, Yahaira Cintron, Lisa Pantano Kane, Wendy 'Bear', Colleen Snibson, Kathy Bankard, Christina Gobin and Bethany Castaneda for being such great supporters and, more importantly, friends.

I'm beyond thankful—in a way I can never fully express—to ALL of the bloggers who do what they do. YOU ARE IMPORTANT! What you do has tremendous value and I thank you from the bottom of my heart. Without you, there would be no this. Period.

Very special thanks to my COPA girls. Our group provides sanity and laughs in this often whacky world of writing. Kristi Webster, Rochelle Paige, Jeanette Escudero, Jay McLean, Cora Brent, Tessa Teevan, Crystal Reynolds, Beth Ehemann, Stylo Fantôme, Mary Elizabeth, Rachel Brookes, Anne Mercier, Elle Jefferson, Tijan, Jessica Ingro Katz, Elle Christensen, Sao Moose, KC Lynn and the rest of the crew—I think you're all AMAZING. Your hearts are as big as your talent. I am proud to call you friends. COPA is my happy place online & I wouldn't have it any other way.

Mad love for SVC Ricketts who always makes me smile.

Special, special thanks to my mom and my nephew for tolerating my erratic schedule and not complaining when I'm roaming around at 5am muttering about my characters. You guys are great roomies.

About the Author

Ella Fox is the *USA Today* Bestselling Author of Consequences of Deception, The Hart Family series & many other sexy and exciting books.

Ella loves music, photography and comedy movies. She's an all around goofball. She grew up loving to read, especially romance. That's not surprising considering the fact that her mom is *USA Today* Bestselling Author Suzanne Halliday.

LIKE me on Facebook & you'll never miss a release or any of my fabulous giveaways!
Facebook.com/EllaFoxAuthor
Follow me on Twitter: @AuthorEllaFox
Visit my website and sign up for my mailing list: www.authorellafox.com

OTHER BOOKS BY ELLA FOX

The Hart Family Series:
Broken Hart
Shattered Hart
Loving Hart
Unbroken Hart
Missing Hart
Finding Hart

The Renegade Saint Series:
Picture Perfect
Twist of Fate

The Temporary Series:
Strictly Temporary Volume One
Strictly Temporary Volume Two

The Catch Series:
Catch My Fall
Catch and Release

The Deception Series:
Consequences of Deception

Made in the USA
San Bernardino, CA
05 May 2016